WHERE THE SHADOW FALLS

Gillian Galbraith grew up near Haddington in Scotland. She worked for many years as an advocate, specialising in medical negligence and agricultural law cases. Before qualifying in law she worked for a time as an agony aunt in magazines for teenagers. She was also the legal correspondent for the *Scottish Farmer* and has written law reports for *The Times*. Her first book, *Blood in the Water, An Alice Rice Mystery*, was published in 2007, and this was followed in 2008 by *Where the Shadow Falls*. A third Alice Rice mystery, *Dying of the Light*, was published in 2009. She lives deep in the country near Kinross with her husband and child, cats, dogs, hens and bees.

WHERE THE SHADOW FALLS

Gillian Galbraith

Polygon

First published in 2008 by Polygon
This paperback edition published in 2009 by Polygon
an imprint of Birlinn Ltd
West Newington House
10 Newington Road, Edinburgh EH9 1QS

www.birlinn.co.uk

Copyright © Gillian Galbraith 2008

ISBN-13: 978-1-84697-106-8

Set in Italian Garamond BT at Birlinn Ltd

Printed and bound in Great Britain
by Clays Ltd, St Ives plc

Acknowledgements

Maureen Allison
John Beaton
Colin Browning
Douglas Edington
Lesmoir Edington
Robert Galbraith
Daisy Galbraith
Hamish Galbraith
Sheila Galbraith
Diana Griffiths
Jinty Kerr
Dr Elizabeth Lim
Aidan O'Neill
Pat Younger

Any errors in the text are my own.

Dedication

To Robert and Daisy, with all my love.

I

His head lolled to the side again and he raised it upright, aware for the first time of its enormous weight. Am I still fully compos mentis, *of sound mind or whatever, James Freeman mused, before concluding that he was, probably, no longer capable of such a judgement. Pouring himself more whisky from the decanter, the old man drank it neat, in a single gulp, determined to dull his brain further, banish all remaining senses. Anything, he thought, rather than stay in this limbo, with emotions heightened and nerves jangling. He had imagined a peaceful journey, a seamless transition from tranquil sensibility to blessed oblivion, with his love by his side. Never mind. Before long this cup too would be taken from him, and impatience at such a time, and with so little left, might lead to damnation. Hellfire no longer seemed preposterous, better play safe than risk that.*

The ringing of the doorbell startled him, causing him to drop his tumbler onto the rug and utter a loud curse. Then realisation dawned, and his spirits soared. Now he would not be alone, despite all his well-intentioned efforts. Neither of them had proved strong enough to remain apart and he, at least, did not regret it. Rising immediately from his favourite chair, he was surprised to find how unsteady on his feet he was, swaying dizzily, the room spinning around him. With a supreme effort of will he straightened up and began to cross the carpet, heading towards the landing. His own momentum helped him down the stairs and he steadied himself on the banister end, resting for a few seconds before preparing to traverse the vast expanse of the hall. A straight crossing was all but achieved. 'Fwiend or Foe,' he whispered theatrically, before opening the door

1

to greet his caller. Without another word, he ushered his visitor in, readying himself to speak, concentrating intently on what he must say and saying it clearly.

The halting speech delivered by the old fellow elicited a reply, but it made no sense to him, sounding like a string of meaningless noises, and his inability to understand made him fearful. It could have been the braying of a donkey or the miaowing of a cat for all it now conveyed to him. Attempting to reimpose order on his befuddled mind, he focussed his attention on the corner of the window, where a butterfly was struggling to free itself from a spider's web. A single silken thread had attached itself to the creature's legs, and as it twisted and turned it bound itself more tightly, manacling its delicate wings, inadvertently parcelling itself up. And then, out of the corner of his eye, he saw the dark form of the spider scuttling towards its prey and could bear to watch no longer. He must intervene. Conscious of the offence he might give, but careless of it, he turned his back on his companion, intent only on freeing the Painted Lady before it was too late.

The first blow to his head felled him and as he tumbled to the ground, his left hand caught the butterfly in her trap, simultaneously releasing her and killing her. And all the angry words that rained down upon him, accompanying each subsequent stroke, landed on deaf ears.

—

As James Freeman was speaking in his drawing room, trying, in vain, not to slur his words, Alice Rice was removing her keys from the ignition and smiling to herself, anticipating her parents' reaction to her unheralded visit. Carefully she disembarked from the car, closing the door without making a sound. The front door of their house was ajar and she crept on tiptoes through the hall, heading in the direction of the kitchen. Unexpectedly, she found the place deserted. Wandering into the garden, she was surprised to see her father at the far end of it, energetically digging in the potato patch, intent on earthing up the shaws. In the Rices' precisely demarcated world, such cultivation was solely her mother's responsibility and never before had she seen her father wielding a spade. Still unaware of her presence, he stopped for a few seconds to catch his breath before returning to his task with redoubled vigour. Softly, she walked across the lawn until she stood, motionless, behind the bent figure, intending to tap him on the shoulder, hearten him with her unanticipated visit. But noticing her shadow on the ground, Alexander Rice turned round to face her before she had even begun to extend her arm.

'Alice! What on earth are you doing here?' He sounded irritated.

She was taken aback by his reaction, momentarily speechless, disappointed that he was not pleased to see her. Her face betrayed her feelings, and immediately he spoke again, this time his tone softer.

'Darling, it's lovely to see you. I'm so sorry, I just wasn't expecting anyone, and to be honest I'm rather on edge today.' He reached for her hand, abashed, eager to soothe any hurt he had inadvertently inflicted.

'Where's Mum?' she asked, still numb from his initial response.

'She's in Edinburgh at the moment, I don't think she'll be back until about seven or so. Let's go into the house, have a cup of tea, eh?'

Carefully, he poured milk into her cup, and then began to tilt the teapot. Glancing down at the resultant chalky mixture, Alice asked gently: 'Dad, did you put any tea leaves or teabags in the pot?'

He lifted the earthenware lid, peered in and then smiled, shaking his head. They sat together at the kitchen table, elbow touching elbow, but not, as was usual between them, exchanging news and chattering easily. Both were discomfited by the continuing silence, but Alice's attempts at conversation soon petered out as her father, preoccupied, failed to catch her drift or answer at all. He was somewhere else altogether. Looking at his familiar face, she noticed that his mouth moved occasionally, saying nothing, as if he was absorbed in some kind of troubled internal dialogue. It was a mannerism he'd never shown before, and it disturbed her.

'What's the matter, Dad?' she asked, hoping that she did not sound as anxious as she felt.

'Nothing, darling. Are you going to spend the night with us?'

She nodded. 'That was my plan, if it suits you.'

'Of course…' He stared out of the window, into the distance, and then turned to her, adding as if the thought had just entered his mind, 'Would you do me a favour, Alice? If you could it would make a great difference to me… well, to both of us, actually. I'm supposed to attend a meeting, an anti-windfarm gathering, at the MacGregors' house near Stenton. I'm the minute-taker for the group. Would you go in my place? I want to speak to your mother about something when she gets back… to be here when she gets back.'

As he seemed so strained, so uncharacteristically tense, she longed to repeat her earlier enquiry, but he had chosen to say nothing, and presumably had a reason for it. Consequently, she refrained from asking anything, conscious that if she did he might withdraw his request, thinking it too much bother. Instead, she dissembled, telling him, despite a headache starting at the base of her skull, that she would enjoy going and seeing such a gathering for herself.

On the overgrown roadside verges the pink campion was dying back, seed pods wizened and stems broken. But among their

4

fading blooms cow parsley was beginning to emerge as the midsummer weeds took over from their early season predecessors. The profusion of leaves on the lime trees transformed the narrow country lane into a tunnel roofed with foliage, dappled light dancing on the road below. Glancing at the clock on the dashboard, Alice saw that it was nearly eight pm and accelerated, conscious that she must not be late. As instructed, she turned left at the bottom of the hill and began a bone-shaking ascent up a drive, once smooth with tarmac, now heavily pot-holed, slaloming between the chasms, anxious to preserve her car's shock-absorbers and undercarriage.

The dilapidated three storey mansion that greeted her no longer boasted any formal gardens, instead it was surrounded by a thin sprinkling of gravel, punctuated by drifts of poisoned dandelions, thistles and ground elder. And creeping ever closer to the building were armies of rhododendrons, their shiny leaves reflecting the evening sunshine, a few guinea fowl pecking disconsolately in their shade. Jagged cracks in the harling on the house revealed glimpses of the cut stone below and an isolated stretch of guttering hung perilously above the front door, its companions to the left and right lying, rusted and broken, where they had fallen. Despite this, the place remained strangely impressive, eloquent of status, if no longer of wealth.

Alice readied herself for the forthcoming ordeal; meeting a band of complete strangers, each known to the other, united by a common purpose, and one completely alien to her. By the time she had located the doorbell, discovered it to be silent and knocked instead, a shower of rain had begun to fall and she shivered, involuntarily, waiting to be let in. Prue MacGregor, when she finally came, matched her description. Mr Rice had warned his daughter to expect a small, bandy-legged creature with piercing blue eyes and an inhospitable manner. Without the usual pleasantries or introductions, a glass of red

5

wine was thrust peremptorily into Alice's hand as her hostess, intent upon answering her mobile phone, marched out of the kitchen.

No one approached the uneasy newcomer, so she looked round, taking in her surroundings, accustoming herself to the hum of other people's conversation. The room was harshly lit by a single fluorescent strip, and suspended from the ceiling was a massive pulley, laden with jodhpurs, patched blankets and overalls, swinging a couple of feet above the visitors. Otherwise, the kitchen contained little furniture bar a large oak table and a miscellaneous collection of ill-fitting cupboards flanked by a gloss-painted Welsh dresser, its shelves bowed with the weight of the *Horse & Hound* magazines piled on them.

Some of the guests began to drift towards the door and Alice followed passively, notebook in hand, as they processed into a dark, musty drawing room. Fifty years earlier the room had been magnificent with linenfold panelling and plasterwork columns, but its glory days had long gone – blisters disfigured the wallpaper and the brocade on the furnishings was threadbare, slits of black horsehair visible beneath. A pair of gilt-framed mirrors, silver peeling, flanked an ornate chimney-piece, in front of which two men sat at a table, facing chairs set out before them as if in an old-fashioned school room. The men looked on apprehensively as the party settled into the seating provided. When Alice's turn came, only an embroidered footstool remained, and she lowered herself onto it gingerly, expecting its woodworm-infested legs to crumble under her weight.

As she was breathing a sigh of relief, sitting safely with the footstool still intact, the younger of the two men stood up and introduced himself as Ewan Potter, Commercial Director of Firstforce, and then gestured towards his companion, Doctor Angus Long, Technical Consultant of the Company. Potter's voice was smooth, assured and resonated with authority, as if used to giving orders and accustomed to obedience, but as he began telling his audience about the company's desire to consult with the local community, to accommodate their wishes, he was interrupted by a thickset woman with unconcealed aggression in her tone. Alice felt the temperature in the room rise a few degrees, and the tension in it, created by the speaker's blatant antagonism, became palpable.

'You want to "consult" with us, do you? "Accommodate" our wishes, eh? But, Mr Potter, you and your company are not wanted here. There is nothing to consult with us about!' the woman shouted. 'To accommodate our wishes you'd have to ensure that none of your twenty-five bloody turbines came anywhere near Gimmerfauld. That's our view, we told you that at the last meeting...'

Following this outburst, Alice glanced around the room expecting every jaw to have dropped in astonishment at this seemingly unprovoked display of fury, but saw, instead, a few heads nodding, as if in approval of the views expressed. For a second she caught the eye of a rotund, bespectacled man, and the quizzical look she bestowed on him was not reciprocated as he patted his knee, as if applauding the speaker's tone.

Doctor Long swallowed, adjusted his tie, then readjusted it, before looking intently downwards at his papers and re-assembling them into their previous impeccable order. In contrast, his companion leant forward over the table and stared hard at his antagonist as if his pugnacious attitude might persuade her to alter, or retract, her cutting words. But the woman seemed oblivious to his display of annoyance and continued speaking, still at an uncomfortably high volume.

'You've seen where we live, Mr Potter, and our hills cannot "absorb" the one hundred and twenty-five metre structures you've planned for them. We've asked you to reduce the height of the towers, the size of the blades, to "accommodate" us, but have you? Have you buggery! I told you and your sidekick the last time, three of your sodding turbines are within two hundred metres of my house. Have you considered for one moment what that might be like, eh? I don't give a flying fuck about you or your company. This is just a job to you; you knock off and then go back to your comfy little house somewhere or other, but your "project" results in the ruination of my home, my sodding life, actually. And don't imagine we don't know what Firstforce's real concerns are. Nothing to do with clean, renewable energy, polar bears and saving the planet… No, it's all about the bottom line, capital returns, dividends for your shareholders…'

Potter cleared his throat loudly in an attempt to halt the apparently unstoppable flow, and his ploy worked, the speaker was surprised into silence, as if she believed that her tirade might bring about his departure, and with it, the cancellation of Firstforce's plans for the wind farm. But in seconds, any such illusions were shattered.

'Thank you, Miss Lamont. We are all familiar with your views by now. You gave us the benefit of them last month and at the gathering before that. All I am trying to do is to get across to you that whilst the fact of our wind farm in this location is non-negotiable, as far as the company is concerned, we may be able to accommodate the wishes of the local community in respect of the proposed layout. Equally, Firstforce intend to set up a community-fund…'

Like a small child, a middle-aged man in a worn green tweed jacket put up his hand to attract attention, and in deference to him the Director returned to his seat.

'I'm in exactly the same position as Sue… uh, Miss Lamont. Your design shows my farm, at least I'm the tenant of it, with six of the turbines within my boundary and the ones marked… uh, ten, fourteen, eleven and thirteen,' he jabbed a thick forefinger at a creased map, 'surround my house. Number fourteen is actually to be built on the catchment area for my water supply.

The same is true at Blaebridge, Miss Kerr's cottage. Her house is supplied by a borehole, and it'll be bound to get polluted if you erect turbine number twenty-three where you've shown it on the plan. Miss Kerr's not here tonight, she's too upset, but she's an old woman who could do without all of this hassle. Couldn't you just re-think the whole thing, find another site?'

The man folded his map, returned it to his pocket and sat down, looking expectantly at Ewan Potter.

To the surprise of the assembled group, Doctor Long caught his colleague's eye deferentially, nodded his head and then rose to his feet to respond.

'Thank you for expressing your concern, Mr... Eh?'

'Dougal.'

'Yes, Mr Dougal. Fortunately...'

'Dougal Thomson.'

'Sorry, Mr Thomson. Fortunately, I think that I can provide all of you with a degree of reassurance in relation to private water supplies and the likely impact our proposal may have on them. We have commissioned independent experts, ECO-Co, to investigate the local hydrogeology, the catchment areas, subterranean water reservoirs and so forth, and every single dwelling within the site boundary has already been surveyed...'

Sue Lamont, evidently unable to control herself any longer, shouted, semi-incoherent with fury: 'No, you stupid... basta... man. They have not. There are thirty-one properties that'll be affected by your proposal and how many of them have received letters from ECO-Co and were surveyed by them?'

Angus Long, aware that the question was addressed to him, looked uncomfortable but did not attempt to respond.

'Shall I tell you then? They've surveyed a pitiful twenty out of the thirty-one. You can't even get that right, and we're supposed to let you construct massive concrete foundations, quarries and mile upon mile of track all around us and be "reassured" that nothing untoward will happen. Why don't you and your tinpot company leave us alone, eh? Pack up your bags, collect your papers and be gone. We all know that the scheme's a done deal, so stop pretending to consult with us and just go…'

The sheer passion evinced by the woman both appalled and enthralled Alice. There was nothing false or manufactured about it, she was speaking from the heart and all eyes were on her, silently supporting her, egging her on. But Ewan Potter, sensing that any vestigial control he had over the meeting was slipping away, said loudly: 'Any further questions from anyone?'

'Your reports—hydrogeology and so on—you say you've received them all now. Can we see copies of them? No reason not to share them with us, eh… in the spirit of consultation and all.' It was a woman speaking, standing up to make sure she was heard.

'Er… No… They're only in draft form, unfinalised—so, no. Any other queries?'

Alice watched as the members of the group exchanged glances as if to communicate to each other and to the two outsiders present their contempt for the proceedings. As they were doing so an old lady, sitting in the front row, eased herself to her feet.

'Aye, I've yin.'

Ewan Potter gestured with his hand for her to continue.

'It's aboot a' the burds…' she began, licking her lips nervously and twiddling her crooked thumbs as she spoke. She had faded brown eyes, the irises encircled by bluish rings, and although she was indoors, her head remained swaddled in a thick, woollen bonnet.

'The eagles, ye ken…'

Potter said, with pretended patience, as if to encourage her, 'And what about… the eagles?'

'Ye've nae mentioned thae burds in yer report, but they'll be the yins tae git chopped up wi' the giant blades. What'll ye be daen aboot that? The buzzards an' that I'm nae sae bothered aboot, there's that many, but the eagles, noo, they're special. An' there's only the fower o' them...'

'We've not mentioned the eagles, because there are no eagles,' Potter replied trenchantly.

'Says who?' came back the startled response.

'Says ECO-Co. They've had independent ornithological experts studying the site for two whole days and seen no eagles.'

'Oh, twa hale days, eh...' The old lady repeated sarcastically and then continued: 'Twa hale days... a' devoted tae the eagles?'

Doctor Long answered, looking less assured than his superior.

'Well, no, actually. Not two whole days for the eagles as such, but for the bird study in general.'

'A' the burds?' The tone was incredulous.

'All the birds, yes. The expert ornithologist we employed saw no signs of eagles or eagle activity in any form.'

The old woman smiled mirthlessly before mimicking Long's reply: '"No signs of eagles or eagle activity in any form". Yon buggers must be blind, then! It's a disgrace... you're a' a disgrace. I've stayed oan Gimmerfauld fer the past fifteen year, and I dinnae ken a' the burds oan it yet. Yous breenge in for twa days an' tell me that there's nae eagles 'cause ECO-Co says so. If I'd nae heard it wi' ma ain ears I'd nae hae believed it. Twa bloody days... that's a' it's worth to yous. Ye'll nae ken aboot the blackcock neither, I'll be bound...'

Doctor Long, chastened by the woman's disdain, said, almost in a whisper: 'ECO-Co say there are no black game present within the site boundary.'

'ECO-Co say... ECO-Co say. They're nae gods, ye ken! Well, tell ECO-Co that there's a lek less than a quarter mile frae my ain hoose and I'll show them ma'sel if need be.' The old lady glared at Firstforce's representatives and then, unexpectedly

11

and as if she could no longer stand the sight of them, sank back into her chair and covered her eyes with her left hand.

'About the community-fund…'

The voice came from a bearded man leaning on a large mahogany sideboard. Before either of the company's representatives had a chance to say anything, Sue Lamont hissed 'Judas!' and the fellow, now cowed, hurriedly made for the door.

Ewan Potter looked at his audience, confrontational in his unblinking stare, and then gathered up his papers and crammed them into his briefcase. Without any further words to the group, he and Doctor Long began to converse in low voices before they took their leave of the drawing room, both walking at an exaggeratedly slow pace, as if concerned to conceal the urge to run.

Alice looked at the old lady. Her blue-veined hand, tendons stretched beneath parchment skin, remained over her eyes, but it was trembling and a tear had escaped down the side of her bony nose.

'They've gone now,' Alice said.

'I ken, but thanks anyway, dear. Ye'll be Mr Rice's daughter, eh? I seen ye in Prue's kitchen, but I wis talking wi' Rab. Ye'll be the policewuman, eh? A sergeant, I've heard.'

'That's right, a detective sergeant with Lothian & Borders CID. I work at St Leonard's Street in Edinburgh. You must be one of my parents' neighbours. Whereabouts do you live?'

'Aye, I'm a neighbour an' a friend an' a'. I stay in the wee white hoose at Crawfourdsden, 'ken on the other side o' the toll road. Tell yer dad that Jessie wis asking aifter him, eh?'

Thinking that she had now completed her duties, and still reeling from the pyrotechnic display she had witnessed, Alice made her way to the door, eager to return to her parents house and ostensible normality. Prue MacGregor, however, had other ideas, and herded her towards the kitchen where the hardliners within the group were congregating in the absence of their enemy, preparing to reconsider their strategy. In the middle of the kitchen table lay a pile of bound volumes produced by Firstforce, and on top of the heap rested a blue and white striped sugar bowl. Sue Lamont removed one of the books and began flicking through it.

'Look at that! Their own ZVIs show that the turbines will be visible on the other side of the Forth. Let's see... they'll be seen practically the whole way up to Perth.'

'Yes, yes, we know that, but the point is what are we going to do?'

The accent was English, and the tone languid. Alice glanced towards the speaker, who had his back to the others, inspecting the fridge for milk. Having found it, the man sat down and continued. 'We should have tried to nobble their mast, convince them that the wind "harvest" would be insufficient, but we didn't. We should have complained to the Police about their trespassing on our ground to put up sound equipment, but we didn't. We should have reported our Community Councillor for not agreeing to a special meeting, but we didn't. All we do is talk and talk and talk, and so far, that's got us nowhere.'

'They stop motorways being built with direct action and, if necessary, I'll take it,' Sue Lamont said. 'Make no mistake, I'll lie down in front of the bulldozers, chain myself to their cranes...'

'But by then the permission will have been granted,' the man interjected impatiently. 'We need to ensure that the council refuses the application. I suggest that we start liaising with other groups, the ones on Lochawe, Lewis, the Ochils, to find out how they're tackling the problem. I heard yesterday that THH's application at Muirness was turned down.'

Conscientiously, Alice continued to record the views expressed in her notebook, hampered as before by ignorance of the names of most of the speakers, attempting to memorise their faces for later identification by her father. Dougal

Thomson leant back in his chair, blew noisily on his coffee and grinned, revealing his broken teeth.

'I've been busy on the computer getting stuff from Companies House. Firstforce are not a big company, in fact, they're not even a Scottish company as they've been pretending. They're just a collection of four individuals from Bradford, all with the surname of "Owen", who have somehow allied themselves to an Italian conglomerate called "Grupposerck". And, what's more, their most recent balance sheet shows a loss of seventy thousand pounds. So all their talk of community funds and guarantees for the dismantling of the scheme after twenty-five years may mean very little indeed. Now, if that's not ammunition I don't know what is. I suggest that at our next meeting, in nine days, on the twenty-first of June, we compose a letter about them to our Councillor and get him to raise it with the planners.'

—

Alexander Rice gazed at the photographs in the album on his knee. His wife, Olivia, smiling and holding aloft their new baby, Alice, with their elder daughter, Helen, standing, bemused, beside her. His eyes rested on his wife's beloved red hair, wild curls encircling her face as if it was haloed by flame. The awful realisation that her wonderful mane, now more white than auburn, would all fall out, brought the tears back and he quickly turned over the page. A single black and white image confronted him. Olivia, still in her wedding dress, laughing, neck outstretched, as he, in full morning suit, genuflected on one knee before her, re-enacting his proposal of marriage. A photograph out of sequence, unexpected, and for which he had not prepared himself. He let out a low moan of sorrow, embarrassed himself by his own reaction and gulped down another swig of the raw whisky from the bottle by his side. The album had been selected to provide him with comfort, but he slammed its covers together, disappointed that it had proved itself to be a catalyst for grief rather than any source of help.

On her return Alice found her father on his own, ostensibly tranquil and composed, reading the newspaper. She noticed immediately the glass with the empty quarter of Strathfillan beside it. Not his whisky, a brand given to him and usually, in turn, quickly given away. Something was undoubtedly amiss.

'Dad—please tell me, I know there's something wrong.'

Without replying he patted the seat of the armchair beside his own, gesturing for her to sit next to him. As soon as she was seated, his arm reached across for his drink, slumping back onto his knee when he realised that the bottle had already been drained of all comfort.

'Please, Dad, tell me what's wrong,' she said again, as seconds passed and he remained silent.

'All right…' he began slowly. 'It's about your mother, I'm afraid. She was at the Murrayfield this afternoon seeing a specialist and… well, she's got breast cancer. That's why I needed, to be frank, to get you out of the house. So that we could discuss it, alone, together. The hospital finally confirmed it today. On Wednesday they plan to take the lump out, and then she'll have chemotherapy…'

His voice tailed off, tears now pouring down his face, eyes tight shut in desperation, oblivious to everything except his all-encompassing grief. Instinctively, Alice put her arms around his neck, but his undisguised distress frightened her as if, as in her childhood, he knew something that she did not; that the battle with the disease was already lost, and any remaining hope futile.

Half an hour later, having attempted to console her father with such reassurance as she could muster, she climbed the stairs to her parents' bedroom and peered through the doorway of the dimly-lit room. She felt the need to be near her mother for a little while, even if she had already fallen asleep, and was completely unaware of her presence.

'Alice?' It was her mother's voice.

'Yes.'

'Come in, darling.'

2

Skimming through a report on the probable time of death, Alice gagged on her egg roll.

'Blowflies had already laid their eggs in a white fluid in the mouth and rectum… maggots, together with a few pupa, were found in the bi-lateral avulsion injuries on the lower limbs.'

She returned the document quickly to its file and made her way to the ladies. The female toilets in St Leonard's Street Police Station were kept scrupulously clean, the air permanently scented by noxious floral sprays that hissed conspiratorially every so often as they discharged their asphyxiating perfume. She dried her hands on the starched blue roller towel while scrutinising her reflection in the mirror. Looking back at her, and equally unsmiling, was a tall, dark-haired woman with hazel eyes and a wide mouth. Suddenly, the tongue shot out at her, only to be as hastily retracted as the sound of flushing became audible from an adjacent cubicle. She departed before her colleague had unlocked the door.

On returning to her office, DCI Elaine Bell looked wistfully around it. Her few personal possessions, no more than a mug, brown with caffeine, and a faded photograph of her twin nieces, were safely in the carrier bag. She wandered over to the window to gaze onto the crescent of Salisbury Crags, their reddish rock now bathed in late afternoon sunshine. A view unequalled in the town, peaceful, providing balm to her troubled soul. From nowhere the ache in her shoulder joints returned, and she retrieved from her desk drawer the last two painkilling tablets, conscious that they now provided no more than the hope of relief rather than relief itself. Five weeks rest, at home, might help shift the ME, the doctor had said, and rather to her surprise her husband had encouraged her to take the time off. Maybe he still cared. However, dread was the principal emotion she felt on contemplating such a period of leisure, all alone, and to be spent in their spotless, modern house in the new estate at Cammo, surrounded by complacent housewives. It sounded like an eternity. Without the adrenalin, the excitement of her work, all those old, unwelcome preoccupations might return to unsettle her. The sound of children's laughter in the street, and on the television, advertisement after advertisement for nappies or baby food, somehow reviving hopeless dreams.

She should never have agreed to see that occupational health quack; after all, she had coped, managed to thole the pains for long enough. And then, to cap it all, she'd had no say whatsoever in the selection of her temporary replacement. If the Chief Constable knew half as much about DCI Robin Bruce as she did, Bruce would have remained in charge of his disgruntled troops at Torphichen Place. In her younger days she had suffered a bruised buttock or two at his hands. The man had been a compulsive bottom-pincher with no desire to be cured. Maybe nowadays the climate of political correctness or, more likely, fear of the law, would have wrought some change in his behaviour. On reflection, perhaps her buttocks were no longer tempting, insufficiently pert. This unpleasant train of thought was derailed by a knock on the door.

'Come in.'

Alice entered the office, carrying a cup of coffee.

'Gather you're off sick for a month or so, Ma'am. We were all wondering… well, d'you know who'll be in charge, while you're away, I mean? The rumour is that it's to be Moira Longman…'

'Over my dead body! Nope, they've roped in DCI Robin Bruce. I was at Tulliallan with him, so I've known him for years. He's been at Torphichen forever, so I should think he'll relish a change of scene. But he'd better not get too comfy in my chair, because I'll be back before he can bloody blink.'

—

The brightest star in the firmament of the New Town is Moray Place, a 12-sided circus composed of pedimented and columned mansion facades joined by simpler, plainer houses. It has a grandeur unparalleled in Georgian Edinburgh, or anywhere else in the city, and yet, within the small and intimate capital, it has not become a haven for commercial corporations or sleek partnerships, keen to display to the world their endless wealth, but remains a home for the cream of the middle-classes and their offspring. Most of them now have to make do with flats, but the privileged few, the elect, inhabit intact, undivided dwellings.

When DCI Bruce received news of a murder at such a location he felt, instantly, a frisson of elation. A dead body within such august portals was unlikely to be that of a vagrant, a death of no more than passing interest to the few, a loss likely to remain unrecorded even in *The Big Issue*. No, the corpse would probably be that of some High Court judge, brewing magnate or elderly neurosurgeon, in any of whom the journalistic profession would have a lively interest. Reputations were to be made where those gentlepeople were found. Elaine Bell would surely have fought tooth and nail to stay if she had but known, and lo, it had fallen into his lap! And this could be the one; the one to revive his flagging career and remind all and sundry of his undoubted talents.

The names of those in his squad, the murder squad, were now public knowledge. Please God, he thought, some competent individuals for this choice task, capable of exposing the truth without frightening the horses. Detective Sergeants Alice Rice and Alistair Watt, their names were familiar as a result of the Mair killings; DI Eric Manson, another known name,

19

although this time from the golf course; and DCs Trotter, Lowe, Drysdale and McDonald, unknown quantities all, were to complete the team. An arbitrary selection of individuals to be beaten into shape as quickly as possible. His much delayed promotion might depend upon it. Catching the killer, too.

—

The interior of the house at Moray Place was as elegant as its exterior, but the building had been furnished by its occupant in an idiosyncratic manner and the atmosphere was reminiscent of a museum rather than a domestic dwelling. Huge portraits, in gilded frames, hung at regular intervals above a stair balustrade that curved ever upwards, most of them depicting military men in red tunics helmeted in Glengarries, Balmorals or Feather Bonnets. Adorning many of the door lintels were bellicose arrangements of crossed swords. On entering the drawing room two yellow glass eyes in a ram's head, severed and stuffed and sitting incongruously on a 'D' end table, caught the light and were, in turn, reflected in the glass of the display cabinets. Inside the cabinets were brightly coloured ribbons, medals and orders, each with an ivory label proclaiming the recipient and the campaign. Mementos from the sacking of Tibet, the Boxer Rebellion and the Indian Mutiny were on show, with prayer wheels, Buddhas, and an elephant god huddled side by side in a mahogany corner cupboard. Framed swatches of weathered tartan hung on either side of an Edwardian mantlepiece, and above it, in pride of place, another portrait, a full-length likeness of an ancestor in the 79th Cameron Highlanders in full Highland dress, resplendent with basket-hilted sword and *sgian dhu*. A few dog-eared rugs overlaid the sanded boards, and the sofas and armchairs were covered in plain blue covers, stained and patched. It was a man's room, unashamedly so, completely devoid of flowers, porcelain ornaments, cushions or the other touches which tell of a female hand.

20

The photographers and fingerprint officers busy in it, although used to working in most environments, seemed subdued, almost reverential, attending to their business in near silence and without the usual cracks and guffaws that kept them sane. And the chatter that usually accompanied the Procurator Fiscal wherever she went was absent, replaced by a tuneless rendition of 'John Brown's Body', hummed under her breath.

The victim was lying on the floor of his study, and Alice, her paper suit crackling alarmingly, bent down to get a better view of the wounds on his bald pate. His skull, exposed and disfigured by three large depressed fractures, looked eggshell-thin, and blood, now congealed, was visible in both ears. His eye-sockets were purplish with bruising and a large area behind the right ear had been blackened too. One flabby, hairless hand rested lifelessly by his face; the other lay twisted unnaturally under one hip. A dark pool of his dried lifeblood surrounded him.

'Is he dead, then?' Eric Manson quipped cheerily. An old joke, endlessly recycled. His gallows-humour knew no limits and, as indiscriminate and compulsive as a flasher's habit, occasionally caused upset to the grieving relatives of murder victims. Reprimands had no effect.

As DI Manson departed the study, Alistair Watt entered it, taking trouble to avoid colliding with his superior on the narrow, paper path that had been provided to prevent contamination of the scene. Gazing around, in the gloom, he marvelled at the book shelves covering three-quarters of each of the walls, the volumes within all bound in leather, buff or dark maroon, and bearing gold letters and numbers on the spine. The lawyer's collection appeared to have absorbed most of the daylight leaking through the gaps in the heavy blinds, and any that escaped was quickly consumed by the drab hessian wallpaper. He made a mental note: extra lighting for the video would have to be arranged.

As he was lost in thought, attempting to familiarise himself with the locus, DC Trotter tapped him on the shoulder.

'The deceased's next-door neighbours can see you now, Sergeant.'

Mr Hamish Gunn was an ungainly figure of a man with a light-bulb for a head, a stalk of a neck, narrow, sloping shoulders and ample, child-bearing hips. By profession he was an investment manager and keen to co-operate to the best of his ability, but showing unmistakable signs of impatience, concerned to get to his office and attend the first of the day's appointments. His wife, Iona, sat on the sofa next to him, a surprisingly low-cut dress revealing her ample, freckled bosom. One hand was placed on her husband's crossed knee, almost as if restraining him, and she seemed languorous, the day stretching before her vacantly and requiring to be filled. A Police interview would do as well as anything else.

'Did you know the Sheriff well?' Alice asked.

'Not really,' Mrs Gunn replied. 'We all rather tend to keep ourselves to ourselves, if you know what I mean. No popping in and out of each other's houses here. I used to see Sheriff Freeman occasionally, usually if we were both leaving at the same time. I don't think, actually, he's ever been in our house, has he, darling?' The enquiry was directed at her husband.

'No. We did once invite him to dinner but he declined, and I don't think we ever received a reciprocal invitation.'

'How long have you been neighbours for?' Alistair chipped in.

'Must be… ten… twelve years, but we must have moved in rather different circles, you see,' Mrs Gunn continued. 'Obviously, Hamish would see him occasionally at the New Club, but he was not a sociable man.'

'Was he married?'

'You know, I don't know! Certainly, I've never seen his wife if he had one, but I don't honestly know. That sounds awful!'

'Did he have many callers, visitors or whatever?'

'Well, Moray Place isn't a curtain-twitching sort of area but… No. I can't say I have seen many visitors. But I have to repeat, we lead our own, rather busy lives, and the comings and goings of our neighbours largely pass us by. Half the time I think he wasn't here anyway.'

'What sort of man was he, Mr Gunn?' Alistair said.

Hamish Gunn blinked several times, theatrically, as if to convey deep thought before replying, and spoke ponderously.

'I'd say he was reserved. Yes, I think that's how I would describe him. I expect he had been good at his job, certainly had a distinct gravitas about him. Naturally, I know some lawyers—it'd be difficult to live in Edinburgh and not do so—but while many of them knew him by name, I don't think that even they knew him socially. A friend of mine in the office once told me that Freeman was a first-class shot. I've a gun in a syndicate on Buccleuch land but, to be frank, I never felt inclined to invite him along as a guest. The few times I have talked to him he seemed rather too dry for my liking, almost as if he had some sort of distaste for his own kind.'

'Remember the fire, darling?' Mrs Gunn interjected.

'Oh yes, he did do rather well then, didn't he?' her husband replied. 'We had a fire in our basement, officers, and he and some of the other neighbours helped us to remove pictures and so forth. He came up trumps then. I invited him to the post-blaze drinks party but, again, he refused us… I think he said he was off on holiday or something. When I think about it, he really would be the last sort of person I'd expect to meet a violent end. An inoffensive man.'

'Did you see anyone coming to his door yesterday or last night?' Alice asked.

'Mmm… I didn't, darling, did you?' Mrs Gunn looked at her husband.

'No, no, I think I can safely say that I never saw a soul. I was at a meeting until, oh, about ten o'clock, and then I walked home. I must have got back here at, say, half past ten, and after that I never left the house. And tonight we'll certainly be barricading ourselves in. In fact, I think I'll get a locksmith to add a few more Yales, maybe.'

'Did either of you hear anything?'

'Goodness, no, the walls are solid stone, not plasterboard. Someone could be screaming blue murder… Sorry, a bit insensitive of me—but I never heard a squeak,' Mrs Gunn volunteered and her spouse nodded his assent.

—

The Sheriff's other immediate neighbour on the other side led the two detective sergeants into her downstairs drawing room. Although a large room with a high ceiling, it had few pieces of furniture within it, and such items as were present were evidently expensive and simple in design. No clutter marred any surface, and the wall-space was devoid of pictures barring one large print, an abstract, placed exactly at eye-level on the wall. Lilies scented the air and two glass vases stood equidistant from the picture, on an aluminium table below it.

The woman resumed her seat, gesturing for Alice and Alistair to sit down by her. She gulped unselfconsciously, and with no urge to offer hospitality, from a tiny liqueur glass filled with golden fluid. The viscous liquid clung to her upper lip, emphasising the dark shadow on it, her full thatch of thick black hair confirming a hirsute tendency.

'Well, what can I do to help, detectifs?' Mrs Nordquist's strongly accented contralto voice betrayed her Scandinavian origins.

Alice launched in. 'We were hoping that you might be able to provide some information about Sheriff Freeman.'

'Mmm, he wass not a doc lover, that I can tell you!' She gave a brittle, intoxicated laugh.

'Jusst a few days ago he wass at me... where's your poopa-scoopa, Mrs Nordquist... always so bothered about the little doc dirt! Still,' she corrected herself, 'that's not what you want to know.' She paused. 'He wass a goot neighbour really, no trouble, but I hartly knew him. Not a goot laugh though, always so serious. I sometimes wondered if he hat any fun in his life. Wheneffer I saw him he was busy, lots of papers... that great big briefcase.'

'Was he married?' Alistair tried again.

'No chans! What lady would haff him? No, no, I don't mean it. Yess, maybe someone desperate... butt really desperate... even more desperate than me!' She cackled heartily at her own joke.

Raising her liqueur glass to her mouth again, she nodded again, as if her visitors could neither need nor want any further information.

'Did you see anyone call at his house yesterday or last night?' Alice persisted.

'I wass in the garten at the back of the houss yesterday, so I wouldn't see anyone at hiss door. Last night? Oh yess, I had my bridge friends around—Lillian, Helen ant Annie. We played until, maybe elefen o'clock, ant then I went to my bed... alone ass ussual.' She directed a rueful smile at Alistair who, on cue, shifted uneasily on his seat. From the corner of her eye Alice noticed a shadow pass the open door, and then Mrs Nordquist's deep voice boomed out, as if she was alone in the room.

'Freya! FREYA! You batt doc. Come in here, right now! I know what you're up to...'

Obediently, a large Weimaraner sloped into the drawing room and sank to the floor by its mistress's feet. A sugar-cube was inserted into its mouth which it crunched noisily, before looking upwards beseechingly for another morsel. Mrs Nordquist's attention, however, had shifted to her own glass and the need for a refill.

'Enough... enough, Freya, my botyguard. We haff guests. Iss there anything else I can tell you?'

Alice shook her head and Alistair asked: 'Can you remember when you last saw the Sheriff?'

Mrs Nordquist adjusted her hair while replying.

'Ass I sait, it would be two or three days ago... we jusst sait hallo in the street in passing.'

'So you didn't really know the Sheriff or anything much about him, would that be right?'

'Thatt would be... yess, we were strangers to each other, really. Neighbours jusst. A fine person, but no fun for me wiss thatt man!'

—

At three forty-five pm, Alice set off at a brisk pace on the downhill walk from the St Leonard's Street Station to the Cowgate. The Police mortuary, a plain modern building constructed of burnt sienna coloured brick, was her destination. She had been instructed to attend the post mortem and she knew that the new DCI would be present too. As she slipped through the door to the inner sanctum, she saw that he had already stationed himself on one side of the body, standing a little distance back from the table. The Chief Pathologist, Professor McConnachie, was craning over the Sheriff's head, apparently examining the man's teeth, and in doing so he was inadvertently exposing his own extensive bald patch. The perfect curve of his undamaged skull contrasted cruelly with the Sheriff's cracked and bloody cranium.

'Natural dentition in the lower jaw... upper jaw natural too. No dentures,' Professor McConnachie muttered, 'no signs of injury to the buccal cavity itself. Tongue grossly normal...'

He straightened himself up, pushed his gold-rimmed spectacles up with his wrist and then turned his attention to the Sheriff's hands, prying the fingers apart to inspect closely the undersides and nails. Beside him the mortuary attendant was waiting, scalpel posed theatrically above the corpse's abdomen, for a signal from the Pathologist to proceed with the incision. Doctor Zenabi gave it, miming the anticipated action as he spoke. 'On you go, Jock.'

Alice shuddered as the blade began to penetrate the Sheriff's unclothed body. His nakedness did not disconcert her, she had assisted in the undressing of the body earlier in the day, and any sensation of shock had long since worn off. She had already observed his long toenails, prior to placing the toe tag, and the massive scar that ran across his chest, suggesting a seamstress, or surgeon, less talented than Doctor Frankenstein. He was just flesh now; aged, faded flesh, heir only to decomposition. The distinct smell of cigarette smoke, sweet and stale, on clothing, wafted in her direction as a Police photographer moved towards 'the head end' as the mortuary attendant insisted on calling it. Jock himself was completely absorbed in his own task, exposing the internal abdominal organs for inspection *in situ* prior to their removal for dissection by the Professor.

'Get one of each of the wounds,' DCI Bruce instructed the photographer. 'I mean each one individually… as well as the whole skull.' He turned his attention to the Professor: 'Presumably a hammer or something?'

Professor McConnachie nodded his head, before saying, almost conversationally, 'Mmmmm. Cranial vault fractures and that one—' he pointed with a bloody finger, 'extends into the base of the skull… The weapon used must have had a relatively small surface area, but had been wielded with considerable force. Not a hammer, mind. Then you get depressed circular fractures. I'd say something rod-shaped—maybe a thick iron bar—something more like that.'

27

A bluebottle dawdled on the Sheriff's hairless thigh. Alice became spellbound by its slow upward progress, its unconscious defiling of the grey corpse, but she was unwilling to swat it, in a quandary as to what to do. A wet, gurgling sound distracted her as the attendant slowly withdrew a single kidney from the exposed cavity and laid it, briefly, on the Sheriff's pelvis before delving back inside to extract its twin. Bile rose to her mouth and she swayed, colliding with a coiled hosepipe, willing herself not to be sick. Not this time, not here, not now, not in front of Elaine Bell's replacement.

She glanced towards the new DCI, aware that he was still talking to the Professor, and tried to concentrate on the living rather than the dead. She noted how small he was, dwarfed by the lanky form of the Professor, and yet, with his arms crossed tightly across his chest, he appeared to be in control of all around him, directing the photographer and, simultaneously, quizzing the principal pathologist. As she watched him she became aware that he had shifted his attention on to her and, for an instant, their eyes met. She quickly closed hers, swept by another wave of nausea, and on hearing the sounds of male laughter, assumed that it was at her expense. Just another fifteen minutes or so, she prayed, let me last another fifteen minutes.

The old habit, inculcated at an impressionable age by nuns, was slow to die. In times of stress she found herself involuntarily mouthing the rosary, although she had not uttered a Hail Mary out loud since her convent schooling had ended over thirteen years earlier. She half opened her eyes for a second, just long enough to take in that the face was now being peeled back and heard herself retching. All her resources would need to be marshalled. I will remain upright. I will not vomit. As she was concentrating, she felt a hand on her elbow gently directing her towards the only bench in the white-tiled room. The powerful scent of nicotine told her that her saviour must be the photographer, and she sat beside him as he changed the lens on his camera.

'It's just another body, eh?' he said, by way of comfort. She nodded, speechless. Another unwelcome thought had entered her head unbidden, and she had seen the surgeon's scalpel on her mother's pale skin.

'Any indication yet as to time of death, Prof?' DCI Bruce asked.

'Well, taking into account the liver stab, the fixation of the livor mortis and rigor mortis, I'd say he must have died some-time between early last night and this morning. Of course, he only had his pyjamas on so I suppose he'll have cooled more rapidly, and the room temperature was fairly low. But, overall, I think that's a reasonable estimate.'

'Can you not narrow it down a bit more precisely than that for us?'

'Well, if you're pushing me—and it's a bloody inexact sci-ence as you know—I reckon, maybe, sometime between seven and ten or thereabouts.'

'AM or PM?'

'PM.'

'And the cause... presumably the hammer, or whatever it was?'

The Professor looked up from his examination of the brain, now cradled in his left hand. 'Some atheroma of the basal vessels...' he muttered almost to himself, before turning his attention to the question. 'Now, the likely cause—blunt force trauma, almost certainly, causing a massive sub-dural haemorrhage.'

Unbeknownst to Alice, she was being watched. In the fi-nal stages of the post mortem DCI Bruce's interest in it had waned. He now knew all that mattered. In common with her, he had shifted his attention from the dead to the living, taking in her good looks, unmistakable despite the greenish hue, and tall, slim figure. Her appearance at least could not be faulted, but he had hoped for a little more stoicism from a member of his squad. Obviously, only the truly bone-headed, those devoid of all imagination, could witness the cutting, sawing, weighing and bagging involved in the procedure and remain untouched by it, but a bit more mettle would not go amiss. On her ability to cope with just such ordeals his advancement might depend, and he had weeks rather than months to make his mark.

Professor McConnachie removed his gloves with a snap and went over to the bench.

'You nearly made it this time, Alice. Must be a record?'

'Yes.' The reply was of necessity, brief.

'If it's of any comfort, DI Oswald passed out earlier today when we were going into a head, and he's a hard, hard man.'

—

At eight pm new statements for marking-up were delivered to Alistair Watt's desk in the detective sergeant's room. Alice, clutching a mug of tea and still feeling weak, wandered over to take a look. As she was picking them up, Alistair returned to the room and noticed her.

'Not a pass, eh?' It was a rhetorical question: a single glance at his friend had already provided the answer.

'No, a fail since you ask. Jock didn't help, slapping organs under my nose. This time it was a kidney that was my undo-ing.'

'You kidney take it, eh?'

'Worthy of DI Manson, Alistair. Have you looked at the results yet?'

'No, and I don't intend to. I am off to get a pie and chips then home. Want some? I'll bring them up for you.'

'I think I'd bring them up myself without any assistance at the moment. Thanks, but I can't face anything at present.'

The phone call must be made and Alice steeled herself for

it. Her neighbour, Miss Spinell, would, in all probability, be thrilled to remain as a dog-minder for Quill on her behalf for a few extra hours, but nothing with the Alzheimer victim was ever entirely straightforward. The old lady's attachment to the collie-cross dog was passionate, but did not extend to his owner who was tolerated, simply, as a necessary evil. Alice dialled the familiar number.

'Hello… hello, how can I help you?'

A tone of bewilderment was apparent in the quavering voice, which had begun to speak before Alice had a chance to introduce herself.

'Miss Spinnell, it's Alice. Quill's owner. I was just ringing to see if it would be all right for you to keep him this evening until, say, ten thirty?'

'Keep who until ten thirty?'

'Quill. There is something on at the station and—' she was interrupted by Miss Spinnell's impatient tone.

'Of course… of course I'll keep the dog, and I'll see you later Alison.'

The last remark, which was followed by the replacement of Miss Spinnell's receiver, sounded like a veiled threat, the sort made by a tetchy headmistress when prevented by circumstances from giving vent to her true emotions.

3

Walking down St Leonard's Street towards the Pleasance, two weeks later, Alice revelled in the warm, summery breeze, its heat so uncharacteristic of the capital that its simple existence allowed the residents briefly to dream that they had been transported to London or Madrid, cities where the air has no sharp edges. Everyone she passed seemed relaxed, happy even, as if like plants they had responded to the sunshine and allowed themselves to unfurl. Even in the deep shadow of the Cowgate it felt balmy, and before too long she was able to bask once more in full sunlight as she turned to her right and entered Old Fishmarket Close. Heels clicking on the cobbles, she zigzagged her way up the hill, past Patrick Wheatley's abandoned office with its jaunty slogan 'A Wheatley defence makes sense', intent upon joining the High Street at the City Chambers.

In Parliament Square a few mourners had congregated by the Mercat Cross, huddling together before entering the cathedral for the Sheriff's funeral. She walked past them into the dimly-lit interior and was handed a copy of the Order of Service. A vacant seat near the Chapel of Youth caught her eye and she sat down, oblivious to the scowl on the life-size statue of John Knox guarding it. Self-conscious at being unaccompanied, she raised her eyes to the stained glass and began examining the depictions of John the Baptist and King Solomon, as if they were of genuine interest. Around her the few remaining seats in the row were being taken and a sudden hush fell over those assembled, as the minister, clad in robes of black and purple, climbed the stone steps to the pulpit. The service began with the hymn 'O Love That Wilt Not Let Me Go'. As the strains of Heward's melody burst forth from the massive organ pipes, she looked about her to survey those within the Kirk. She had expected St Giles to be packed to the gunwales, standing room only, but the elderly congregation filled no more than twelve rows. The female members of the establishment present seemed to favour wide-brimmed hats, velvet berets and veiled pill-boxes to cover their white locks, and their few remaining spouses wore Crombie overcoats to a man, some sporting sombre black ties, others regimental stripes. Gathered beneath a large marble relief of embattled warriors was a discrete group, clad exclusively in black and white, the uniform of the legal profession on duty. On further scrutiny Alice recognised the faces of Lords Cairncross, Darling and Thorburn, their features branded onto her memory from her High Court trial appearances as a witness. One of the women seemed familiar too: Lady Schaw, the trial judge for the Gravestone Rapist.

A second hymn, 'Immortal, Invisible, God Only Wise', started up, and the sparse crowd did their best to breathe life into it. While fumbling for the correct page, Alice became aware of an alien aroma, brandy, and as she was speculating on its origin an elderly man shuffled past her, extending his stride on reaching the northern aisle. There, he raised his head, lifted his shoulders and marched, as if on parade, towards the pulpit.

His accent was that of the former ruling class, with clipped vowels and staccato sentences, and his voice boomed out in the cavernous space, magnified unnecessarily by the sound system. The address that he gave was short, factual and without frills or any sign of emotion. It was more like the Sheriff's entry in *Who's Who* than any kind of funeral tribute. The congregation was informed that James Henry Freeman had attended public school at Wellington College, Berkshire, where he excelled academically and had been captain of the rifle team. At Edinburgh University he had achieved a first class degree in

Law, the foundation for his subsequent meteoric career at the Bar. For five years in the sixties he had been the Sheriff in Haddington prior to obtaining his shrieval post in Edinburgh. On the bench his reputation was for a keen mind combined with a kind manner, and his industry, in this office, was second to none. The speaker paused briefly, re-adjusting his notes before continuing in the same authoritative tone. James had been a bachelor to the end, and had been sustained throughout his life by his strong Christian faith, albeit not as a churchgoer. He was, in short, a true Christian gentleman, and his premature death, a little more than a fortnight earlier, represented a great loss to the legal profession and, of course, a great personal loss to his only remaining family, his younger brother Christopher.

After the old fellow had cautiously descended the stone stairs, the minister resumed his place in the pulpit, neck now shrunk into his robes like a tortoise's in its shell, and gave the briefest of addresses, excusing its slightness on the basis of his lack of personal acquaintance with the deceased. He ended it with two stark announcements. Firstly, all donations were to be made to the Earl Haig Poppy Fund, and secondly, a luncheon had been laid on in St Andrew's Church Hall at Holy Corner, and all who wished to attend would be welcome to do so. On cue, the organ began to play the introduction to the final hymn.

Listening to the first few bars, Alice began to relax. Her unspoken fear that the service might provide too forcible a reminder of her mother's mortality had proved groundless, the tissues remaining dry in her pocket. And then a beautiful soprano voice rang out, heart-rendingly pure, shattering her complacency and all but undoing her. She concentrated, as intensely as if her life depended upon it, on an inscription on a brass plaque, until she could be sure that the moment of weakness had passed, that she would remain the owner of her face.

As the mourners filed out, the Gunns, both dry-eyed, were

at the front of the queue attempting to manoeuvre themselves round a small man who was stationary, sobbing unashamedly. Nearer the middle was Mrs Nordquist, her face partly hidden by the brim of her straw boater, but her eyes were exposed, red and tear-stained. Alice caught up with her by the Signet Library, where she had paused to slip on a pair of dark glasses. Recognising the policewoman, she spoke, as if sensing that some explanation for her condition might be required.

'Funerals! It could be a deat ratt in the box ant I'd be weeping… I'm off home now for a goot, strong drink.' But her breath suggested that she had refuelled already.

⸺

Few made the journey to the Church Hall, and a desultory affair the wake turned out to be. Metallic Women's Institute-style teapots were in service, and the food would have disgraced a post-war austerity street party, consisting entirely of white bread egg-and-cress sandwiches and angel cakes. Its unabashed stinginess contrasted uneasily with the ancient splendour of St Giles and the evident affluence of most of the guests.

The host appeared to be the Sheriff's brother, Christopher, and Alice watched him as she took sips from a mug of bitter Indian tea. His leathery skin suggested a twenty-a-day habit, all deep lines and furrows, and white stubble shone in little, isolated patches on his chin, confirming, with the crusted blood on one cheek, the use of a blunt razor. His clothes were those of the no longer well-to-do of his class: frayed collar, elbow patches and a dark pin-stripe, glistening with wear. Only his brogues were impeccable, black and shiny, as if rarely liberated from their shoe-trees.

She noticed that his heavy-lidded eyes were scanning the room, checking who had turned up, and occasionally he chatted animatedly to a guest, pressing an angel cake on them as if it was Beluga caviar.

After an hour the numbers dwindled further as the old brigade took their leave, kissing each other's powdery cheeks before heading slowly back to their well-polished cars. While farewells were still being exchanged, a woman busied herself scooping the sandwiches off the plates into polythene bags, and putting the remaining cakes into a Tupperware box.

'They'll do for the dogs,' she said to her husband as he passed her, carrying a pile of stacked white plates into the scullery area.

'Good thinking, darling, they'll wolf them down.'

As Christopher Freeman was washing dishes at the sink, Alice introduced herself to him and he extracted a hand from the soapsuds to shake hers.

'I didn't know you people attended funerals, too, but thank you for coming.'

'We usually do, sir, as a mark of respect, you understand. Also we've had such difficulty in speaking to you, we need information if we are to find out who killed your brother. I've phoned your house numerous times but…'

'I know, I know,' he interrupted, 'I'm sorry, I've been busy making arrangements… you know, like funerals, wakes, that kind of thing. I did say after I'd identified the body, that poor Mop woman being well nigh hysterical, that I'd get back in touch with you.'

'I appreciate that, sir, and I really do apologise for intruding at such a time…'

'Don't worry, you're not "intruding at such a time", actually, but Sandra and I really do have to go. I simply cannot speak now, we're off to a dentist's appointment, and before that this place has to be cleaned up. You can come to the house, tomorrow, say at three o'clock. You've got my address in Frogston Road West, right?'

'Yes. Thank you, sir,' Alice said wearily, eager to leave and not in a position to object.

DI Manson lay sprawled across his chair, hands clasped behind his head and feet crossed on the desk. He had just returned from the forensic laboratory, where he had learned that despite the murderer's attempts to clean up after himself, traces of the Sheriff's blood, tissue and hair had been found adhering to an enamelled truncheon retrieved from Moray Place. He snuffled idly in his bag of crisps, examining the crevices for any further salty crumbs to extract, and then licked his fingers. He was bored, unwilling to rise and annotate the white board with the new information.

'Alice, dear, would you do me a favour?'

She looked up from the statement that she was marking, nerves on edge from the very word 'dear'. Little he said to her was not topped or tailed by 'dear', 'love', 'pet' or some other term of affection—used, she was convinced, to belittle her or deliberately irritate her. And as he had calculated, she had never remonstrated with him, feeling the slight to be too intangible, petty even, so he used the terms freely, watching as his little jabs went home.

'Sir?' At least she did not sound rattled.

'Would you write on the clean board some information for me? Under "weapon" put "truncheon"—ironic or what—and then add "traces of the deceased's hair, tissue and blood".'

'Anything else, Sir, before I sit down?' She knew his tricks.

'Well, yes, Alice. Put in "Alien DNA (A) on two doorknobs: drawing room door—external and internal: front door—external and internal. Within the house Alien DNA (B) present throughout the house".'

She resumed her seat, picked up her marker pen and began to re-apply her brain to the paperwork. Just as she was again lost in concentration DI Manson spoke, once more breaking the spell, his timing perfect to annoy.

'By the way, Alice, I'm coming with you tomorrow. To Frogston Road, I mean. It's been actioned by the boss. I don't know why, you could have handled it yourself,' he paused, '...I expect. Mind you, he'll be twitchy. Two weeks gone already and sweet Fanny Adams to show for it. Nothing will be left to chance now.'

The pool car had all the signs of being unloved, nobody's car, the passenger floor littered with sweet-wrappers and the air freshener, a little set of traffic lights, overwhelmed by its task, unable to cloak the smells of stale smoke and body odour. DI Manson was at the wheel, displaying his usual mixture of un-provoked aggression and unexplained hesitation, and Alice mused on the conclusions to be drawn from the way a man drives to the way he'd make love. Only a ghastly experience could be anticipated from this quarter; no thoughtfulness, no smoothness, no rhythm... the list of 'nos' was endless. And then, as if reading her thoughts, the inspector said casually: 'Has the vacancy been filled yet, Alice?'

'Which one, Sir?'

'Don't be coy, dear, you know very well. The "Tall, slim young lady, cultured, intelligent, GSOH, seeks... anything male".'

She attempted a good-natured laugh, playing for time as if no answer was called for, but he persisted.

'Well? I hope you don't mind me asking...'

It was all too close to the bone. Attack might well be the best form of defence.

'You seem strangely well acquainted with the vocabulary of the Lonely Hearts columns, Sir. Mrs Manson back from her Easter holiday yet? I heard it's another long one... she left in, must have been February, wasn't it?'

DI Manson brought the car to a sudden halt, using the

handbrake for the final few inches of momentum, and Alice was hurtled forwards; they had arrived at their destination.

The front door was opened by the woman Alice had seen collecting sandwiches at the funeral, and two black standard poodles rushed out of the bungalow to greet the visitors. They jumped all over the Inspector, dark eyes invisible in their black fur and their unclipped tails waving like mediaeval banners in a strong breeze. One of them then scampered across the pavement and began leaping up to the window of a parked Volkswagon Polo. The white car was unwashed and decorated with stickers on the back window proclaiming allegiance to the RSPB and support for 'Vertenergy—Wind Power for a Clean, Green Future'.

'Off our car, Pepe, come on, sweetie,' Mrs Freeman cooed in an unnaturally high register, her Essex origins still discernible in her voice, and, unexpectedly, the poodle's claws clattered off the vehicle as it rejoined its mistress.

If the furnishings of the house at Moray Place looked as if James Freeman had inherited them from an unbroken line of well-heeled ancestors, the furnishings in his brother's bungalow looked as if they had been acquired, cut-price, at a warrant sale of household goods. But in amongst the bric-a-brac a discerning eye would have detected some anomalous pieces. A solid silver Georgian sugar bowl sat on the Formica-topped kitchen table, an ornate-framed pier glass hung on a wall in the narrow hallway, and in the sitting room there was a bureau-cabinet veneered with satinwood, empty now of Meissen or Dresden porcelain, filled instead with slant-eyed kittens rolling balls of wool and be-hatted donkeys pulling carts, all made in China.

Christopher Freeman seated himself at the kitchen table beside his wife, leaning towards her as if to inhale the smoke from her cigarette. Against one of the walls a pile of carrier bags, full and from Jenners, John Lewis and Hamilton and Inches, lay waiting to be unpacked.

Taking the initiative, DI Manson pulled out a seat and gestured for Alice to do the same.

'Mr Freeman, thank you for seeing us.'

'Major Freeman, Inspector.'

'Well, sir, Major, what we need is information, just general information about your brother. Some indication as to the sort of life he lived, the sort of man he was.'

'Mean,' Mrs Freeman giggled.

'Now, Sandra,' her husband said, in a semi-jovial remonstration, before continuing: 'My brother, Inspector, was... now, let me think,' he paused. 'Well, to be entirely frank with you, we didn't see eye to eye. Haven't for years. I used to see him at family funerals but rarely otherwise. He was a lawyer, moved in that sort of society, I think. He didn't have much time—'

'—for a feckless wastrel,' his wife interjected, giggling again.

'... for me,' the Major continued, 'or I for him or his kind.'

'You never met him even socially?' DI Manson asked.

'No, we never met him at all,' Mrs Freeman chipped in. 'He didn't like me, or Chris, for that matter. He'd got everything he needed, and that didn't include us.'

'Got everything?' Alice enquired.

'You know, the eldest son, primogenitals... what's it called, Chris?'

'Primogeniture,' the Major corrected.

Mrs Freeman continued. 'So, James scooped the lot. The house in Moray Place, most of the money, all of the farms...'

'No, no, we share Blackstone Mains, darling.'

'Just as bloody well, too!' she said hotly, drawing deeply on her Silk-cut.

Before her husband had a chance to reply, DI Manson intervened again: 'Was the Sheriff ever married... did he have any children?'

'Goodness, no! Far too uptight to form "a welationship"

40

with anyone—any woman for sure—a stranger to "lurve",' Mrs Freeman said disdainfully.

'My brother couldn't say his "Rs",' the Major explained, grinning.

'When did you last see him?' Alice asked.

Mrs Freeman answered. 'Cousin David's funeral, I think, and that would be over seven years ago... maybe six years ago, what do you think, Chris? It was certainly before you lost that little job with those estate agents, showing people over houses.'

'Who should we talk to, to get some impression of your brother?' DI Manson asked impatiently.

'I really don't know,' the Major replied. 'We communicated largely by letter, Christmas cards and so on, or the odd telephone call. He must have had friends, maybe some of the people at the funeral? Mind you, most of them were old friends of the family, not of him personally. Best try his work colleagues, if any of them are still alive.'

～

That evening in the cramped back room of the Clearwater Diving School Alice sat next to her friend, Bridget, filled in the register and passed it to the man on her right.

'Who's Mrs Norton?' she whispered to her.

'Me, obviously.'

'Why on earth?'

'I'll be more mysterious as a divorced woman. I'm too old to be a sodding spinster. I'm not signing in as Miss Norton or Msss bloody Norton. Are you Miss Rice tonight?'

'Of course. I thought half the point of the classes was to meet available men.'

'Well, this crew's much better than the car maintenance lot, I can tell you that for nothing,' Bridget said. 'These ones can speak, the mechanics just grunted at each other, and that one… is not bad-looking.' And she pointed a finger, unobtrusively, on her lap at a man sitting opposite them.

Once they had all changed they were paired-up for manoeuvres in the pool. Alice waddled, practically doubled-up, to the water's edge, weighed down by a massive lead belt and cylinders and encased in an unflattering skin-tight wetsuit. Tripping on a flipper, she smiled weakly at her companion, a balding surveyor from Leith, as they began to practise the hand signals that they had been taught for 'OK', 'distress' and 'danger', prior to immersion. As she lumbered into the water, she noted through her mask that Bridget had been buddied with the last person to join the group, a man too beer-bellied for any of the available wetsuits and who, when asked to introduce himself to the class, had described himself as 'a successful entrepreneur in waste management'. While Bridget was flopping into the pool, the man continued talking to her until she disappeared below the surface in a whirlpool of bubbles, swiftly followed by him.

On meeting her friend underwater at the deep end, Alice flourished an 'OK' hand signal at her and nearly choked on her regulator when Bridget turned sideways to face her and then, gesturing at the entrepreneur, signalled 'tosser' in a speedy hand movement.

Quill played with a piece of greasy wrapping paper on the floor of the kitchen as Alice emptied the remains of her fish supper into the bin. She poured herself a glass of white wine and went to phone her mother.

'Mum, how are you tonight?'

'The wound's still a little sore, darling, but so far so good, no swelling in my armpit and we got wonderful news today. They've checked the lymph nodes and they're all clear, so I've only got radiotherapy now, no chemotherapy.'

'I'm so glad, I can't tell you how pleased I am. Dad must be thrilled too.'

'He certainly is, and so am I. We found a bottle of champagne in a cupboard and it's finished already. I'll have to go back to the Western in a month or so to get inked up for the radiotherapy, but I've only to have five weeks' worth of doses, so with luck I'll be all clear by my birthday. How was your first sub-aqua lesson?'

'Fine. Fun. I'll persevere and try and get my open water certificate, I think. I don't know if Bridget will carry on though, she's already talking about electrical engineering courses.'

4

He brushed the bee, nonchalantly, off his bare hand and lifted the first layer from the hive. Every year the supers seemed to get heavier, and yet, paradoxically, they contained no more honey. Fitting his hive tool between two filled frames, Sir Archibald Learmonth levered one loose and then carefully raised it to examine the white seal covering either side. Nowadays, he strained to see anything through the fine gauze of his bee veil, and he cursed modern beekeeping equipment; it made the beeman's task well nigh impossible. He swung the frame forwards and backwards in order to see if any honey would escape from the few remaining uncapped cells. No, the sticky fluid remained inside, so he added the frame to his pile for extraction. Next, the checking of the brood boxes to see what the varroa was up to. Picking up his capping fork from the roof of a nearby hive, he raised his trembling hand over an area of drone brood, before stabbing the fork into it and examining the larva impaled on its tines for any signs of the mite. Good, not a single black speck to be seen, those expensive strips had done their business. Carefully, he wiped the whitish goo off the fork onto the bird table. Another treat for the blue tits.

Under his broad hat he gradually became aware of a tapping sound, and looked round to see his wife at the window signalling for him to come in. Blast her! The job was only half done, and he'd just put a new cardboard cartridge inside the smoker; most of it would be wasted now. What on earth could be so important that it could not wait until the whole job had been done? He would have to explain to her, again, that the bees did not like being disturbed, and therefore any operation that had to be carried out on them must be allowed to be completed in order to avoid too many disturbances. Crossly, he re-built the hive, replacing the queen-excluder, stacking the supers, topping the whole with the crown board and the roof. He gathered together his full combs, swept the few remaining bees off with a large feather and headed towards the back door, his morning ruined.

Inside the kitchen of his Heriot Row house, the former Sheriff Principal of Lothian and Borders pulled off his hat and veil and then collapsed into an armchair, extending his legs and allowing his wife, wordlessly, to bend down and pull off his green Wellington boots. Hairy woollen socks encased his legs, and the elderly woman casually flicked a bee off one of them into a glass tumbler, before releasing the creature back into the garden.

Alice introduced herself and the old fellow, now mollified with a cup of tea and a biscuit, turned his attention to her.

'I've come to see you in connection with the death of one of your brother Sheriffs, James Freeman. I understand that he was under you until he retired about ten years ago. I wondered if you could tell me anything about him,' she began.

The Sheriff nodded benignly, crunching his mouthful of ginger snap, before replying: 'Perhaps you could be more specific, Detective Sergeant Rice. What sort of thing exactly would you like to know?'

'Just about anything you can tell me, Sir. His job—was he good at it, for example?'

'I couldn't fault him. He was absolutely first rate, always completely reliable, never shirked anything, including the residence stuff or even crime. His judgements were routinely well written and well reasoned, and he was very rarely overturned. Of course, he loathed our administrators, everyone does, but he took his turn on committees and so forth. As you are probably aware, for most of his time in Edinburgh, I was in Perth, but he was one of my Sheriffs for his last three years up until his retiral.'

'Did you know anything about his personal life?'

The Sheriff looked keenly at Alice from beneath his unruly eyebrows, and when he spoke he sounded wary.

'Very little. In fact, only what James chose to tell me. Obviously, as an unmarried man, albeit elderly, there were rumours—there always are—but I paid scant attention to them. I have been the subject of gossip in my time, plenty of it, so I don't place much credence on such tittle tattle... however entertaining it may be.'

'And what did Mr Freeman choose to tell you?'

'Almost nothing. Simply that he had never married and would now never marry.'

'And the rumours?'

'Surely you can imagine?' the Sheriff said impatiently. 'Girls, boys, sheep—two legs good, four legs better—that kind of thing. It must happen in your own workplace. Certainly, the idle tongues waiting to be exercised in the ordinary Court enjoy nothing better than clacking about the orientation of those around them, any new liaisons or break-ups, no-one's safe, but it's all pretty harmless.'

'I know Sheriff Freeman retired a good while ago, but can you think of anyone who might have a grievance against him, having been locked up by him or whatever?'

The retired judge sighed. 'No. Most of the young neds he sentenced will be middle-aged men with their own children in tow now. Maybe even householders. Anyway, he didn't end up with much crime. You see he was happy to listen to endless debates, complicated skirmishes over contractual terms and the like, civil proofs; and many of his brethren were less amenable to that sort of thing so they tended to get... well, the crime. Furthermore, any malcontent dealt with by him would have waited a very long time for revenge, and frankly, as a motive I find it pretty implausible.'

'Did you ever visit his house in Moray Place?'

'No, nor did he ever come here. I never went to Geanbank either. We weren't friends in that way.'

'Geanbank?'

'It's his house in Kinross-shire, somewhere near Carnbo. Deep in the countryside, I believe. Maybe you'd even get heather honey there…'

A precious afternoon off and here she was supping with the devil in a seedy bar in Roseburn. It had come to this. Alice savoured the taste of the white wine on her palate, oblivious to the incessant chatter of the man by her side. She sensed his eyes on her, uncomfortably aware that his real object was to possess her, not just any information she might choose to impart to him. It was nothing personal, any woman would do. And this time she had nothing to tell him and, worse, he had lured her to the pub on false pretences; he had no news either and his bar-room patter was no substitute. What the hell. They both understood the value of their relationship; the need to nurture and preserve it. Her companion, a pasty-faced crime reporter, finished his cheese toasty, offered Alice a refill and, when she declined on the pretext of her imminent return to the office, snatched up his jacket and hurried off in order to catch the four thirty at Musselburgh.

As she raised her glass for the final swig, Alice became aware that the newly vacated seat beside her had become occupied. Turning, she found herself looking into the dark brown eyes of Ian Melville and saw him flinch as their eyes met; he had not expected to meet her in O'Riordans. Perhaps he had not expected to meet her ever again, and his disquiet on doing so could not be disguised. No wonder. Not so long ago he had been a murder suspect pursued by her, interrogated by her, afraid of her, and now here they were sitting together, side by side, like old friends. As she made to rise, he spoke.

'Stay, Alice, please. I didn't mean to disturb you. If it bothers you I'll move… there are plenty of other tables.' It sounded genuine.

'Thanks for the offer,' she heard herself say, 'but there's no need to go. I'd welcome the company.'

And it was true. His company would be welcome, but she had, somehow, expected her brain to bridle her mouth as it usually did, keep back the truth and give only some anodyne reply, nothing as forward as a welcome. It must be the drink. But he had remembered her name, and no longer required, in using it, to preface it with her rank, and she had remembered his. The sparring that they had engaged in during those tense interviews the previous year meant, in some bizarre way, that they knew each other. No. Correction. The truth was that she knew a fair amount about him, but he knew little of her. He was a painter, a good one; he had proved himself, ultimately, to be an honest man. He was rational and loyal. And, to his eternal credit, he had taken an immediate dislike to DI Manson and had, without difficulty, routed him. Finally, she had always found his irregular, angular features alluring. Others could feast their eyes on fair-haired men with perfect, symmetrical faces. They left her unmoved.

Forty minutes later they left the pub together and strolled down the steps that led to the walkway running alongside the Water of Leith, inhaling the scent of brewing effluent and lime blossom that accompanied the river on its winding course through the city. Deep in conversation they passed through the cold shadow cast by the Belford Bridge, high above them, their words echoing eerily within the archway, past the Dean Village and on to the final stretch that led to Stockbridge and their immediate destination. Opposite the Rotunda of St Bernard's

Well their hands linked, though neither of them was conscious of having taken any initiative.

—

The sign for Geanbank was nailed to the picket fence that marked the entrance to the driveway on the Carnbo to Cauldstones Road. The drive itself was flanked on either side by wild cherry trees, giving the place its name, and the fields beyond contained Highland cattle, long-haired and red-coated, their tails flicking incessantly to ward off the summer flies. Swallows chattered under the eaves of the house, their nests clinging perilously to the deep arches of the gothic windows where the mud used by them had splashed onto the soft yellow render of the building. The double front doors were locked, so Alice followed the perimeter of the house to the back door, but received no response when she rang the bell.

Stretching behind the house was a large walled garden and she looked in wonder at its perfect order. A caged area for soft fruit: raspberries, strawberries, black currants and red currants; straw laid lovingly beneath them all. Apple trees, espaliered, and row upon row of neat vegetables, each bed provided with the additional shelter of a dwarf privet hedge and not a single weed in sight. A feat that could surely only have been achieved by an Edwardian staff of gardeners. The shrill cry of a cockerel drew her attention to the farthest corner of the enclosed ground and she moved towards the noise—maybe someone would be feeding the chickens. On arrival, she saw a group of Light Sussex hens scratching up the earth and, occasionally, pecking at a stray grain of corn. All sure signs of life, but still nobody about.

She returned to the front of the house and noticed, for the first time, a figure in the distance, busy at the far end of the lawn tending to a wide herbaceous border. By the time she reached the man she was breathless. He was dressed in faded dungarees and a battered cap protected his head from the sun.

'Excuse me, are you one of the gardeners here?'

'Yes, I do the garden.'

Her enquiries were interrupted by a call from Detective Inspector Manson on her mobile phone. The tone of his voice conveyed urgency, that this was to be a monologue to which attention must be paid. If she had checked out Geanbank then she should return to the office immediately, as DCI Bruce had ordered the whole squad to attend the next meeting, re-scheduled for two pm. If she left now and put her foot down she'd miss nothing.

——

This village shop, Alice thought irritably, should have gone out of business long ago with the rest of them. The days when shopkeepers could lean on their counters exchanging local gossip with every shopper, however paltry their purchase, were thankfully over and their replacement with brightly-lit, soulless supermarkets could only be a cause for rejoicing.

'Well, ma lass, what can ah dae fer ye?'

'Just the crisps and the Irn Bru, thanks.'

The old lady fingered the crisp packets and can before placing them slowly in a carrier bag and, smiling up at Alice, apparently quite unconscious of her customer's impatience, she continued with her chat.

'Ye're just visiting, eh?'

'That's it.' Such brevity should convey the hint.

'Who were ye seein'?'

None of your business. 'I was at Geanbank. I just saw the gardener there and now I've got to hurry back to Edinburgh.'

'Gairdner, there's nae gairdner there. Just Nicholas.'

'Sorry? What did you say?'

'Ah says there's nae gairdner at Geanbank. Just Nicholas... well, ye ken...'

'I'm sorry, I'm not sure what you mean.'

'Och, he's a fine man, dinnae git me wrang. But he's no' the Sheriff's gairdner, no, no. He daes the gairden a'richt. Daes it well, an a'. But he's no the man's gairdner... He's his—well, ken, his wife, ye could cry him. Ma sister cleans their hoose. They've separate rooms but—ah kent the both o' them fer the last ten year since they moved... Well, ye can tell, eh? Live an' let live, ah always say, but Nicholas's nae the gairdner.'

'What's Nicholas's surname?'

'Lyon. Ah always thocht he wis mair the lioness though...' She chuckled merrily, pleased with her own joke, before her laughter turned itself into a bubbling cough.

⎯

Nicholas Lyon did not put down the string he was weaving around the peonies when he saw the Astra return to the gravel sweep. He wound another length of it between their reddish stems and then tethered the twine, finally, to a thin metal support. It had to be done. Otherwise a strong wind could come at any time and destroy the plants, never mind the damage the rain would do, rotting their glorious crimson heads while they were still tight in bud. He had done all he could to protect them and, if he had the time, he'd stake the delphiniums too. James loved delphiniums, 'delphiniums (blue) and geraniums (red)' and neither of them had ever tolerated chrysanthemums in any colour. The woman approaching him seemed to be quite young, the same one he had seen before; her leaving had seemed too good to be true.

'Mr Lyon? I'm Detective Sergeant Alice Rice of Lothian and Borders Police. Could we go inside the house? I'd like to talk to you.'

Looking at the elderly gentleman putting the kettle on the Aga in his kitchen, Alice cursed her own stupidity. Of course the face was familiar, she could place him now. He was the fellow she had seen at the Sheriff's service, sobbing, overcome by grief. The image of him had remained fixed in her mind simply because at the funeral he had been almost the only one, bar Mrs Nordquist, to exhibit any kind of sorrow.

'Mr Lyon, I need to talk to you about the Sheriff, James Freeman.'

The old man nodded his assent as he poured out the tea into two mugs. But his eyes never met hers, they flitted nervously to the floor, to the ceiling, left and right, and all the while he blinked copiously.

'I understand that you lived together?'

The question had come, as he had known it would. Nicholas Lyon thought long and hard before replying, although he had already allowed himself ample time to rehearse any response. 'Lived together.' He knew exactly what was meant by this apparently innocuous phrase. That he and James lived together as homosexuals, inverts, nancies or whatever... There were few such objectionable epithets with which he was not familiar. People must have known, of course they must, but never the people that counted. Or, if those people had known, then it had not mattered as James had been so discreet. He, both of them, had never chosen to venture out of the closet. Maybe it was claustrophobic inside, but, fortunately, they had only ever needed each other and, anyway, it had been necessary. Many, no doubt, had found it suffocating, undignified certainly, but they had coped and nothing in James' private life had prevented him from becoming a QC nor, eventually, from being elevated onto the Shrieval bench.

If such involuntary incarceration had been the price for his career then they had paid it. And when the militants had gone mad and smashed the closet doors around them to sawdust, he and James had declined to join in, having become accustomed to their private retreat and the double life that society had, once, enforced upon them. It was too difficult, breaking

52

the habits of a lifetime. Of course, James had been a master of the half-truth, the distraction. He was a verbal-impressionist: a single well-chosen word and the inquisitors would create for themselves some unsuitable female consort for him, her non-appearance immediately explicable to them, and they would secretly pat themselves on the back for their perspicacity in the face of such subtlety. Others again, just assumed that he was asexual, had no 'passionate parts', and, insulting as it was, he let it pass. 'Confirmed bachelors' were not threatening and needed no further investigation.

It was just a case of triggering expectations, people seeing what they expected to see despite the truth staring them in the face. And with his simple assent their well-worn carapace would be stripped away, never to be replaced. Still, no harm could now come to James or his career with such an admission, and pretence would be futile, maybe even dangerous. A private life was a thing of the past.

'Yes,' Nicholas replied baldly, interlinking his fingers to control the shaking that had begun in his hands.

'For many years?'

'For forty-five years and three months exactly.'

'Why didn't you come forward to help us... when the Sheriff was killed? You must have known; it was in all the papers.'

Another simple question to which no simple answer could be provided. Difficult to think where to begin, but a start must be made somewhere. The incompatibility of their early relationship with James' advancement, perhaps? Or the motor neurone disease? The amitriptyline, even? Something must be said, seconds were ticking by. But Christ, what? He felt like a snail being torn out of its shell, soon to be exposed in all its vulnerability.

'I'll tell you, Sergeant, as best as I can.' She appeared sympathetic; maybe she would listen, even comprehend. Certainly, silence was no longer an option.

'My relationship with James has never been public. If it had been you would have been here much sooner. We are just an old married couple really… but nobody, well almost nobody, knew that. I mean KNEW that. Some suspected, maybe others guessed. James' career had to be protected, you see, and to be honest, his privacy, our privacy… what business was it of anyone else? But the tabloids would have taken a prurient interest in James—gay Sheriff found dead—in both of us, I suppose. Now? Now, maybe it is acceptable, but then it wasn't, and we got used to things the way they were. Why should he, or I, put up with being called an "old poof" and all the other far more unpleasant things that go with such a label? Why should we, on sufferance only, be allowed into polite society? And what a misnomer that is! We managed very well without them all.'

'So, you didn't come forward as you didn't want the nature of your relationship to become public?'

'Yes, that's partially true. It was part of the reason, but there was another, too, which you may or may not understand…' His speech ended, nervousness having drained him of all energy. It felt so unreal, listening to his own voice laying bare their lives, exposing secrets that should have gone to the grave with them.

'Go on, please, Mr Lyon.'

'About eight months ago James began to have difficulty with his words. Not in remembering them or anything like that. More, in articulating them, his voice changed and his speech seemed to become slurred. Sometimes badly so, especially when he was tired. Next thing, he couldn't swallow his food, kept choking, and it frightened him. It frightened me, too, actually. I had to learn the Heimlich manoeuvre, for all the good it did. Eventually, I bullied him into seeing a neurologist, and the man carried out various tests, scans and so on and then we got the news…' The old man paused again as if reliving the moment.

'The news?' Alice prompted.

'The news that he had motor neurone disease, a form of it anyway, something called "progressive bulbar palsy" to be exact. James's intelligence would remain unaffected but, slowly, inexorably, crucial muscles would cease to function until, eventually, he wouldn't be able to breathe unassisted.'

'Why would that mean that you wouldn't come forward when James was murdered?'

'I am coming to that,' the man said reproachfully, twisting and untwisting his hands. 'James was a very determined man, you know. I would have nursed him until the end, I didn't care. But he decreed otherwise and was implacable. He decided that he would end his own life. The thought of God's reaction troubled him for a bit, but he concluded that no benign deity, worthy of such a name, would expect any creature to suffer a slow, terrifying death if an alternative quick, clean one was available. Even if that alternative death was suicide. So, he began planning his end. He did it meticulously, like everything else he did. He didn't fancy Switzerland, that… er… Dignitas set-up. He chose the house in Moray Place. He used the house, particularly, during the week, and I think he saw it as the home of his ancestors in an almost Japanese way and thought it would be fitting to return—to wherever—from there. Also, and crucially, he didn't want me involved in any way.'

'Involved in what respect?'

'In his suicide. If he had done it in Geanbank then… well, that was ours. Our home. I almost never went to Moray Place. It had always been his, whatever other houses we owned. He was going to take my amitriptyline—old stuff, I got it when my mother died—and the Brahms double violin concerto. Said he'd like to go listening to celestial music with a dram or two for company. I suspected when he left here on Monday afternoon that he'd determined to do it that evening. He'd choked at lunchtime and some of the muscles in his tongue had begun to twitch. Anyway, it was so different when he said goodbye. He didn't cry or anything like that, James almost never cried, but he looked hollow... lost... it's hard to explain. I tried to talk to him about it, but he wouldn't. He said if I had no involvement, knew nothing about it, then I'd be quite safe from the Police. I phoned the house the next morning and there was no reply. I was in the process of collecting my things to go there when Liv called.'

'Liv?' Alice interrupted.

'Liv Nordquist, our neighbour. She knew—about us, I mean. James trusted her completely. She knew about the disease too. She told me that James had been murdered... and that you, the Police, were already involved. So I've been waiting for you to come.'

Finally, Nicholas Lyon looked into the policewoman's eyes and she nodded her head for him to continue.

'That's it, really. Why I didn't come forward. In the papers it wasn't "Gay Sheriff found murdered". No. No-one could speculate about some homosexual crime of passion, or any of that sort of thing. And, yes, I believed that James was going to die that night but not... that he was going to be killed. I reckoned you'd come to me in the end. You see, James had lived as straight in the world, but my very existence made that a lie. And all I cared about, then, was that he was dead. Nothing else mattered.'

——

After the policewoman had gone, Nicholas Lyon wandered into the rose garden, desperate to calm himself, to restore his shattered nerves and dispel the fears that seemed to have taken control of his mind. A momentous change had occurred and it had happened against his will. Now, the known had become the unknown; the familiar, unfamiliar; and in this new, unwelcome environment he would have to survive.

'Tuna fish today—nice chunks of greasy... eh, flesh. How would that suit you, Quill?'

Miss Spinnell opened the cupboard above the sink and scrabbled blindly inside, delving for the chosen tin. Two forefingers landed in a pool of oil and she withdrew them quickly, smelling them before reaching back inside and extracting the opened can.

'They've done it again,' she muttered to herself, 'drinking the very milk from my cartons, and now the very... dog flesh... from my, eh... eh... tinister... boxes.'

Quill's dish was soon full of a strange assortment of ingredients from the store cupboard, but he gobbled it down greedily before lapping up the bowl of Ribena that had been thoughtfully laid out for him.

When Alice arrived and knocked on the old woman's door she was surprised by the silence that greeted her before Miss Spinnell's thin voice could be heard. Where were the usual clanks, clicks and rattles that always heralded the relaxing of her domestic security, appropriate for a nuclear reactor, protecting her Broughton Place flat ? The door did not open its usual ten inches, a single chain remaining, for inspection of all visitors.

'What do you want, caller?' The tone sounded surprisingly aggressive.

'It's just me, Miss Spinnell, I've come to collect Quill.'

'I'm afraid that will be quite impossible tonight, I'll have to keep him with me. I have been locked in here by those rogues. My door, simply, will not... out... ehm... open.'

Alice sighed. Work had been arduous enough without having to endure the additional burden imposed on her by her neighbour's gradual loss of all remaining wits.

'Perhaps, if you undid the locks, the internal ones, you could free yourself?' she said slowly, attempting to keep the

57

impatience she felt out of her voice, reminding herself of her beholden state.

The reply sounded querulous, doubtful: 'I'll give it a try, this once.'

The usual cacophony of metal on metal could be heard before the door swung open to reveal a slightly startled, blinking, Miss Spinnell with Quill sitting beside her, restrained by a lead.

'Your dog must be tested,' the old lady said stiffly.

Alice was baffled. 'Tested? Tested for what?'

Miss Spinnell's bulging eyeballs, in unison for once, travelled heavenwards. It was all so obvious. How could this so-called policewoman (God help us all) not understand?

'His hearing. A hearing test. Men—men—I repeat, MEN... have been in my flat and locked the pair of us in, but was there so much as a howl, a growl, a bark even, to warn me? There was not. This... this,' she struggled for the word 'this... eh, horse...this hound... has a hearing problem and a carefree... er, caring owner would have detected it eons ago. Things could, possibly, then have been done, but it will be too late now. Poor Quill must be stone deaf.'

So saying, she patted Quill's soft head before blithely issuing her order, 'Off you go, boy.'

The phone rang in Alice's flat. It was Alistair. Thankfully, no effort would be required.

'Did Bruce have a go at you, too?'

'Yes. I missed the meeting completely. I gather you did too. Not a great start, eh?'

'Nope. How did you get on at Freeman's other place?'

'Well, it's a long, long story. I met the Sheriff's other half and I reckon that the plentiful alien DNA in Moray Place will turn out to have come from that source.'

'Why on earth didn't she come forward?'

'Because she's a he.'

'Oh, really! Do you...'

'Hang on, there's more. On the night he was killed the poor bastard was attempting to do away with himself.'

'Christ! Why?'

'Nicholas, his partner, told me that the Sheriff had motor neurone disease and didn't want to wait and let the illness take its natural course.'

'And did you believe the man?'

'Yes, I did. Why wouldn't I? I'm not sure what I'd do if I found out I had something like that. Freeman, apparently, took an overdose of amitriptyline. I think I might well choose to opt out, too.'

'Maybe, but when his partner was killed he didn't appear, didn't help us in any way whatsoever, and that's bloody odd, I'd say. He might have told you about the amy... whatever, in the knowledge that an explanation would be required—for the drug I mean. Any idiot would know there'd bound to be a PM.'

'True, but there was nothing at the post mortem to suggest that the Sheriff had been forced to ingest anything. Anyway, I'm due to speak to Lyon again, but, remember, if this was the dead man's widow we wouldn't be quite so quick in assuming that she'd done it. We'd all be falling over ourselves, trying to understand her predicament. Comfort her, even. He didn't abscond, disappear or anything, he simply waited for us to find him at the home he shared with Freeman. That's not such suspicious behaviour in their particular circumstances.'

'I'm not convinced. Don't forget, there was nothing in the post mortem report about any disease at all, and the drug could have been added to food or drink. And who'd give a stuff about the Sheriff being gay nowadays? I don't think it hangs together at all.'

'Well, Professor McConnachie was pretty sure about the cause of death, and it looked convincing enough. The big holes in the skull. I think we should go back to him and see if there was any evidence, from the brain, spinal cord or whatever, about motor neurone disease. If the old man had it, then his partner's version of events could be possible.'

She paused, thinking, and then continued: 'Certainly, there'd be no need for Lyon to whack him over the head if he knew the Sheriff was already full of a fatal dose of amitriptyline... and, like I said, there's no evidence of any force-feeding. Anyway, even if the old fellow was wrong about any press interest in their relationship, as long as his belief was genuine then it would still explain his action—or inaction. Wouldn't it? By the way, Alistair, why did you miss the meeting?'

'Because DI Manson noticed in your report on the funeral that you described Mrs Nordquist as tearful, and he thought she ought to be talked to again, the tears suggesting something other than neighbourly feeling. This being Edinburgh and all. Also, he said DCI Bruce asked her to ID the body in the mortuary, before we managed to contact Christopher Freeman, and she'd been completely unbothered by the prospect. Odd, with her weeping at St Giles.'

'And did you find anything?'

'No. Mrs Nordquist had been imbibing again; actually I'd say she was drunk this time. Anyway, I couldn't make head or tail of what she was saying, with her accent and all, and she kept trying to press that liqueur stuff on me. She got furious when I wouldn't join her and then edged towards me on the sofa and started crying. We'll have to go again, or on reflection, perhaps, just you.'

5

DCI Bruce whirled round at speed in a full circle on his revolving chair. It could have been simply *joie de vivre*, but Alice sensed that the man had done it to proclaim his dominance over his territory and over the only subordinate present, herself. Returning to his place at the front of his desk he pressed the ends of his fingers together, as if praying, and began to speak.

'That's very useful stuff, in its way, Detective Sergeant. Almost, but not quite, makes up for missing my meeting...' he smiled with no warmth. 'Anyhow, the toxicology report should make entertaining reading, so I suggest that you go off and harry the lab for me. It's over three weeks since the post mortem and this case, surely, deserves some priority.'

'Yes, Sir.'

'And when you talk to Nicholas Lyon again, bring him in here, eh? Just to let him know what he's got himself into.'

'What has he got himself into, Sir?'

'A murder enquiry, remember?'

'I hadn't forgotten that, Sir, but he's not really a suspect at present, is he? Mr Lyon's the... the... well, the bereaved. He lived with the victim for over forty-five years. We've got nothing to suggest that he was involved in any way, and I'd much rather see him in his own home; he'll be more relaxed there.'

'Get real, Sergeant! He didn't come to us, did he? We had to go and winkle him out, and that speaks volumes in my book. He's a suspect as far as I'm concerned! So let's give him a dose of reality and bring him in here "to assist us". In fact, I'll do the interview myself to make sure we get everything we need.'

The Professor's desk was almost invisible beneath the array of empty coffee cups and polystyrene mugs stacked on it, and the man's expression betrayed irritability when he looked up from his computer screen as the policewoman entered.

'I've tracked the report down, Alice.' He sounded defensive. 'It's with Doctor Zenabi for his signature. We were going to email it to you later this morning, but if you want to pop in and collect it, his room is further down this corridor, third on the left. He should have signed it by now.'

'There were one or two things I need to ask you, first, if you've got the time, Professor?'

'When have I ever got the time on a lecture morning? But fire ahead. I can give you until eleven o'clock, and then I'm off to give a talk on "Paradoxical Undressing". Law students on this occasion. No, we'd better make that quarter to eleven, in order to give me time to get to Old College.'

'I've spoken to the Sheriff's partner and he told me that on the Monday night, Freeman planned to take an overdose of amitriptyline…'

'He?'

'He.'

'Well, the toxicology certainly confirmed that,' the Professor said, gathering together, as he spoke, a couple of lever-arch files from a desk drawer. 'It was an unexpected finding—that it was in his system, I mean. There was none among the drugs swept from the various cabinets and drawers in Moray Place. Did he tell you where the man got it from?'

Alice nodded. 'From their other house, in the country, in Kinross-shire. Nicholas, that's the Sheriff's partner, had some. He told me that he was given it a while ago when his mother died, and that he'd never got round to throwing it out because…'

'Mind you,' the Professor interrupted, 'it wasn't the cause of death. He was undoubtedly alive when he was attacked. After all, we took over 150 millilitres of sub-dural blood from the brain, a massive haemorrhage. But it was certainly a fatal dose, the amitriptyline, I mean.'

'What sort of condition would the Sheriff have been in between, say, about seven o'clock and ten or thereabouts?'

'Well, you've got to remember that he'd been knocking back alcohol a bit—not that much—about fifteen milligrams, no more than a few double whiskies, I suppose. By that time, seven onwards, I'd say that most of the effects he'd be feeling really would be from the drink. Maybe his speech would be a little more slurred with the two in combination… he might have been a bit slower in thought, too. Unsteady. As the evening progressed the effects of the drug would begin to kick in.'

'And there was no sign of him having been forced to eat or swallow anything? I'm thinking of the pills?'

'No. Certainly, the oral examination showed nothing unusual.'

'At the post mortem you never mentioned any motor neurone disease, Professor?'

'No. Did he have it?'

'Well, Mr Lyon said that he was diagnosed with it about eight months ago and had begun to experience some pretty unpleasant effects; largely difficulties with speech and swallowing. That kind of thing.'

'I'll take your word for it.'

'Would it be possible to look again? I mean, to check to see if he did have the disease?'

'No, probably not. We released the body for the funeral and I think we'd be short of blocks. I'm not sure we'll have taken enough from various areas of the brain. We might also have needed tissue from the tongue and I'd probably have had to involve Professor Donaldson, the neurologist but—' he hesitated.

'I wouldn't advise going down that route anyway. There's no point, we know already the cause of death. The Sheriff could've had motor neurone disease in its early stages and nothing would necessarily appear on post mortem, but his general practice records are being sent to the department. Why don't I phone Maureen and see if they've got here? If a diagnosis of MND was made during his lifetime it'll be in there and more reliable, in all probability, than any made at post mortem. In life, you see,you get fasciculations, clear symptoms, signs etc. Let's phone Maureen and ask her to bring them if they've arrived, eh?'

The secretary bustled into the office bearing a thick brown folder and pointing at her watch.

'You'll need to get a move on, Professor, or you'll be late for the students.'

Professor McConnachie nodded non-commitally, and began to examine the file, pulling aside clinical notes and charts until he reached the correspondence section.

'Here it is, Alice. The Sheriff went to the Murrayfield and saw a neurologist there. I know him, actually. A chap called Kennedy. He seems to have made a fairly confident diagnosis— let's see... slurring of speech, excess saliva... history... electromyalgic results, CT scans... fasciculations. It's all there.'

'And the date of the letter?'

'Er... 4th November 2005.'

—

'A thoussand pieces you know, not the bikkest I haff effer done but, well, pussles relax me.' Mrs Nordquist twirled a minuscule jigsaw piece between her fingers and then began to concentrate intensely on the puzzle tray on the table before her. Surreptitiously, Alice attempted to make out the image being formed. Upside down, it seemed to be no more than a mass of squiggles, possibly in the form of an alien with multiple auras encircling it.

Without looking up Mrs Nordquist inserted her piece, took

a sip from the little glass beside her and said conversationally, 'The Scream... do you know? Munch's masterwork? It's one off my faforites. But I can eassily talk at the same time, so you jusst carry on, Detectif Rice.'

'Well, perhaps I should begin by letting you know that I've met Nicholas, Mr Lyon.'

'Yess?' Mrs Nordquist did not appear to be disconcerted by the news.

'Yes. And I got the impression from him that when you told us that you and the Sheriff were strangers to each other, that was not quite true.'

'Well, maybe, but I also said he wass a goot neighbour.'

'In fact, you were friends?'

'Yess.'

'Why didn't you tell us about Mr Lyon? You must've known that such information was exactly the sort of thing that we needed.'

Mrs Nordquist sighed deeply and slowly put down her next jigsaw piece.

'Becoss I knew what James would haff wanted ant what he would not haff wanted. The Police, anyone, really, to know he wass gay. He wass very olt-fashioned. I could haff told you, but it didn't seem right. So I jusst made jokes, I wass nervouss. It wass his secret to impart, not mine.'

The woman's speech stopped abruptly as her housekeeper entered the room bearing a tray with lunch on it. After it had been placed on the coffee table in front of her, Mrs Nordquist said, 'Ant the bottle, Mrs McColl—where iss the bottle?'

Mrs McColl looked defiantly at her employer, but on being met with an equally unblinking stare, she signalled her defeat by shaking her head and muttering 'It'll be the death of you... your precious aquavit!'

Her servant vanquished, Mrs Nordquist began to poke at her food idly, and then continued: 'James wass my friend.

Nicholas too. James wass deat. What difference does it make, eh? Effentually, you'd find Nicholas. It's your jop.'

'Why did you phone Nicholas that morning?'

Mrs Nordquist stabbed a piece of asparagus and raised it to her mouth.

'Wouldn't you haff? The man's luffer wass dead, for heffen's sake. Kilt!'

'What exactly did you tell him?'

'That James had been murdered, ant that you were all ofer their houss.'

Holding Alice's gaze as she did so, and to show that she had now lost all appetite, Mrs Nordquist flicked the green spear off her fork onto the cream carpet below her, and Freya's muzzle emerged from its hiding place under the sofa to snap up the titbit.

—

DCI Bruce looked into the mirror compact that he had found in his desk drawer. A fine-looking man, he concluded. No-one had ever actually paid him such a compliment, or likely ever would, but its absence had never dented his belief in the truth of such an observation had it been made about him. Red hair and blue eyes. An excellent Celtic combination. Today, maybe, the skin looking a little pallid and freckled, but more than made up for by the manly auburn moustache. At the afternoon press conference he would photograph well again, any pallor being put down to overwork, and such an impression could only do him good.

The unannounced entry into his office of the Assistant Chief Constable, Laurence Body, jolted him out of his reverie and he dropped the mirror back into its hiding place before rising from his seat.

'Well, DCI, I hope you have some progress to report. There seems to have been precious little to date.'

Thank God the Detective Segeant had phoned. 'I do, actually, Sir. I heard from DS Rice that the toxicology report confirms that the Sheriff took a fatal overdose of that drug—am... whatever.'

'The amitriptyline?'

'Yes, Sir.'

'So?'

'Er... so what, Sir?'

'So, do we know whether the Sheriff was already dead when he was hit over the head or whether the drug killed him? Whether only a corpse was battered?' Body's irritation coloured his voice.

DCI Bruce cleared his throat, trying to gain time to think. This possibility, now so obvious, had not previously occurred to him. He would rely on Professor McConnachie's post-mortem remarks.

'The cause of death was the blows, the Prof told me that at the mortuary,' he said, trying to sound confident.

'And did the Professor have the toxicological results to consider then?'

The Chief Inspector was just formulating an evasive reply when Body answered his own rhetorical question. 'Of course *not*. He wouldn't then be aware of any competing cause. For Christ's sake!' He sighed with exasperation before continuing, 'And we have no suspect as yet, I understand?'

'Actually, I'm just about to see one. The Sheriff's partner.' The day had been saved.

—

Nicholas Lyon leant against the window-sill and looked out through the smeared glass across St Leonard's Bank and the broad sweep of Queens Drive and onto Salisbury Crags beyond. A scene so carefree and sunlit that it seemed to belong to his past, not to this dreary, painful present. All his life he had been protected by the law, by James and James' knowledge of it; and here he was in the front line, unprotected and under attack. And all because of James. Even his own body was letting him down, palms clammy and sweat trickling down his brow. He closed his eyes, slowly breathing in, trying to blot out the alien world in which he found himself, with its institutional smells and unashamed ugliness.

Suddenly, the door of the interview room was thrown open and a small red-haired man entered, shoulders back, head erect, with the now familiar policewoman following behind him. Nicholas sensed that this time there would be no gentle preliminaries, no charade of 'assistance'. The manner of the entrance proclaimed that an interrogation was about to begin, however it might officially be described. He could feel his heart-rate rise, the pounding in his chest audible to him, if not everyone else.

'So, Mr Lyon, the Sheriff took the amitriptyline himself, did he?'

'Yes. He must have done, if you found it in his blood, and as he had planned, in Edinburgh.'

'And you knew all about it?'

'Yes. Well, no... not exactly.' The old man was becoming flustered, 'I mean, I knew that he intended to take it and I thought that he was going to do so on Monday night, but I couldn't be sure. You see, it's difficult to explain, but James didn't want me to know... when, exactly, I mean.'

'How did you discover that he was dead?'

'Like I said to the Detective Sergeant, our friend, Liv Nordquist, phoned and told me.'

'And why, in God's name, didn't you immediately make yourself available to us for the purpose of our enquiries? The Sheriff had, after all, been murdered.'

It was difficult to explain. More than that. Maybe impossible, or at least impossible to explain to this strange martinet. But, again, he must try.

'James was dead, Chief Inspector, and he never liked people to know that he was gay. He came from a long line of military men, generals and brigadiers, that sort of thing... Service people. You know the sorts of views they tend to have about people like us.' Seeing the DCI's expression of surprise, he corrected himself quickly. 'James and me, I mean. Anyway, most people didn't know that he was gay, or that he had a partner. If I had turned up... well, that would all be over, wouldn't it? And word of his homosexuality would get out, it would have, wouldn't it? Into the newspapers and everything.' He glanced up at the policeman, seeking his reaction, expecting agreement but not finding it.

'Not nowadays. You'll have to do better than that, Mr Lyon.'

The old man, sensing that he was not being believed, looked dismayed. His words began to tumble out, a new note of desperation in his voice.

'But I knew you would find me... I suppose if I had come forward sooner you'd have got whatever information I can give you sooner, but, you see, I don't know anything. I have no idea who killed James or why anyone would want to. If I can't help now then I couldn't have helped then either.'

'Did the Sheriff have other lovers?'

'I'm sorry, what are you talking about?' The old man appeared bemused by the question.

'Lovers. Other gay lovers. Other than you. It's simple enough. Did the Sheriff have other gay lovers?'

No. I was his lover, his friend, his companion for over forty-five years. I was all he needed.

'No. I don't think so.'

'What about when he was in Edinburgh, with you left in the country?'

'No, I don't think so.'

'But you didn't know?'

'Does anybody know what their lover does every minute of

every hour of every day sufficient to know for certain that they are faithful, Chief Inspector?'

'So the simple answer is that he could have done so?'

Of course, he could have done so. I could have done so but, you foolish man, I knew his heart. He would not have done so any more than I would have done so. A truth apparently beyond your imagination or experience.

'Yes, he could have done so.'

'And are you aware whether anyone might have any kind of grievance against him due to his job?'

'No. He retired over ten years ago, but even when he was on the bench I never heard of anything like that. Once, ages ago, I remember him telling me that a woman pelted him with an egg as he left the Sheriff Court in Haddington. Otherwise, I can't recall anything or anyone.'

Interfering Scottish fucking Executive. Them and their bloody rules, DCI Bruce thought to himself. I NEED a cigarette. I don't just want a cigarette, I need one, and without one all that I can think about is a smoke and where the next one is coming from. Something to calm my shattered nerves and stop the constant re-running in my head of the meeting with the ACC. No less than a sodding fiasco, and a further obstacle on the road to promotion. When would DCI Bell be returning, indeed! As if the man could not wait to replace him. But a little nicotine would restore his confidence, restore his self belief. Oh, it was intolerable! This interference with the rights of individuals, particularly individuals doing important and responsible jobs and who needed, physiologically, needed a good drag to function at top level. Without it he could not listen to this drivel for a second longer.

'Perhaps you could take over now, DS Rice?' DCI Bruce said as he rose, departing with unconcealed haste, intent on achieving his single, easily accomplished goal. And it would not be, ignominiously, behind the bike shed either.

'Mr Lyon, maybe we could continue this interview at Gean-bank in a few days' time?' the policewoman asked.

'That would be fine. Thank you, I'd prefer that.'

—

Alice looked at the exam paper.

'(12) There are several factors that may affect underwater vis-ibility. Tick those that do:

A – Weather.

B – Water movement.

C – Ambient pressure.

D – Suspended particles.'

The weather must, surely. Bright sunshine could only make things clearer. Tick. Water movement? If there are lots of waves, then stuff, like sand, would be mixed into the water. Tick.

Ambient pressure? Christ knows. Leave it out.

Suspended particles? Of course. Tick

'(13) Almost all injuries caused by aquatic life are attributable to (fill in space) action by the animal. Tick, as appropriate:

A – Unpredictable.

B – Unprovoked.

C – Defensive.'

Alice racked her brain for an example. A shark attempting to bite a lump out of a diver. That would do. Let's see; thoroughly predictable and therefore, possibly, avoidable. Routinely unpro-voked and offensive in nature rather than defensive. Tick 'unpro-voked'. She wished she had read 'Knowledge review – Module 3' of the *Open Water Diver Manual* last night instead of another chapter of Ishiguro's bleak novel, which had reduced her to tears. As she began to scrutinise Question 14, at first sight com-pletely incomprehensible, she became aware of Bridget craning over her question sheet. The invigilator had left the room.

'Well, what's the answer to Question 12?' Her friend murmured.

'No idea, I've opted for A, B and D.'

'And 13?'

'Again, I haven't the faintest, but I'm going for "Unprovoked".What's the answer to 14, Bridget?'

'I've put "Establish buoyancy; Drop weight belt; Stop; Think; Act relaxed and signal". I had it all written down on my palm.'

'My palm wouldn't be big enough!'

The urgent whispering in the room ceased as the invigilator returned, bearing a cup of coffee for himself.

'Now, students, your time's up. If you exchange sheets with your neighbour we will correct the exam.' Before Alice had a chance to pass her sheet on to the man on her right Bridget snatched it from her grasp and thrust her own onto Alice's lap, wheedling conspiratorially, 'Last week, 90%. This week 92%? Eh? Top o' the class for me?'

'These things matter!' hissed the waste disposal entrepreneur.

'I know,' nodded Bridget before adding blithely, 'that's why I intend to come first.' And then she muttered to Alice, 'water off a Dux's back, eh!'

6

The woman's carmine lipstick glistened moistly in the light. As always it had been immaculately applied, DI Manson decided, while he watched, transfixed, as she inserted a cashew nut into the flawless Cupid's bow of her mouth. Oh, and her eyebrows were thin and perfectly arched, her nails long, manicured and pearly pink. Blonde hair, too. This is exactly how a woman, a proper woman, should look, and then men, all men, certainly this one, would give her whatever she desired.

'A gin and tonic for the lady and, eh… a pint for me,' he said to the barman, before adding 'make it a Bitter and Twisted, eh?'

Turning his attention back to the journalist perched on the bar-stool beside him, he smiled broadly at her and was nonplussed when she displayed signs of dictating the pace of the meeting.

'So, Eric, what exactly d'you want?'

The Inspector attempted, as usual, to disguise the disappointment he felt at the sound of her voice. It was a high-pitched squawking noise, and whenever he heard it, he recoiled, dismayed by its ugliness. As if an exquisite bird of paradise had opened its beak and screeched like a magpie. She should have made a low, purring sound, perhaps, with the slightest hint of a lisp; and he had wanted the illusion of a social drink between friends to be maintained just a little longer, but so be it. If it had to be down to business, then fine, she would be impressed with his offering whenever it was laid before her.

'It's not a question of what I want, love, more what you'll want.' He winked, inwardly congratulating himself on his answer. Flirtatious, intriguing even.

'Don't play games with me. I've not got all sodding night. If you've got something to say, then just say it, eh? I'm needing the loo and I've better things to do than lounge around the friggin' Balmoral all evening.'

'It's about Sheriff Freeman.'

'The murdered one?' Her voice betrayed rising interest.

'Aye. The murdered one,' he nodded, tantalising her.

'Well?' Another squawk.

'Well. Wait for it… he was gay!'

The semblance of a smile. 'How d'you know?'

'Because we had his partner in the station, at St Leonards. Another old bloke, lived with Freeman for years and years.'

''Tell me he's a suspect?' Her eyes now glittered with excitement.

In for a penny, in for a pound, the Detective Inspector thought, replying: 'Aha. He certainly is!'

The woman uncrossed her long, shapely legs and leant towards the policeman. A little notebook was extracted from her shoulder-bag and she began, for the first time that evening, to bestow her full attention upon him.

'Go on then, Eric… talk to me. For you, pet, I've all the time in the world.'

DI Manson drained the dregs of his pint, swallowed a burp, and allowed his left foot, accidentally, to brush against hers.

⚊

Shortly before three o'clock in the afternoon, Nicholas Lyon put up his umbrella and set off to walk to the village shop to collect his bread and milk. A soaking was just what the ground needed; the soil had become dust-dry and the lawn was disfigured by leprous yellow patches where the grass had died.

He squelched through the puddles on the drive in his boots, breathing in deeply to inhale the pungent scent of aniseed released as the rain sank into the parched earth, slaking its summer thirst.

Reaching the store he cast his eyes over the billboard propped up against the plate glass window. Most days it was of little interest—'Fife Councillor on the Take', 'Road Bridge Toll to Go Up', or 'T in the Park – a Record Success'. Once in a while someone else's tragedy had become news: 'Local Boy Dies in Motor-cycle Crash' or 'Mother's Coma Vigil'. He had ruminated over the incidental cruelty involved. A private grief magnified to assuage the public's insatiable appetite for 'human interest' stories. And then the relatives' reaction, exacerbated by the news coverage, might, in itself, provide more columns of newsprint. This time the hastily scrawled black lettering on the white background spelt out 'MURDERED SHERIFF'S GAY LOVER NOW A SUSPECT'. On reading it he was swept by an overwhelming feeling of dread, a sensation of fear, unmistakably physical, like nothing he had ever experienced. Cold sweat rose on his forehead and acid seemed to be seeping into the pit of his stomach. What would everyone think? And then, and worse still, came the conviction that, somehow, he had let James down. In death, James Freeman had become cheap, tabloid fodder, a source of vulgar amusement at best, infuriated disgust at worst. And the easiest label of all would now be bestowed upon him, that of hypocrite.

A hand tapped on his shoulder and he opened his eyes to see the plump form of the shopkeeper beside him.

'Ye all richt, Mr Lyon?'

He nodded, embarrassed, incapable of speech, afraid that if he attempted to say anything he might break down and weep, and then be unable to stop himself.

'Come in oot the rain eh? Dinnae worry yersel aboot yon board. S'only up the day an' it'll be doon afore tomorrow morn. Fish 'n chips frae then oan. We a' ken you, an' aboot the Sheriff an' a.'

—

'Yes! A result!' Eric Manson slammed down the receiver and punched the air. Alice caught Alistair's eye. Should they indulge the man in his excitement, ask the inevitable question or, sadistically, let the seconds tick by, force him to wait for a bit? Even say nothing at all and twiddle their thumbs before another exhibition was staged in an attempt to whet their curiosity further? DC McDonald, unaware of the tensions within the squad, resolved their unspoken dilemma.

'What is it, Sir?'

'Only a lead. That's all! Some poof's been boasting in a gay bar, the Boar's Head down Leith way, that he was having it off with the Sheriff. Come on Alice, turn off the computer, we're going to…'

Before DI Manson had finished speaking his phone rang again, and he snatched it up impatiently, annoyed at being delayed.

'Yes! Oh, I see, Sir. Of course, I quite appreciate that. I'll come through right away. I had been on my way to check out something urgent in Leith, a boy we need to see there. Maybe I should go there first?' He grimaced at Alistair. 'Yes, Sir, Alice and DS Watt could easily go in my place. If the Assistant Chief Constable needs a report then, obviously, that takes priority. I'll attend to it now.'

—

The traffic on Leith Walk was gridlocked, moving little more than a few feet every minute and, in the still, warm air, the stench of exhaust fumes was overpowering. But no escape presented itself. A bus driver hooted his horn angrily, and in vain, at two parked cars blocking his lane, and a stationary taxi-cab, immediately ahead of them, disgorged its overheated passangers. The two Police officers wound up their windows simultaneously, desperate to preserve such fresh air as the Astra contained, knowing that they would now swelter in its furnace-like interior. By the time they reached Salamander Street both of them had, somehow, stuck to their plastic car seats. They immediately flung the doors wide, enjoying the cool sea breeze, preparing to peel themselves off the vinyl.

A few tables, sporting faded parasols, littered the pavement frontage of the newly-decorated pub, and a shaven-headed bulldog of a man turned out to be the inspector's contact. He seemed pleased that they had been sent in Manson's stead, and led them through the bar into the back kitchen, shooing out two pale youths who were occupied stirring, lethargically, the contents of a gigantic aluminium tureen. The snout was helpful, eager to provide such information as he could, but scrupulous in distancing himself from any accusations potentially associated with it. The press had already been sniffing about the place, he explained. Georgie was the name of the customer who had been boasting; a flamboyant, middle-aged extrovert who revelled in being the centre of attention. But, the bull-dog cautioned, maybe the boasts had been no more than empty talk, a bid by Georgie to upstage a popular raconteur, who had been regaling the regulars with tales of his adventures as a transvestite fire-eater. In any event, he said, he was simply passing on the guff for what it was worth. He did not know the fellow's surname, only that he worked in a small second-hand bookshop on Nicolson Street, up near the University. They would recognise him by his shock of blond curls and his invariable buttercup-coloured tie. Oh, and he was a smiler.

—

Back in the Police pound, the two officers piled out of the car, thankful to leave its close atmosphere, only to find themselves immediately separated, DI Manson summoning Alistair to the office. But Alice had no intention of waiting for him and delaying following up such a promising lead. He might be able to join her later in person, and the shop was within easy walking distance. A stroll in the bright sunshine, on her own, down the Pleasance and along Drummond Street, would have been a joy even if she had not been getting paid for it.

Their quarry was discovered, less than twenty minutes later, perched on a high stool in his bookshop, nose deep in a leather-bound copy of *Court Dress through the Ages*. Georgie was so engrossed in his book that he appeared unaware that a potential customer was at his elbow until a discreet cough alerted him. On seeing her, his face lit up as if he had encountered a long-lost, and very dear friend, and his bonhomie was catching. Alice felt herself smiling warmly in return, until she recollected the real purpose of her visit and, assuming a more appropriate, business-like expression, showed him her card.

'And what can I do for you, my lovely?' he asked, inserting a till receipt to mark his place in the book.

When she asked him about his reported boasts, deliberately affording him an opportunity to deny them, he chose not to do so. Instead, he maintained, with a degree of exaggerated indignation, that he had, indeed, slept with the Sheriff. Their only tryst had taken place a few days before the fellow's death, in Georgie's flat in Cumberland Street. He volunteered that while he might have been slightly intoxicated on the night, incapable of recollecting all the evening's events with complete clarity, the essentials remained clear, including his pick-up's identity. After all, he had seen the judge's photo in the paper within days of their meeting. Anyway, he said, now in mock anger, he was not in the habit of fabricating false liaisons, someone so delectable had no need to do so.

When questioned on his whereabouts on the night of the murder, he replied that he had been, as far as he could remember, on his tod, attending to the accounts for the business and parcelling up a few books for mail-order customers. His bookshop, he said proudly, had cornered the market in fashion and footwear literature, dispatching stock all over the country and beyond. He seemed unconcerned by the gentle interrogation he was undergoing, untroubled in admitting his recent encounter with a murder victim, and, incongruously, pleased with his involvement in the whole affair. It appeared that the limelight was irresistible, whatever it illuminated. She left him as another customer arrived, noting that his face showed as much pleasure on seeing the stranger as it had done when first she interrupted his reading.

———

The hall carpet in Geanbank had been partially covered by a dust sheet. In its folds, in disarray, were cut stems, sprays of leaves and a few crumbs of Oasis sponge. Above the sheet, on a bow-legged table, was a vast flower arrangement with pale blue irises, delphiniums and cream, full-bloomed roses. Nicholas Lyon led the policewoman past it, and Alice smothered the impulse to congratulate him on its perfection. On entering the drawing room he went straight to the window and drew the curtains tight shut, excluding the prying eyes of the Press, now camped en masse outside. He poured her China tea from a silver teapot and offered cake, apologising as he did so for the lack of biscuits and explaining that, for the moment, he was unable to leave the house to get more. Alice braced herself for his reaction before dutifully warning him that the Press interest had probably not reached its zenith. It was possible that reports might appear, fed by those claiming close acquaintanceship with the Sheriff, reviving the story, artificially expanding its lifespan. The old fellow listened to every word, blinking furiously and occasionally giving an almost imperceptible shake of his head.

'Did James know anyone called Georgie, a bookseller…
a second-hand bookseller up past the Bridges?' she asked,
tentatively.

'No. Nor did I.'

'Did he ever go to a pub, the Boar's Head, on Salamander
Street, Leith?'

'I wouldn't think so, he didn't really like pubs any more,
couldn't hear in them. I don't think so. Why do you ask?' he
looked genuinely puzzled.

'Nothing. We have to follow up everything, however unlikely it may be. I wondered,' she continued, keen to change
the subject, 'whether you'd had any thoughts, you know, if you
knew of anyone that might wish James harm?'

Her companion sighed, and then asked ruefully, 'In life,
you mean?'

'In life, yes.'

'I have thought about it. And I'm not sure that I'm much
further on, but perhaps you can be the judge of that. I found
these…' He handed over a cardboard box containing a number
of sheets of paper. 'I knew about them, of course. James told
me about the letters but I'd never actually seen them before.
I wish I had, then I could have shared the worry better, but I
had no idea that they were so, well… threatening. James made
light of them; he said a lunatic had begun a one-sided correspondence with him and would, likely in his own time, bring it
to an end. Maybe he was protecting me. He knew how I hated
dissension, hostility of any kind.'

Alice lifted a single piece of paper from the box and read:

'I hope you die in hell, you selfish bastard. Thanks to your
greed, my life will be ruined. You don't even need the money.
You have no excuse. You don't live there so you don't care. You,
and the rest of them, will pollute everything. Can you imagine
that? No-one will want to come. Stop it or else I'll stop you.'

The words were written in green biro ink in an elaborate

italic hand, and some of them, 'selfish', 'greed' and 'ruined', were underlined heavily twice. Although the content of the message was intimidating, its appearance was artistic, oddly beautiful. She removed another letter in the same hand, this time in red biro ink.

'Stop it, bastard. You can stop it still. It's your land. You have the access strip. I know who you are and I know where you live. If you go ahead you will destroy me and my family. It's only money, for Christ's sake! End the whole thing or I will put a stop to you.'

The paper was cheap, lined and textured as if recycled. The other messages were in similar vein, sometimes pleading, sometimes threatening, always desperate in tone.

'Have you any idea who sent these, who wrote them?'

'No, I don't, and James didn't either. You can see, they're all anonymous. He hadn't a clue who the author was.'

Alice nodded. 'But what about their content? Do you know what they're about? What exactly was James proposing to do that the writer wanted to stop?'

Nicholas Lyon blinked rapidly before he began to speak.

'I think—well, we knew—that it was to do with Blackstone Mains. It's a farm that James and his brother owned jointly. Christopher persuaded James to offer it to one of those re-newable companies, Vertenergy, to put up turbines on it. All the land's tenanted at the moment. It's to be part of a gargantuan wind farm on the Ochils. I think there are to be thirty turbines or thereabouts. Massive things too, maybe one hundred and twenty metres high. The wind farm's to be called "Scowling Crags". The company's still seeking planning per-mission from the Council, a decision on it's not due until the end of September.'

'Are any of the letters dated?'

'No. But the last one was received, maybe, a week before James died. They were always addressed here, in James's name, and he'd open them and tell me that it was just another crank missive.'

'And you've no idea who sends them?'

'Sorry. As I said, I don't think James knew either, but, you see, he never took them seriously. So obviously I didn't... and I'm kicking myself now. He said he'd come across this kind of thing in his job, he believed that the type of person who writes them never actually does anything more. He or she gets it out of their system on paper and then that's it. James said they were usually sad, inadequate creatures, capable only of venting their spleen with words.'

'What does it mean, "the access strip"?'

'I think, though I'm not sure, that Blackstone was the access strip. A ransom strip, actually. For the whole development I mean. Blackstone's on the main road, and none of the farmers round about it were prepared to allow their land to be used by the company. The ones at the back, on the hill, were really keen and that's where the wind is anyway, but the developers needed land downhill, with access to the road, if the scheme was to go ahead. The Mains, Blackstone, provided access for the whole site and without that land, then it couldn't go ahead. I was never for it in the first place, the wind farm, I mean, and I told James that too.'

'Why? Why were you against it?'

'Well, if you really want to know, because they're ugly, inefficient things and the equation only comes out in credit if no value whatsoever is placed on beauty, the beauty of unspoilt scenery I mean. The answer isn't to generate more, it's to use less. We used to argue about it sometimes. Actually, I think I'd almost succeeded in persuading James. Maybe even the letters played a part. All I know is that he was less enthusiastic about the whole venture than he had been. I suppose Christopher will just go on with it though.'

'I'll need to take the letters if that's all right, Mr Lyon?'

'Nicholas. Please. I thought you'd want them. Take them in the box. I racked my brain after the conversation with the inspector and I couldn't think of anything, anyone who'd want to harm James. And then, really by chance, I've found these things. Reading them chilled me, I can tell you. They were in one of his desk drawers together with something that I think must be his will. It's addressed to his lawyers and I'm seeing them tomorrow.'

Alice walked quickly to the Astra, keen to avoid the attention of the Press who, like vultures, had spotted her and were now closing in, flapping towards the car. No sooner had she slammed the door shut than a rosy-cheeked young man pulled it open, suggesting, with a charming grin, that she might like to speak to him. Before she had time to answer, another figure insinuated himself into the same space to demand information about the Sheriff's lover. Within seconds three more reporters had bent down, thrusting their heads towards her, each shouting, trying to outdo the others. A loud knocking had become audible on the driver's side window, and she turned her head, briefly, to see DI Manson's crony smiling seductively at her and gesturing at her notebook, apparently expecting a favour or some sort of preferential treatment.

Alice closed her eyes and breathed out. The creatures must be dealt with, although in their merciless pursuit of an old, heart-sick man, they had all but lost her sympathy. No. Like burying beetles, they had a place in the scheme of things. So, she must not indulge herself and give way to the overwhelming urge rising within her to shout expletives, put her foot down on the accelerator and shower them all with gravel. Temporarily calmed, she gazed at the woman and then, slowly and purposefully, drove off, watching in her rear view mirror as the reporter's smile faded into her habitual scowl.

Another button missing but it could wait, the last one at the bottom of the blouse. No more than usual would be revealed. She folded it up, put it on the pile and began to iron a sheet, lost in Corelli's Concerto Grossi and enjoying the clean scent of washing powder rising from the heated fabric. Was it Concerto No. 4 or No. 7? A repetitive clicking sound signalled grime on the disc, and she left the ironing board to go and wipe the CD. The telephone rang and she knew, intuitively, that it would be Ian Melville. The answer machine was on. Maybe she would listen to his voice, see what he wanted and then, if she chose and could pluck up the courage, return the call. Her recorded speech on the tape sounded unnatural, like some low-voiced stranger.

'This is Alice Rice's answer phone. Please leave your message after the beep.'

On impulse she dashed across the room and picked up the receiver.

'Hello.' She sounded breathless.

From the more than momentary silence that followed she recognised the caller's re-adjustment as he prepared himself to speak to a human being rather than a machine.

'Alice, hi, it's me. Ian. I thought you must be out.'

'I've just got in.' A whitish lie.

'I was wondering if you'd be free tomorrow… tomorrow evening? Maybe join me on a walk? We could go to the beach at Tyninghame or somewhere. What d'you think?'

I would love to. I would really love to. 'Mmm… that sounds fine. What sort of time were you thinking of?' Without alcohol a measured, less-truthful response.

'How about six thirty? I could pick you up in Broughton Place and we could have a meal afterwards, after the walk, I mean.'

Perfect.

'Thanks, yes, that'd be great. See you then.'

He had called again. She had hoped that he would, but prepared herself in advance in case it was not going to happen. Now she could relax, luxuriate in the knowledge that he wanted to see her once more. He must feel a little, at least, of what she felt.

7

Eric Manson yawned, took off his jacket and slung it across the back of his chair. Then he rolled up his sleeves and wandered towards the nearest window, intending to open it. Straining loudly, he pushed upwards on the lower half but, despite the veins now pulsating in his neck, achieved not an inch of movement; it was glued fast with paint. All the other windows in the room proved equally resistant. He took a sip from his bottle of water, switched on the fan nearest to his desk and settled down to read his newspaper.

The voices of DCs Trotter and Drysdale could be heard, arguing loudly, as they clattered up the stairs, exchanging heated views in a medley of tenor voices. Davie McDonald followed close behind them, mouth full of bacon roll, unable to participate in their row. On entering the murder suite he made a beeline for the coffee flask, emitting a stream of curses on finding it empty. DCI Bruce glanced down at his watch. Three minutes to nine and only four out of the expected six had appeared. The absence of DC Lowe, he decided, should be viewed as a cause for celebration. The moron held everything up, needing instructions endlessly repeated or clarified, and the sooner he was returned to the uniform branch the better. Let the doctor put up with his vacuous prattle for a change.

'Morning, Sir,' DS Watt said cheerily, switching off Manson's fan as he passed it and taking a seat beside the vacant chair usually favoured by Alice Rice.

'Anyone actually seen Ms Rice yet?' the Chief Inspector said testily.

'Yup,' Alistair Watt replied. 'I saw her heading off towards the Ladies', less than a minute ago,' and before he had finished his sentence his friend swept through the door to find all eyes on her and DCI Bruce tapping his watch. She glanced at her own. Nine o'clock on the dot. A triumph, in itself, to arrive on time, given Miss Spinnell's uncharacteristic garrulousness on Quill's handover. With an effort she managed to smile at DCI Bruce.

'Morning, Sir, just in time for your nine o'clock meeting.'

The Chief Inspector slid his buttocks off the desk and handed out to each of the members of the squad a copy of the most recent anonymous letter sent to James Freeman.

'We need to find the writer of this,' he said. 'He or she's now our best suspect. So I expect everyone to concentrate on it. Alistair, did you get a chance to check out the rest of the letters in the box?'

DS Watt nodded. 'Yes, Sir. They're all very similar in tone and content. Vague threats or pleas. But I didn't see anything in them to provide us with any additional clues on the author's identity. All that seems to emerge is that the writer doesn't want the wind farm development to go ahead as it'll "destroy" him and his family if it does. Presumably they must live somewhere near the site or, at the very least, have some interest or other near it which will be damaged if it gets the go-ahead.'

'I've handed over the principals to the graphologist, Sir,' DC Trotter interjected eagerly, 'and they're looking at them the now. They'll let us know if any of them were written by a different individual. Forensics are going to check out the paper after that.'

'Good. Now do any of you know anything about sodding wind farms or wind farm activists?' the Chief Inspector asked.

'I do, Sir,' Alice replied. 'I've learned a little about both from my father. He's involved in a group. I think that there are a number of ways for us to find out who's been putting pen to paper...' she tailed off, conscious of a certain presumption.

'Go on then,' the DCI said encouragingly, 'we're all ears.'

'Well, there'll probably be a particular group who have banded together in their opposition to the Scowling Crags development. The group could be made up of just a few individuals or quite a sizeable number. They're usually composed of those most immediately threatened...'

'Threatened? How threatened?' DI Manson demanded.

'Threatened by a wind farm around their house or in close proximity to it or their business or whatever. They'll organise themselves...'

'Hang on, hang on,' Eric Manson butted in again, 'how the hell is anyone threatened by a wind farm! We're talking about a murder here, right?'

Alice sighed. She had anticipated scepticism in some form.

'It's difficult to explain, Inspector, but I'll do my best. I've seen it at first hand. A couple of weeks ago I went to a wind farm meeting—never mind why—and I can assure you that the protestors loathe not only the developers but also the landlords benefiting from the schemes. I've rarely witnessed such raw emotion on show in a supposedly civilised gathering. Some of the group could hardly contain themselves. If you'd seen it I don't think you'd doubt that they feel threatened. They love the countryside. They don't expect radical change to happen round about them...'

'They're just bloody nimbys then,' the DI said.

'Maybe. Anyway, well, I'm just trying to explain. OK?'

'On you go, dear,' Eric Manson said, as if in charge, unperturbed by the look of annoyance that passed over his superior's face.

'Even if they own very little land they consider that, in some sense, they also have a claim on the ground beyond. On their view. Ordinary agricultural work on it by the landowners is fine, expected, even welcomed. In any event…' she paused, grappling for the right word, 'understood. But the imposition of gargantuan machines with all the infrastructure required for their erection and maintenance… that's something else altogether. The anti-wind farm protestors are passionate, truly passionate, in their belief that the desecration of the countryside, as they see it, is wrong. Morally wrong. Completely unjustified.'

'As I said,' Eric Manson cut in again, 'sodding nimbys.'

'Whatever. The only…'

'All right, Alice. Speech over. Can you get on with telling us about the organisations?' DCI Bruce enquired.

'Of course, Sir. Sorry. I expect there'll be a group of those immediately affected by the development. There usually is. Then there'll be associated groups, friends of the area, walking associations, equestrians and so on and, finally, there'll be the individuals, each acting completely independently. Usually, all of them, groups of whatever nature, individuals, shower the local Planning Authority with letters, emails, objections in a variety of forms…'

DCI Bruce interrupted again. 'OK. Eric, I want you to contact the local Planning Office—Perth I suppose—and get a list from them of anyone who's objected to the Scowling Crags wind farm application. And make sure and ask for any letters they've received, handwritten stuff particularly, and we'll pass it on to the graphologist and forensics. You could pick it up while you're at their offices.'

'OK, Boss.'

'Alice, how would you go about contacting the… er, local group?'

'Sometimes they've a website. We could put "Scowling Crags" into Google and see what comes up. If we've no luck with that, then the easiest thing to do would be to go and visit someone living in the houses in the centre of the development or as close as possible to it. And James Freeman, Christopher Freeman too, both of them, are almost bound to have been supplied with copies of the information that the developers have to submit to the Council in support of their application. They could give us that information. I need to see Christopher Freeman anyway and I could collect the stuff from him. He may have been getting letters too.'

'Yeh,' the DCI agreed, 'yeh, you do that. If the Sheriff's been threatened it's possible his brother's been too. I want to know if he's been getting the same shite through the post. Alistair, see what you can find on the computer, eh?'

The waiting room of McCowan, Cheyne & Little in Abercrombie Place was plush. Redolent of corporate wealth, landed private clients and a thriving trust department. Only Dundas Street separated it from Heriot Row, one of the most desirable addresses in the whole of the New Town, and its front windows overlooked Queen Street Gardens, providing a view of trees deep within the professional heart of the capital.

A grand portrait in oils of Torquil McCowan, WS, founder of the firm, stretched from the top of the mantelpiece to the ceiling and on either side of it were more modest portrayals of lesser men, recent senior partners meriting only depictions in crayon. Copies of *Country Life*, *Homes & Gardens* and *Scottish Field* were strewn artfully on the heavy oak sideboard, and none of the magazines was out of date. Nicholas Lyon perched on a hard upright chair by the door inspecting his still slightly grimy fingernails. He wished he was somewhere else, at home maybe, in the garden. There was plenty to do there. Both the black and the red currants needed pruning, the Cosmos daisy seedlings could be planted out to give them a good start and the henhouse was in need of a clean.

'Would you like any coffee or tea, Mr Lyon?'

The enquiry from the elegant young receptionist, clad stylishly in a blue linen suit, returned him to the sedate waiting room and he declined, politely, wishing all the more fervently that he was somewhere else. This was James' milieu, and he was impressed anew by the ease with which his partner had inhabited two such dissimilar worlds. One quintessentially urban and urbane and the other rural, simple and organic. No sooner had the young lady gone than she returned, addressing herself to him again.

'Mr McKay can see you now, sir.'

As Nicholas Lyon loped through the door of the solicitor's office he witnessed its occupant tossing a grape up into the air and then catching it, seal-fashion, in his mouth. Neil McKay, on seeing his visitor, immediately dropped the bag of grapes onto the floor and swallowed the morsel hastily as if to conceal his circus trick. Seeing the futility of this approach, he said sheepishly, 'The grape diet, you know. Apparently, they're almost entirely composed of water. I've had too many business lunches.' And he patted his well-rounded belly fondly before gesturing towards a chair and muttering, 'Take a pew.'

Nicholas laid the envelope on the solicitor's leather-covered desk and watched as the man opened it and quickly scanned the document within.

'Thank you, Mr Lyon. The letter simply contained a codicil to James Freeman's will; a small bequest to a charity. Nothing too important. I had intended to get in touch with you once I became aware of the Sheriff's death. Pressure of business I'm afraid...' He looked up apologetically before continuing. 'You and I are to be his executors, in terms of his will, I mean. And, as you probably know, you're also the Sheriff's principal beneficiary. His estate is being left, almost in its entirety, to you.'

'But what about his brother, Christopher?' Nicholas asked.

'Provision has been made for Major Freeman. He's to have a legacy of twenty thousand pounds, together with certain of the contents of Moray Place. Let's see… he's to get…' Mr McKay fingered the Sheriff's will, 'Mmmm. Well, in essence, most of the regimental stuff and a few of the family portraits.'

'James left me the land?' Nicholas enquired in wonderment.

'Yes, he did. And Moray Place and his half-share in Gean-bank. Who owns the other half-share?'

'I do.'

━

Alice's reception at Frogston Road was cool. She had phoned earlier to arrange a meeting, but on arrival she was informed by Mrs Freeman that her husband had just left and was not now expected back until one o'clock. Evidently, the couple had squabbled and the woman could not conceal her anger. Alice sat at the kitchen table awaiting the man's return as his wife smouldered, banging cupboard doors shut and clanging knives onto the table, making the forks on it vibrate and jump. In the ten minutes before his return Mrs Freeman consumed three cigarettes, one lit by the stub of the other, as she prepared a meagre lunch of cold ham and chips.

A strange yodelling sound mixed with strains of 'Some Enchanted Evening' announced Christopher Freeman's entry. He glided speedily into the room, blew a theatrical kiss at his wife and slumped wearily into a chair, a miasma of whisky fumes surrounding him. Without waiting for his wife to join him he picked up his cutlery and began to eat. After his first mouthful he turned his attention to his guest.

'So, Sss… ergeant, what exactly can I do for you?' he asked.

'I've been talking to your brother's partner and…'

'Sorry, sorry,' a look of exaggerated disbelief passed across her host's face. 'Stop right there, please. My brother's what?'

'Your brother's partner…'

'What on earth are you talking about? My brother had no "partner". He was partnerless.'

'Er... the Sheriff did have a partner. A male partner, called Nicholas Lyon. You must have seen the stuff in *The Scotsman* and the *Evening News*, surely?'

'Bloody hell!' Mrs Freeman sniggered, 'so he was still at it, eh? Still at it after all those years!'

'Quiet, Sandra,' Christopher Freeman barked. 'We've been away—down south. Partner... how do you mean, partner? Presumably just a pick-up? That's how those kind of people operate isn't it? Nothing permanent in their world, eh, Sergeant?'

'Well, your brother and Mr Freeman have been together for over forty years.'

'That's bb... bollocks! Bull's bollocks!' Christopher Freeman said, dropping his knife and fork onto his plate. 'I'd have known. He was my brother, for Christ's's sake! They don't mate for life, you know, they are not like us or... eh... ducks, swans. I always knew that James had had a predilection for men but... this just has to be nonsense!'

'No, sir, it's not, and it's also not what I came to talk to you about. Your brother was receiving threats. Well, threatening letters...'

'Never mind that, Sergeant. I've not finished. This Nicholas Lyon man, are you saying that he was a ff... fixture, that he'd—well, that they were married or whatever?' Major Freeman's words were slurred.

'I don't think they'd been through a Civil Partnership ceremony if that's what you mean, Major, but they seem to have been as married, in effect, as any heterosexual couple. Now, going back to the letters. Your brother was receiving threatening letters...'

'About being a poof?' Sandra Freeman giggled, putting her hand over her mouth.

'No, Mrs Freeman. Not about that. The letters seemed to be concerned with the Scowling Crags wind farm. Someone didn't want it to go ahead. Have you received any letters, threatening or otherwise, about the wind farm, Major Freeman?'

'No. Not a dickie bird from anyone about it. Should I have? Mind you, I don't suppose anyone much knows that I have any involvement in it.'

'Why's that, sir?' Alice asked.

'Because James does everything. To do with Blackstone, I mean. My only contribution was the idea. The tenants have been there forever, and I mean forever; there are no written leases or anything. If something had to be done then James saw to it. Actually, he didn't exactly trust me, but that was fine by me. As it happens, I didn't exactly trus… sst him either, but he's… efficient.'

Christopher Freeman turned his attention to his wife. 'Are you not going to eat, my honey? You'll fade away!' he said smiling, patting a chair and beckoning her to sit beside him. Her resentment visibly dissipated, she sidled across to him, pecked him on the cheek and began to eat her meal.

'Perhaps,' Alice said, 'I could show you a copy of one of the letters in case you recognise the handwriting?'

'On you go, but we won't, will we, darling?' the man said, winking at his wife.

'No, we won't,' Mrs Freeman answered, inspecting the copy letter with no real curiosity.

'Could I borrow the material that Vertenergy produced in support of their planning application, please, sir? I understand that you'd get copies of most of it from the company.'

'You'd be welcome to it if I had any, but I don't. I told you I've had nothing to do with the scheme. It was just my idea. James organised everything with everybody, including the company.'

Mrs Freeman placed her knife and fork neatly side by side on her plate before gathering it and her husband's crockery up and depositing them both in the sink. From the fridge she extracted a highly coloured trifle and showed it, lovingly, to her husband.

'Sweetie,' he purred, 'my favourite.'

She laid it on the kitchen table, returned to her seat and lit up a cigarette. 'Light one for mm… me, eh, love?' her husband pleaded, dipping his spoon in the trifle and scraping off a layer of cream. She pouted at him, extracted one from its packet and lit it from her own. Major Freeman leant back on his chair, stretched an arm around her and inhaled deeply. Alice lifted up the box and prepared to leave.

'One more thing, Sergeant,' Christopher Freeman drawled.

'Yes?'

'The poof. Nicholas… whatever. I never saw him in Moray Place. Did he…' the man's question tailed off as he started on his pudding again.

'Did he… what, Sir?'

'Oh never mind, Sergeant. I forget.'

'Have you been to Moray Place recently, Major?'

The man shook his head, still savouring his mouthful.

—

Tears coursed down the old man's face, slipping off his jowls and tainting the coffee that he was trying unsuccessfully, with a trembling hand, to drink. Nothing he did seemed to staunch the flow and his eyes felt gritty, an ache in their very sockets. Twice the kind waitress had approached him to check that he was all right, and twice he had tried to allay her anxieties with a silence and a nod of his head.

I never wanted money, land, anything, he raged to himself. Just James. And I would lose every penny I ever had for him to stay here with me. That bloody motor neurone disease. Without it he would never have chosen to die. I know, he told himself, I *know* that the disease forced it on him, but what about me, left on my own?

But worse still to witness James' suffering and be able to do nothing. And what kind of God confronts his creatures with such an impossible choice? What kind of God, after such a choice has been made, allows a murderer to make it meaningless and transforms a peaceful end into a terrifying death? Couldn't he just have been allowed to slip away in his sleep as he had planned?

The sight of a gold-tipped black umbrella resting on a nearby table delivered another blow. It was identical to James' brolly. Everywhere he looked there seemed to be reminders, ambushing him and overwhelming him. The effort of hiding his emotions, ostensibly functioning as normal, left him exhausted, drained of all life. And now, today, for the first time, he realised that he no longer looked forward to returning to their home. It was no more than an empty shell without James. What did it matter if the weeds grew tall? The lawn remained unmown? They would never again walk, hand in hand, enjoying the beauty of the garden that they had created. Somehow, the conversation with the solicitor, Mr McKay, had impressed upon him, as nothing else had, the finality of his lover's departure; and an endless line of grey, cold days stretched before him. A new half-life, or existence; one devoid of all warmth and colour.

8

With a thud a large, sealed box was dropped onto Alice's desk, startling her and causing the tea in her cup to spill onto her opened newspaper. She looked up, annoyed, into the smiling face of DC Lowe.

'Special delivery for you, Sarge. Nicholas Lyon dropped it off yesterday and the DI said to pass it on to you, as the expert, like. The boss knows you've got it and he wants it checked out immediately. The *Evening News* is planning a front page spread on the Freeman murder and he's shitting himself because he's got nothing to fend them off with. I overheard him on the phone to Charlie at Fettes trying to postpone the next press conference. Not like him, eh?'

Opening the flaps of the box Alice looked inside and found eight ring binders, all devoted to the Scowling Crags wind farm proposal, produced by Vertenergy. She pulled out the topmost one and flicked through previous felling plans, site layouts, habitat maps and visibility diagrams. Nothing of any use there. The next volume was headed 'Environmental Statement', and she scanned a paragraph entitled 'People and Safety':

'13.02—Under certain combinations of geographical position, time of day and time of year, the sun may pass behind a rotor and cast a shadow over neighbouring properties. When the blades rotate, the shadow flicks on and off; the effect is known as Shadow Flicker. It occurs only within buildings where the flicker appears through a narrow window opening…

'13.04—Shadow Flicker frequency tends to be related to the rotor speed and the number of blades on the rotor and this can be translated into "blade path frequency" and measured in alternations per second or hertz. Two main concerns have been raised regarding the effects of Shadow Flicker and they are not exclusive to wind turbines: (1) they may cause seizures in people who are photo-sensitive and (2) they may cause considerable annoyance to people.'

Further down the same page was a table headed 'Detailed Dwelling Assessment' and in it each property scheduled to have a turbine at 11.5 rotor diameters to the east, south or west of it, was listed. In all, eleven houses were named: Foxhill Farm and Farm Cottage; Blaestane Cottage; Cockers Toll Cottage; Ballinder Farm and Farm Cottage; Wester Broadhill Cottage; Easter Broadhill Cottage; Struieford Cottage; Gowkshill Farm and Scowling Crags Farm. Another nearby page showed proposed turbine locations on an enlarged section from the Ordnance Survey map with all of the nearby dwellings marked with a red star.

Eric Manson strolled past Alice's desk to his own and emptied a black bin bag, full of correspondence, onto it, sighing deeply as he did so.

'Could I have a quick look, Sir?' Alice asked.

'Be my guest, doll, I'm off to talk to the boss and then I'm going to see what Forensics has come up with, if anything.'

She combed through the pile, item by item. It was composed largely of e-mails, typed submissions and a few pre-printed postcards; and, diligently, she wrote down the names of all the senders. A few of them kept recurring: Angus Kersley, Joanna Hart, David Oxford, Gavin Logan and Morag McTear. Morag McTear's contribution was contained in a slim folder and her address was marked, together with her name, prominently on the first page. She lived in Gowkshill Farm and her date of birth was also marked: 11th January 1920. An old lady. For Angus Kersley two addresses had been given: Wester Broadhill Cottage and 'Barleyknowe' in Ravelston Dykes, Edinburgh.

Hundreds of the e-mails had come from another source, jhcocker@cockerstoll.com. Enough to be going on with.

—

When Alice rang Angus Kersley he was, by her good fortune, in Ravelston, suffering from a broken ankle, instead of at work, attending to his legal practice in his Alva Street office. Home turned out to be a half-timbered mock-Tudor mansion in the middle of the comfortable suburb. Even the garage had been decked with dark horizontal beams, and the front garden showed signs of slavish adherence to current gardening trends, with alarming clumps of black-leaved plants, tussocks of arid grasses and not a flower in sight. The delay between the pressing of the doorbell and the door being finally opened was explained by the large plaster cast encasing the man's left leg and foot. He guided her to his study, his leaden limb dragging against the deep pile of the carpet, leaving a broad trail behind him.

The sight that met her eyes on entering the room amazed her. It was like gaining access to some kind of military headquarters. Pinned on the walls were large-scale maps, most of them of the Scowling Crags wind farm area. Each one displayed something different. One mapped out the turbine locations relative to the houses within the development. Another showed the system of tracks required for the wind farm, together with the 'borrow pits' from which the track construction materials would be quarried. Others showed the hydrogeology of the area and others still depicted the principal archaeological sites either within the development or close to it. Part of one wall was devoted to lists, each written in a neat, workaday hand with no pretension to style. They contained the names of the members of the local Council and the names of the members of the various committees of the Council. The names of those on the Planning Development and Control Committee were all underlined in red. Vast piles of pre-printed postcards lay strewn about the floor, together with blank sheets headed 'Petition Against Scowling Crags Wind Farm'.

Kersley's computer was on, and Alice noticed that some of the material that Vertenergy had produced appeared to have been scanned into it.

'A day off?' she said conversationally, as he closed his study door.

'A day off paid work,' he corrected her, in his distinctive Morningside accent. The telephone rang and he picked it up.

'Sorry, Alistair, I'm busy just now. We'll speak at the big meeting and I'll bring along forms for your group then. Have you discovered how much the Post Office charge for a drop? Mmmm. OK. Speak to you later.'

'I need to…' Alice began. The telephone rang again and, once more, he picked up the receiver.

'David. OK. I can't talk now. I suggest that you contact the RSPB to see if their ornithological data about the geese is correct. No, I haven't got a number for them. You'll have to fish it out yourself. It'll probably be in the book.'

'Sorry,' the man said, turning his attention back to Alice. Yet again the telephone rang.

'Nope. It's Councillor Garth you need to speak to, and you can forget the Community Council, they're hopeless. I'm afraid I've got someone here so I must go. Bye.'

So saying the man took the phone off the hook and they both, momentarily, enjoyed the silence before Alice attempted to re-start the interview.

'It's about the Scowling Crags wind farm, Mr Kersley. You seem to be part of the group, quite possibly its leader judging by the stuff your study's now filled with, and all those telephone enquiries…'

'I am, for my sins. Absolutely,' he replied. 'I've a house within the proposed development, Wester Broadhill, and I'd planned retiring there. But the place will be ruined if the developers get their way. How can I help you, Sergeant?'

'First of all, can I ask you where you were on Monday 12th June between, say, seven pm and ten pm?'

'Easy. I was here, preparing for the next day. I'm a solicitor. I had a complicated fatal accident enquiry in Glasgow Sheriff Court, all about a suicide in a mental hospital. I had to work on it until about two am to try and master some of the more arcane stuff about staff rotas and so on.'

'Was there anyone here with you?'

'Aha. My wife, Angela. She can confirm it for you if you want. She'll remember all right, because we had a blazing row that night as we were supposed to be having dinner with friends and I said I couldn't go. Caused some unbelievable fireworks.'

'Those lists on the wall, the Councillors and so on. Is that your handwriting?'

The man looked bemused. 'Yes. It's mine.'

Alice handed over a sheet bearing examples of the anonymous letter writer's script.

'Can you tell me, do you recognise that writing, Mr Kersley?'

The man examined the paper carefully before handing it back.

'No. It's very distinctive. Artistic looking. Why?'

Alice ignored the question. 'Would it be possible for you to give me a list of all the people in your group?'

'No problem. Anything else you need?'

'Thank you. Do you know who the landlords are, I mean those allowing Vertenergy to put up the turbines on their land?'

'Yes, of course. I tried, personally, to persuade some of them not to go ahead. Let me see... they're mainly absentees, of course. Well, there's Tony Theobold, Kenneth Winston and the retired Sheriff, James Freeman. The dead one. Is that why you're here?' A look of anxiety passed across his face.

'Was Sheriff Freeman one of the ones you met with?'

'So that's what this is all about. I see,' he smiled weakly. 'My leg's been in plaster for over six weeks, Sergeant, so I couldn't have killed him even if I had wanted to. And I didn't, by the way. Either want to. Or kill him. Yes, I met with James Freeman at the cottage. It must have been months and months ago. Spring, I think. The daffodils were certainly still out. He was polite, as you'd expect, but obstinate. He lectured me about clean, renewable energy, although, to be fair, he did listen to my counter-arguments. It was all very civilised.'

'Forgive me for asking, but are there any members of your group who feel particularly passionate about the development, stopping it, I mean?'

'I wouldn't know where to begin. They all, I repeat, *all*, hate it. Really hate it! Would any of them kill someone to stop it? I don't know. No-one sane for sure. But why don't you come and see for yourself? There's to be a big meeting in Perth Town Hall, four days hence, on Sunday 9th July. There's no admission charge and virtually all of us plan to attend. There's supposed to be groups from all over the country.'

'Will Joanna Hart be there?'

'I'd be surprised if she wasn't. She's one of the speakers.'

—

The PM programme was just starting on the radio, so time was plentiful. She turned on the cold tap with her big toe, reducing the temperature of the water until it was just above tepid. The air in her flat, like that in the street outside, was warm. It would dry her without the need for a towel. Resting on the bath was her glass of white wine, all but empty, and she drained its dregs, relishing the taste on her tongue. While so thoroughly relaxed she should, she thought, plan what to wear. If they were going for a walk by the sea then her black jeans would do and, maybe, her red tee-shirt. No, she would have to think again. That tee-shirt was still in the wash, and with it her second favourite top, a light-blue short sleeved blouse.

Eddie Mair's voice, interviewing the latest Secretary of State for Defence about the campaign against the Taliban in Afghanistan, re-directed her thoughts away from clothes and back onto an old and well-worn track. Women had been oppressed in that country for years and years, and no-one in the West had given a stuff. Scant bloody Radio Four coverage of their suffering then. Now thoroughly annoyed, she rose from her bath and stomped off to her room to dress.

At six-thirty on the dot the doorbell rang, and the tall form of Ian Melville, slightly out of breath from running up the tenement stairs, stood before her. 'Let's go to the Dean Cemetery and have a look around it, eh?'

Not what she had planned. 'OK. I've certainly never been. Have your got your car?'

'No,' he looked slightly uneasy, 'the exhaust's fallen off, but I thought, perhaps, we could walk there? I'm really sorry. Quill could come on the lead.'

Again, not what she had planned. 'That'll be fine. But do you mind deciding on our route? I'll follow happily, but I've had enough decision-making today.'

As they emerged onto Broughton Place the tinny, discordant chimes of an ice cream van could be heard on the windless air. The sun was high in the sky, and on the pavement, in places, the tar seemed sticky. They strolled down the hill towards Canonmills, intending to use the Water of Leith Walkway as a route across the city. A thin mist hung above the turbid waters of the river, making its characteristic scent more pungent and, in the dense shade of the overhanging trees, the atmosphere was unexpectedly dank and humid. Quill, eager to run, strained on the lead as if an invisible hare was half a metre in front of his nose, and by the time they reached the Colonies, Alice's arm ached. Half of Stockbridge seemed to have decided to promenade along the river that evening, and the couple strolled together, hand in hand, amongst the others, occasionally lurching unpredictably to the left or right, following Quill's whim like puppets.

They arrived at a discreet back-entrance to the cemetery, having left the river at Bells Mills, retraced their steps up Belford Road and crossed the grounds of the Dean Gallery. A 'No Dogs' sign immediately confronted them. Alice tied Quill's lead to a tree and tried to ignore his piteous yelps, as he railed against the division of his pack and, in particular, her desertion of him. As they entered the consecrated ground, a massive, pink granite pyramid stood on their right, a strange cave hollowed out of one side, making the structure imperfect and profoundly pagan. Still holding hands they meandered past memorials, grand and grander, until, on reaching the apotheosis of grandeur, Buchanan's Monument, they watched in amazement as a pair of grey squirrels frolicked all over it, using it as a gymnasium, unabashed by the disapproving chorus set up by the magpie residents in the canopy above.

Having torn themselves away from the display, the couple came across a tall sculpture and stopped, rapt by its eccentric charm, the delight of each enhanced by the presence of the other. The base of the piece was composed of winged lions supporting a pedestal with rams' heads on it and they, in turn, supported spindly pelicans.

As they examined it the Dean Bell tolled mournfully and, as if on cue, a few raindrops began to fall, rapidly followed by a heavier downpour. Dropping Ian's hand, Alice raced off towards the pyramid, tearing breathlessly past deceased lawyers, engineers and architects, and on reaching it crouched down in the hollowed-out section. Within seconds he had joined her, and Quill, sensing their closeness, began howling afresh. And in the grounds of the Necropolis, surrounded by the remains of the great and the good, they kissed.

The grandfather clock chimed nine. Alone again. He looked around the drawing room, surveying it as if seeing it for the first time. In his youth its grandeur had both impressed and appalled him until, as the years passed, he had become accustomed to the strange collection of family relics it contained and ceased to shiver on finding himself looked down upon by the stern warriors arrayed on the walls. Slowly he walked upstairs, crossed the landing to James' room and pushed the door open. The scent of his lover hit him immediately, unexpectedly and powerfully, and he buried his face in the pillows, painfully conscious that with time even this slight comfort would disappear. By the bedside was a framed photograph of himself, laughing on holiday in the Alps, and he turned it over, face down, onto the cabinet. It belonged to the past, and somehow, somehow, a new future would have to be forged, one in which he could live each minute of every hour as if it mattered, until, finally, he, too, would be released.

Removing his key from the lock he descended the stone steps to the pavement, watching, as he did so, a troupe of starlings bobbing up and down, bickering with each other on the black railings encircling the gardens. As he began crossing the cobbles, a screeching sound cut through his head, and he turned to his left, attempting to locate the noise. Then there was an ear-splitting bang. The impact of the car sent him flying, hurtling through the air as if he weighed nothing until, everything having slowed down, he slammed into a parked jeep with a strange crunching sound and felt himself sliding down the bonnet, crumpling onto the ground below.

I am still alive, he thought. He tried to open his eyes, to shout, call for help, but nothing happened. The blackness remained and no voice came from his lips. Blood trickling into his eye tickled the edge of his nose and, in his mind, he moved a hand to scratch it, but the itch remained and his fingers felt none of the warm, sticky fluid that was streaming from his forehead.

Someone had come, was leaning over him, shouting, crying, and he recognised, in the warm breath on his face, the smell of alcohol mixed with perfume. Liv. She was speaking to him, pleading, sobbing, and in his head he answered her, comforted her, but it seemed to have no effect. She carried on, screaming now, shouting, inconsolable. Her hair brushed against his face, tickling it unbearably, and he strained to turn to his side, prevent it happening again, maybe even to scratch his skin on the road surface. But another strand swept his cheek.

He shivered. When had it become so cold? The air had seemed kind earlier, hot in the late afternoon. Where had this chill come from? Seconds later he sensed a blanket being laid over him, rejoiced in its weight, waited for warmth that did not come. He could feel the woman close by, beside him, her hand in his below the rug.

9

DCI Bruce's complexion, usually pale, was clay-coloured and his lips seemed to have been drained of blood. His tie had come loose and he was manically pacing up and down the murder suite. Once the entire squad had assembled, chattering together uninhibitedly, he stood stock still. The hum continued unabated.

'Shut up, people!' he commanded, and, electrified, every mouth closed.

'Thank you and not before sodding time. I've just heard that last night, 5th July, probably at about nine o'clock or so, Nicholas Lyon was run down in Moray Place. The car driver didn't stop and no accident's been reported by any driver at that location. In other words, an effing hit-and-run, one likely to prove fatal to boot. An ambulance was called and he's currently in the Western. The traffic department are still scouring the scene. We've no way of knowing, as yet, whether the Sheriff's death and Mr Lyon's accident are connected, but it would seem a remarkable coincidence if they weren't. Accordingly, that probability needs to be considered. Alice, how did you get on with Major Freeman?'

'OK, I think, Sir. He hadn't any letters and seemed completely unaware that his brother had been subject to threats in any form…'

The DCI interrupted her. 'Eric. I want you to go and liaise with traffic. All information must be shared, chat up the redhead in charge—what's her name—Yvonne something or other. Tell her all about the connection between the two victims.'

'Aye, aye, Sir. Yvonne Woolman's her name,' DI Manson said, stirring his coffee but remaining seated.

'Well, move your arse, Inspector, and get on to it now. This very minute, OK?'

The policeman left the room, mug in hand, looking uncharacteristically chastened.

'Alistair, how did you get on checking the stuff on the computer?'

DS Watt shook his head. 'I didn't get much, I'm afraid. I've discovered that there are hundreds of environmental protection groups, landscape guardians and so on, some of them general and some of them associated with particular wind farms or wind farm clusters, but there are no organisations that I've been able to find connected exclusively to Scowling Crags. I don't think we're going to get anything much from that source.'

'Bugger. Alice, go on with what you were saying about Major Freeman?'

'Just that he hadn't received letters or threats. However, I did get the Vertenergy stuff from Nicholas Lyon and I've made contact with one of the anti-wind farm activists, a chap called Angus Kersley. He doesn't seem to think...'

She stopped in mid-sentence noticing that DC Lowe had put up his hand.

'Yes?' the DCI said, looking menacingly at the constable.

'Sir, I missed yesterday's meeting, so I may be well out of order, but couldn't the Sheriff's murder and the hit-and-run on Nicholas Lyon be about... well, their homosexuality? Maybe someone's got a grudge against gayboys. One of these fundamentalist Christians or something. That boy, Georgie...'

'Thank you, Lowe,' Bruce said coldly, cutting the man off mid-sentence, and then turning his attention back to Alice.

'Go on then, Sergeant.'

'He, Kersley, gave me the impression that he didn't think that anyone in his group would have killed Freeman, but there's a meeting on Sunday and I'm going to go and see what's what.'

'OK. I want DCs Lowe, McDonald and Trotter to go and help with the door to doors round about Moray Place. No doubt there'll be uniforms there too. Someone must have bloody seen something. Speak to the officer in charge, Sergeant Joseph.'

'Sir?'

'Yes, Alice.'

'Who reported the accident? Got the ambulance?'

'That Nordquist woman. By the way, I want you to check on garages within the city. See if any vehicles have come in this morning, eh? Liaise with the traffic department.'

Alice nodded her head.

'Should we get protection for Mr Lyon, Sir?'

'No. He's past that I reckon, in intensive care, so never mind him. After I leave here I'm seeing the ACC and he's not going to be pleased. Trust me. We've got nothing—except a second sodding body! You are all going to have to re-double your efforts… I'm not carrying the can for this one.'

The intensive care unit was intimidating, leads and monitors beside each bed and frail lives depending upon them. The staff, however, seemed relaxed, busy measuring out the medications for the evening, so familiar with proximity to death as to be blasé about it. If they had been employed on a confectionery production line in a sweet factory they could not have looked less troubled, more at ease in their own environment. But the air was not scented with chocolate or peppermint, it had an astringent quality, the smell of disinfectant and mortality.

Alice peered at the beds through the windows of the locked double doors, but was unable to make out Nicholas Lyon's figure. Her view was obscured by two closed sets of curtains in the middle of the room. Like oversized shrouds, she thought. And suddenly, the sight of the whole set-up filled her with such despondency, such a feeling of leaden hopelessness that she weakened, and began searching for an Exit sign. As she was wandering down the corridor she noticed a single room opposite the 'Care of the Elderly' ward and decided to investigate it. If he was not there, then she would go, she had done her bit, done her best. Peering round the door gingerly, she recognised the old man in a solitary bed, accompanied only by a single monitor, and came to stand beside him. Little evidence of the injuries he had sustained was visible. One side of his face was livid with bruising, his temples sunken. And his complexion had become colourless, near translucent, as if he had been sculpted in pale marble. The only sign of life in the room was the flashing of a little red light monitoring the flow in a tube running between the patient's hand and a drip pack. Briefly, she watched it pulse, mesmerised.

'Who are you? Are you family? Only family are allowed now.' A nurse had entered and looked disconcerted to find her charge with company.

' Yes, Mr Lyon's daughter.'

On impulse it had emerged; a clear, conscious and defiant lie. But without her he would be alone, and she sensed that he was near journey's end. The nurse left the room discreetly and Alice remained, on tenterhooks in case of her return, unwilling to leave him on his own whatever the proprieties might be. A few minutes later, Nicholas Lyon let out a deep sigh, as if of relief, and it was immediately followed by the mechanical scream of the monitor, signalling that his heart had ceased to beat.

10

The call to his flat had remained unanswered, but he had told her that she was free to come to his studio any time of the day or night. A visit from her would not constitute a disturbance whenever it took place. He would welcome it. And, anyway, where else could he be?

She entered the crumbling building by the Henderson Row doorway, and feeling the cool air of the place she remembered the last time she had gone there, less than a year earlier. Then it had been in the depth of winter, early December, and the mist of her breath had been visible in its freezing interior and the space had seemed threatening, entirely alien to her. Ducking under the grimy bed sheets that formed a makeshift barrier between the two studios, she recognised Kathleen Ferrier's low tones, singing Mahler's 'Das Lied von der Erde'. Nature would renew itself once more, she thought, but not for Nicholas Lyon to tend or tame, and a picture of the gardens at Geanbank, rank and overgrown, appeared before her eyes.

The unplastered brick walls of the dilapidated studio were covered, as before, with sketches of human figures, cavorting at the circus, riding bareback, or performing exercises within a gymnasium. Her study of the drawings ended when her attention was caught by the sound of the hammer and she saw Ian Melville, seated on a sofa in the corner of the room, concentrating hard, absorbed in fashioning a picture frame and blithely unaware of her entrance. She began to move towards him, but stopped at an easel to view the drawing resting on it. A light pencil sketch of a naked woman reclining on a bed.

The work betrayed tenderness; imperfections recorded but not dwelt upon; a portrait, not simply a ruthless exercise in observation. Looking at the head, she started on recognising her own face, felt momentarily rattled to find herself scrutinising someone else's image of her, as if she was indulging in some form of extreme egoism.

'When did you do it?' she asked, her voice sharper than she had intended.

The man looked up and she watched as his face reddened, suffused with blood, more embarrassed now than ever when naked, as if his drawing of her had exposed something far more personal than his own unclothed body. He recovered quickly.

'When do you think? Early in the morning when you were still asleep. D'you mind? I'm just making a frame for it, to give it to you.'

A quick succession of unwanted thoughts flitted through her head before she answered. Had he drawn all the other women that he had slept with? Was the picture a form of record of a conquest, like the notches on a Spitfire's wing? Would it have been worse if he had photographed her, unconscious and asleep, instead? She glanced again at the picture and found that what she saw allayed the sudden panic that had risen within her. It was not some stolen glimpse of a meaningless encounter; rather a depiction that could only have sprung from genuine intimacy, true sympathy with the subject.

'No, I don't mind. I've just come from the hospital. Nicholas Lyon's dead. He died less than an hour ago.'

She had not expected his death to affect her as it had, but somehow in her mind his fate had become linked with that of her mother. If he could just survive, then she, too, would survive. And the sadness she had felt, gazing at the still, small figure in the hospital bed had, to her shame, expanded, swollen and consumed her, releasing all the anxieties she had been trying to control, to make her day-to-day life possible. But all she could think about then, and now, was her beloved mother in the shadow of that evil disease.

⟨⟩

The next morning Alice was swearing to herself, unable to find the paper copy of Doctor Zenabi's report in among the midden of papers covering her desk. Alistair plonked a mug of tea on her diary.

'You heard?'

'Heard what?' she asked, irritation at this interruption clear in her voice.

'The Sheriff's partner. He died last night.'

'Yes, I know.'

'How come? Anyway, apparently, he's got a child. A grown-up daughter actually. The boss wants us to spend the morning tracking her down.'

'Well, Bingo!' Alice said, abandoning the search and taking a sip from the mug, 'we've done it already!'

'What on earth are you going on about?'

'Yesterday night… I spent some of it with the old fellow at the hospital. A nurse came in, just before he died. She would have shooed me away unless I claimed to be a family member. So I said I was. He couldn't be left to meet his Maker on his own.'

'Jesus Christ, Alice. You could have mucked things up nicely! Anyway, haven't you got a home to go to?'

She smiled at him. 'I have, thanks, and I can do without the lecture. Don't worry, pal, I'll speak to the DCI about the phantom child. By the way, I've just been on the phone to traffic. Dan there says that they've found a few flakes of paint. It seems the car was white and, they reckon, probably, one of the smaller, cheaper makes. Some of the slivers are with the lab now, so they think they'll have a better clue as to the exact type before too long. They're attempting calculations on the tyre marks as well, and the photographers are busy at the scene. Dan also said that some uniforms brought in a few shards of broken glass but they're not sure if they've come from the vehicle we're looking for. Apparently, the fragments are dirty, as if they'd been at the locus for a while. After I've seen the boss and explained things, let's go and see Mrs Nordquist again, eh? '

'Certainly. With you as my chaperone.'

Beside her, as always, stood a small glass, filled to the brim with golden fluid. It rested within a hand's reach of the striped deckchair, which sagged beneath the weight of the solid Swedish matron. She did not rise from it to greet the two detectives when they were shown into her paved back garden. Instead, she pulled up the rug that concealed her naked body until it almost reached her chin. On one side, however, an expanse of pink flesh was visible. Conscious of their surprise, she said to her visitors in a matter of fact tone: '…the sowna. I haff von in the basement.'

Both officers towered over the seated figure, feeling awkward and ill at ease, unsure of the etiquette in this situation. Their hostess, in contrast, seemed unflustered, relaxed even, despite the unmistakeable tension of her visitors and her own relative undress. Eyes half closed, she said: 'Why don't you both jusst sit on the ground, officers,' before adding, as an afterthought, 'I haff only von deckchair ant I neet it.'

And so the interview began with her interrogators squatting at her feet, each wishing that they had taken the initiative earlier and requested, or even demanded, that the session be conducted indoors. Alice, painfully conscious that any authority she might once have possessed had evaporated on finding herself at eye level to a bare knee, began: 'I understand that you were the first one to find Mr Lyon on Wednesday night. Is that right?'

114

'Yess.'

From under the rug Mrs Nordquist found a cigarette, and endeavoured, ineffectually, to light it while preserving her decency.

'Can you tell us how that came about, you finding him, I mean?'

The remaining lobster-red arm extended itself to grasp the glass, and a large swig was consumed before any answer was forthcoming.

'Waal, I wass upstairs in my betroom actually—it faces the street—ant I heard a car. The noiss of sutten acceleration... high speet. From nowhere. Then there was the sort of... thut... ant then the sount of the car drifing away. I looked out,' she stopped momentarily and sighed before continuing, 'ant there he wass. Nicholas, I mean, lying on the copples, blut all around him. Sso I put down my hairbrush ant ran out to see him. His eyes were clost. I shouted "Mrs McColl, Mrs McColl! Nine, nine, nine." She gott the ambulance ant brought blankets to keep him varm. I state with him... but he nefer opened his eyes or spoke.'

Alice looked up at Mrs Nordquist's face. Her lower lip was trembling and she was blinking copiously, fighting to keep control of her emotions. Wordlessly, the policewoman passed her the glass of aquavit and wordlessly, she drank from it, draining every last drop.

'And when did all this happen?' Alistair asked.

'The night before lasst. Oh... say, nine o'clock, possibly, a little after when I heard the noisses.'

'But you didn't see anything happen? The collision? The first thing you saw was Mr Lyon, injured on the street?'

'Yess. I nefer saw the car. Most probably, it must have been parked in Moray Place or something. It wass the sutten acceleration that first... well, that seemed so ott.'

Freya padded through the French doors to join her mistress, and stood expectantly in front of her. Gently, Mrs Nordquist raised both of the dog's ears in her hands and then sank her face into its warm head. As the detectives began to rise from their prostrate position, it stared at them with its sinister yellow eyes and let out a long, low growl which stopped them in their tracks. The noise only ceased when Mrs Nordquist came up for air and relaxed back into her deckchair. And then, and only then, did her visitors exit her domain.

Mrs McColl, an Aberdonian Scot and as conventional as her Scandinavian employer was unconventional, sat with her knees tight together on a leather-covered stool in the state-of-the-art kitchen. In fact, the place was more of a food laboratory than an ordinary, domestic kitchen, the stainless steel and glass units lending it an air of sterility. Oddly, the housekeeper was wearing a nylon housecoat, a garment completely at odds with her space-age workplace, an environment which would more harmoniously have suited a skin-tight silver one-piece rather than this incongruous throwback to a gentler age.

'When did you first become aware of the accident, Mrs McColl?' Alice enquired.

'The time? Och, mebbe about half nine or thereabouts I'd say. I was doing the washing up—we've a Miele, quiet as a mouse you know—and I heard her shouting, screaming something. I ran upstairs, looked out the door and saw her in the street, bending over someone who's been knocked down. I phoned the ambulance right away. Then, after that, for you… the polis, I mean.'

'Did you see the car involved in the accident… anything?

'No, I'm sorry. All I saw was the man, Mr Lyon, lying in the street. I recognised him when I went out with the blankets.'

'Had you heard anything before you became aware of your employer shouting?'

'No. I'm really very sorry but I was busy putting away the supper things. I only heard her voice because… well, she was screaming, she sounded hysterical.'

116

'Did you know Mr Lyon or Sheriff Freeman?' Alice persisted.

'No,' the woman looked her inquisitor in the eye. 'I didn't know either of them. Mrs Nordquist does, so I have seen them both, on occasions, when they've visited here. I saw more of the Sheriff. The little I saw of them... well, I liked them. Mrs Nordquist was always very pleased to see either of them, and the Sheriff, you know, helped her a lot after her husband left her. And not just with the legal stuff; as a real friend, I mean. I think, and I may be speaking out of turn, but I think he was helping her to get off... well, the drink. She almost never touched the stuff in the old days. My life was a great deal easier then, when she was happy, I mean.'

—

'Alice, love, I've left a little note on your desk,' DI Manson said cheerily to her as she passed him on her way to the La-dies. The ill-suppressed glee in his voice forewarned her that its contents would not please her. Sure enough. It contained an instruction from the DCI that she now telephone all the garages round the edge of the capital; places like Musselburgh, Tranent, Penicuik, Portobello, Ratho and so on. Sheer unadul-terated drudgery, probably given to her as a punishment for her unauthorised impersonation and, more damningly, the lack of remorse shown by her for it. At their meeting earlier that morning, Robin Bruce had impressed upon her his disappoint-ment and disapproval of her conduct. And he had conveyed something altogether more sinister; that if the matter were to be taken no further she would, in some intangible way, be in his debt.

'DS Rice, apart from anything else, scarce resources might well have been wasted in the search for Mr Lyon's non-existent daughter.'

'I know, Sir. I'm sorry, too, but I don't think that's very like-ly. Tracing the woman would have fallen to the murder squad, so I'd have heard about it and immediately explained that she didn't exist.'

'And if you hadn't heard… because, say, you were out of the office attending to something or other?'

Good point, she thought, but said only: 'Well. As I say, Sir, I'm sorry. But Mr Lyon had nobody. I knew that he had nobody. And he was, obviously, dying. If I hadn't pretended to be a member of the family the nurse would have kicked me out.'

'Before you went to the hospital you didn't know he was dying. What the hell were you doing there anyway?'

'It sounded, from your report, as if he was close to death's door. You said it was "likely to prove fatal" after all, and traffic was involved. I knew him a bit. I liked him. To be honest, I wanted to see him. It all happened in my own time.'

'Well, we're lucky that the Infirmary isn't making more of a fuss about the whole thing. As far as I am concerned you can visit whomsoever the hell you like, in your own time, but do not, I repeat, DO NOT ever impersonate a relative like that again. Is that clear? This is a murder enquiry and you—you nearly sent us off on an expensive wild goose chase.'

'Yes, Sir. Sorry, Sir.'

'Oh, and Alice?'

'Yes, Sir.'

'For the moment, at least, this'll go no further. Be our little secret, eh?' And he winked conspiratorially.

—

And looking at the Yellow Pages she felt genuine penitence; 'Boswell's Garage', 'Butchart Motors', 'Chas's Auto Repairs', page after page of similar entries. But not for holding the man's hand as he died. Jaded already, she picked up the receiver and dialled the first number.

'Hello, is that Allanton's Auto Services?'

'Aha.'

'This is DS Rice of Lothian and Borders Police. We need to know if any cars have been brought into your premises this morning, following an accident, for repairs. Or if you've had any phone calls asking if any such vehicles could be attended to in the near future?'

'Eh?' Apparent incomprehension.

'This is the Police. Can you tell me, have you had any damaged cars brought in this morning for repairs?'

'Eh? Damaged cars?' Had she somehow lost the ability to speak English, she wondered.

'Yes, damaged cars. Have any been brought into your garage this morning to be mended?'

'I've nae idea. Derek! Derek! Come and speak, there's a lassie on the phone...'

After three hours of non-stop calling, all she had to show for it was a black transit van in Loanhead, a motor bike in Ratho and a minibus in Port Seton, and none of them seemed likely candidates for the Moray Place accident. DI Manson rose from his chair, stretched and yawned and ambled over to her desk.

'Alice, dear, I've just heard from the DCI that you are to prepare the press release for the witness appeal. It seems you've been on the phone for ages so he told me to tell you myself. Also, he wants you, for some reason, to draft something in case there's to be another television appeal. He'll do the appearance, obviously. Now, I'm just off for my tea. I could get you something only... I'm off to the pub after that. Oh yes, and you are to make arrangements for text messages in connection with the appeal. And... no, that's it.'

❦

Maybe the woman would be late, held up by a benevolent deity, Alice thought. But the ominous sound of the cleaning trolley, mop clanging against the bucket, confirmed the nuns' claim that He moved in mysterious ways. Mrs McLaren pushed her chariot towards the bank of wastepaper baskets and began tipping the rubbish, untidily, into a black bin-bag. An organic, vinegary odour clung to her, occasionally masked by drifts of air-freshener or furniture polish, and as she propelled the cart onwards, using it as a makeshift Zimmer, wafts of her overpowering perfume were dispersed throughout the room. The job bored her; she was not one of nature's domestics and her own home would not have borne inspection, too much of a busman's holiday for her to flick a duster in any of its nooks or crannies. Lavatories alone provided her with job satisfaction; immaculate porcelain and glistening mirrors. So unlike offices, veritable death-traps of cables, usually attached to expensive machines.

'No' still here are ye, pet?' she said conversationally, smiling warmly at Alice's presence. But her prey was wary, unwilling to engage in conversation, knowing only too well where it would lead, and nervous of participating in their well-rehearsed dance, having suffered bruised feet too often.

'I am indeed,' Alice responded, trying to sound cheery, ebullient enough to deflect any further probing.

'Still no man then, eh?'

There had been no preamble this time; none of the customary circling around the subject; the pretence that anything else about the Sergeant was of any interest. The woman's touch was sure, as ever; she had managed to destroy, bring crashing to the ground, her listener's self-esteem, although minutes before it had been fine, high even. Alice immediately found herself wondering how to describe Ian Melville. She could say pertly, 'No, I have a boyfriend now,' only it sounded defensive, oddly undignified too, as if they were the stuff of teen magazines. But to say, 'No, I have a lover now' seemed over-explicit, an unnecessary whiff of carnality, the hollow boast of a desperate exhibitionist. Seconds passed like minutes as she perfected her chosen reply, all the while mocking herself for doing so.

'I have, thanks.'

Nicely judged, she thought, before castigating herself again for wasting time on the semantics of an unwelcome exchange. The door banged open and DCI Bruce rolled in, eyes slightly glazed, bumping the edge of a desk before reaching his target. Alice.

'S'at woman not finished yet?'

He gestured wildly at the cleaner who, over-sensitive to the hint, gathered her tools together and departed, shaking her head at the man and mouthing, mid-exit, a single word. 'Fu'.' And it was true, the inspector had been drinking; drinking to celebrate the end of the day's work, drinking to celebrate his birthday, and drinking most of all to forget the lack of progress in his case. Companions had come and gone, few occupying the nearby bar-stool for any length of time. He sat down heavily on his subordinate's desk and looked at her, saying nothing, gazing into her eyes. His face was only a few inches from hers. Had his gait or unnerving proximity not given away his intoxicated state, his beery breath would have, but he was neither aggressive nor threatening.

'Alice... Alice... Alice... you—you of all people should not be working late.'

Nor would I be but for your sodding orders, she thought bitterly, but said, soothingly, 'Nearly finished, Sir,' while logging out and collecting her keys and purse from a drawer. Then she bent down to pick up her bag from the floor and, simultaneously, he reached over to touch her hair, but finding no resistance, toppled downwards, eventually smiling up at her from her own lap. Gingerly, as if handling an unpredictable beast, she lifted his head up, until, equilibrium temporarily restored, he was able to right himself. Before he had a chance to lunge at her again, she sprang out of her chair, and made a dash for the door. Heels clacking down the stairs, she sped away angry, irritable enough to spit at her own shadow.

'He's nae worth it, hen, trust me!' shouted Mrs McLaren, sweeping the steps and innocently salting the wound.

II

All around Perth City Hall a crowd was gathering, growing from minute to minute as yet more latecomers arrived from each of the four points of the compass. And still the doors remained locked. Faded tweeds rubbed shoulders with track-suits, and cardigans with crop tops, everyone good-natured, patient, united against a common foe. At seven o'clock exactly the bells of the nearby Kirk sounded, and as their peals died away the assembled mass were, finally, allowed into the dingy public building.

The back third of the hall had been reserved for exhibitions by the participating groups, and the chosen centrepieces favoured by most of them were displays illustrating the immense size of the second generation structures proposed by the more rapacious developers. Pathetically inept scale-models had been constructed, usually juxtaposing pylons and turbines, and in the comparison the pylons looked comfortingly familiar, out-dated and gothic beside their vast, streamlined, sky-hugging neighbours. Protesters from all over the country had furnished their stalls with the same things, the essential armaments in the battle against the might of the big companies: petitions to be signed by any sympathetic passer-by, and pro-forma post-cards containing objections to the granting of planning per-mission, every card ready stamped and addressed. Everywhere there were photographs of the targeted wind farm sites, showing idyllic sylvan glades, peaceful lochside retreats and heather-clad hills. Each one a beloved tract of countryside, free from man-kind's recent depredations and their accompanying detritus. In stark contrast were the images of the 'farms' in the course of construction, with Somme-like fields of mud, roads gouged through acres of felled trees, raw gashes left by drainage ditches and the unsightly pock marks created by borrow pits. Three of the Perthshire groups had executed wildlife surveys highlighting the creatures imperilled by the schemes. Endearing posters of pine martens, otters, badgers, red squirrel and hare were lined up beneath a banner stating 'Protect Tayside's Biodiversity'.

And everywhere ordinary, but desperate people steeled themselves to accost passers-by to persuade them to sign anything and everything if they showed the slightest flicker of interest.

At seven-thirty on the dot the lights dimmed and the Chairman opened the meeting with an introductory speech. Alice crept into a seat near the back and stealthily unwrapped her bundle of fish and chips. Extracting a piece of haddock in batter, she endeavoured to eat it silently, conscious that the woman on her left was grimacing, showing her displeasure at the aroma now rising from her newspaper-covered lap.

Joanna Hart took the podium to resounding applause. She appeared entirely self-possessed despite being the centre of attention, and some of the reasons for her sublime confidence were immediately apparent to all. The woman was black, statuesque and blessed with heavenly good looks. If that dusty platform in the small northern city had been a catwalk in Paris she would have ornamented it. She stood erect, hands placed lightly on either side of the lectern, and silently surveyed the hall and the multitude within it. Only when the clapping had ceased completely did she begin to speak, and then in measured tones. No over-hasty delivery, stammering or stuttering for her, rather the performance of a virtuoso, revelling in her mastery of her subject and the known sympathy of those to whom her speech was addressed. It was dry stuff: International Policy on

Climate Change, National Planning Policy, Guidelines, Advice Notes and the Regional Wind Energy Policies. But delivered by her, the abstruse became clear, interesting even, and the dullest texts acquired some sort of spurious excitement.

Next she turned her attention to the approach taken by the developers: their disregard or token regard for the planning system and the ruses they deployed in order to 'play' it. Seamlessly, this merged into an analysis of the fortunes to be won by developers and landlords in the rush for wind. Rents in excess of thirteen thousand pounds per annum for each turbine, and ground, barren, windswept wild land, transformed in value from a few hundred pounds per acre to hundreds of thousands of pounds per acre, simply by the addition of planning permission for the turbines. It was, she explained, a bonanza. The massive subsidies payable by the government meant that the costs involved in submitting planning applications, appealing decisions and obtaining representation at public enquiries were as nothing compared to the size of the prize at the end. She finished on a popular note, contrasting the bottomless pockets of the development companies with the meagre funds scraped together by the little bands of protesters, and then she reminded her now enchanted audience that David had triumphed over Goliath.

'So David prevailed over the Philistine with a sling and with a stone, and smote the Philistine, and slew him; but there was no sword in the hand of David.'

The next speaker was a small man, dwarfed by the lectern, and his task in following the goddess was impossible. Dr Mungo MacGowan was a shy academic, intimidated in a cosy lecture theatre by his own students, and, somehow, he had to compete with an orator capable of changing peoples' minds and rousing crowds. He licked his lips nervously and then made a hurried preamble before attempting to rely on modern technology. But his Powerpoint presentation ceased within seconds, 'NO

SIGNAL' flashing ignominiously across the screen. Feverishly, he attempted to remedy the hitch, sweat glistening on his forehead, until, unable to do so, he abandoned his props and turned, once more, to face the crowd. To his evident surprise his ineptitude had not been met with boos or hisses, slow handclaps or heckling, and the essential goodwill of his onlookers appeared to revive him. Gradually, he began to get into his stride, speaking almost animatedly about the landscape surveys carried out throughout Scotland, the approach taken by the consultants charged with the task and the requirement for developers to take into account the topography of the chosen area. The piercing whine of feedback from the microphone startled him momentarily, but he soldiered on, soon rewarded by being reunited with his electronic assistant, a technician having fixed it in the interim. Eventually the Chairman gestured at his watch, indicating that Doctor MacGowan had overstayed his welcome, and, smiling delightedly, the little fellow gathered up his equipment and vacated the stage.

The final speaker, the Chairman announced, had been billed as David Stein QC, a lawyer familiar with the planning enquiry system. Unfortunately, a message had been received from him that he would be unable to attend, his car having broken down in South Queensferry. By great good fortune, however, a last minute substitute had been obtained: Mr Kevin Wylie, a well-kent local anti-wind farm activist. He had volunteered to fill the gap.

His appearance, the organisers later agreed, had been a mistake. He was, at best, a rabble-rouser, loud-voiced and passionate, but short on facts or any semblance of balance. His rant lasted for ten minutes; confused, repetitive and structureless. Seeing the audience beginning to fidget and shift in their seats with embarrassment, some whispering mutinously to their neighbours, the Chairman ended the unscheduled contribution prematurely, turning the lights on and relying on the need for a coffee break before starting the Question and Answer session.

Clutching a handful of leaflets, Alice left the Dalmellington stall and headed for its neighbour, a higgledy-piggledy group of tables under a banner proclaiming 'Save The Ochils'. She scanned their photographic display, panning past Little Law and Mellock Hill and the other proposed wind farms, until she reached Scowling Crags. Another unspoiled area, with rolling hills fed by rushing burns and blessed with groves of ancient woodland. Pictures had been created showing the site with the threatened thirty turbines in place on it, and the scene had been transformed from one of quiet, pastoral beauty into a quasi-industrial landscape. Pinned up below the photomontages was a drawing showing the size of the turbine blades, each one equivalent to the wingspan of a Jumbo Jet.

'Hello, Alice.'

She turned and saw the ruddy complexion of Prue Mac-Gregor, her gruff hostess at the anti-wind farm meeting held near Stenton. Before Alice had time to respond the woman continued: 'I knew your father wasn't coming tonight, but no-one told me that you were. Perhaps you could relieve Mrs Sinclair at our stand unless you have something better to do.'

She was nothing if not direct.

'I'm afraid I can't this evening. I am here on Police business. But maybe you could help me. I was looking for...' she fished in her pocket for the photocopy of the specimen italic handwriting, found it and held it under the nose of her interlocutor, 'for the writer of this.'

A pair of spectacles was extracted from the grease-stained blue husky jacket, and Prue MacGregor peered at the proffered sheet, putting her face close to it as if nearness to the paper might force it to reveal its secrets. Whilst she was still engaged in her minute examination of it, mouth forming silent words, her mobile went off and she picked it up immediately.

'No! No! We arranged it. I'm going to go to the Parliament. You deal with the newsletter this time. It's too late to change everything around. Incidentally, I noticed that some bastard has been tampering with our signs, so that they now read "More Turbines on the Lammermuirs". The initial No's been painted over. Get Neil to sort that one out tomorrow.'

Having despatched her caller, she handed Alice's sheet back to her.

'Nope. Can't help you... Ah, Joanna.' Her attention shifted to the tall, elegant figure who was collecting a cup of coffee from a nearby table. The speaker joined them, and Alice saw that she was holding in her left hand the handwritten notes for her speech. They were heavily annotated and revised, all in a distinctive copper-plate hand. Quickly becoming aware that the two women wanted to talk exclusively to each other, she drifted back to the Ochil stall. Ten of the photos had captions below them, but each one had been printed using Arial font.

An electronic alarm bell rang informing the audience that the Question and Answer session was about to begin. Alice resumed her original seat, noting that her neighbours on either side had disappeared, and then, disconcertingly, she spied both of them at different locations. The session proceeded much as she had expected. Sympathetic enquiries were directed at the speakers and sympathetic answers bounced back. The converted were preaching to the converted, reassuring each other with every exchange. Only at the very end did any sense of theatre materialise. The Chairman, relaxed and jocular, a glass of whisky in his hand, enquired benignly if there were any developers present and, if so, did they wish to contribute to the evening. The hall fell unusually silent as its occupants looked around, craning their necks to see if any of the enemy was present. After a short interval, a single hand was raised and the Chairman, surprise unconcealed, invited this Daniel to address the lions.

It was Ewan Potter of Firstforce, and spurning the putting of his question from the floor, he edged himself to the end of his row, strode to the stage and, more importantly, the microphone. Standing behind it he looked at the stunned audience, defiant and unbowed.

'Yes, Mister Chairman, I have a question. We've heard, tonight, all the myriad reasons why there shouldn't be wind farms in, as far as I can make out, any part of Scotland including the islands. So, what I'd like to know is...' he waited for a few seconds, his sense of timing perfect, 'where exactly in this country should the land-based wind farms be sited, bearing in mind global warming, government policy and so on?'

At first, his query was met with an anxious silence, until his old adversary, Sue Lamont, stood up and faced him.

'How about, Mr Potter...' she began, voice a little shaky, 'how about fifteen turbines, maybe more in the second stage, at Lawsmoor—you know, by Lanark. There's a good wind harvest there, eh? Little birdlife, willing landlords, no peat... it's got everything. All the prerequisites are met there. How about Lawsmoor?'

Ewan Potter's expression changed as he digested her words. Seconds before it had beamed a sort of aggressive self-satisfaction as if he had checkmated an army of opponents. Now his brow furrowed, uncertain of her next move but wary all the same. The man made no attempt to answer, and aware of her advantage Sue Lamont continued: 'I understand that there's an application in for Lawsmoor, not your company, of course, but one of your bigger rivals. And you know what, Mr Potter... well, I heard that—well, that you live there, and...' she waited—he was not the only one who could work a crowd—'that you are one of the objectors to it. In fact, that you started up the "Lawsmoor Protection Group". Would that be right, now? So, how about there? Would you choose that place?'

Peals of laughter erupted from the floor, mingled with the hum of excited whispers. To his credit, Ewan Potter did not take advantage of the crowd's brief distraction to slink off the platform, but stayed, waiting for the noise to die down, and then replied: 'No, not Lawsmoor. But my view that such a location would be unsuitable simply means, Miss Lamont, that either we are all nimbies, every single one of us, you included, or that there, genuinely, is nowhere appropriate within this land... even though it is blessed with an outstanding potential wind harvest. So we'll all just let planet Earth burn, shall we?'

So saying he strode off the stage, facing his onlookers, leaving them still digesting his response. Discreetly, Alice collected a few fallen chips from beneath her chair, added them to her fish supper packaging and joined the throng making for one of the exits. Stuck in a queue, she passed the time examining the stand closest to her, one devoted to the prevention of the Devonbridge Development. All the usual props were present on it and a middle-aged man was busy packing up the exhibits in cardboard boxes and polythene bags. A blown-up photo of the sun setting behind the summit of a hill caught her eye, and she looked at the simple caption below it: 'Sunset on Devonhill'.

And, immediately, she recognised the handwriting. Extricating herself from the shuffling line of people, she worked her way to the stand and managed to catch its keeper's attention. Busy dismantling the exhibition, the fellow appeared exasperated by her late show of interest.

'Look, if you are needing postcards, or whatever, for the Council, you'll find them on the way out, OK? I've put all of mine away. They cover all the sites, including Devonhill.'

'No,' she replied, 'I've got as many as I can use, thanks. Could you help me with just one thing, though, can you tell me who wrote the caption beneath the photo?'

'You mean "Sunset on Devonhill"?'

'That's it.'

'Yes, it's my cousin, Colin. Colin Norris. Why do you ask?'

'I'm from Lothian & Borders Police, and we may need his help. Can I borrow it?'

'The photo?'

'The caption. Just for a few days, if that's all right with you. Where does your cousin live?'

'He stays in a wee cottage, up from the farmhouse at Blackstone Mains. In Kinross-shire, by the Scowling Crags boundary, if you know what I mean.'

'Thanks. I know what you mean.'

12

Sound travelled unhindered in the open-plan room, and any sneeze, burp or hiccup coming from a member of the squad was heard by all. Consequently, very few private telephone conversations took place within it, and everyone knew everyone else's business. Whispering or a lowered voice alerted all to the possibility of a confidential exchange, and the listeners then re-doubled their efforts to make out what was said. If it had to do with the investigation they wanted to know, and if it did not, then, sadly, they discovered that fact too late.

When a young, solidly-built woman entered the murder suite, most of its occupants registered her entry, together with the fact that she was striding, purposefully, in Eric Manson's direction. Her quarry was sitting with his feet up on his desk, nose flattened against his newspaper, chewing loudly on a sausage roll. His entire attention was being bestowed on a half-naked model, and he let out a gasp of admiration on reading her vital statistics. A sharp rapping on the front of his paper made him drop his shield but his face lit up immediately on recognising his visitor. As he stood up to greet her, arms extended for a hug, she sat down on the chair beside his own. Unable to disguise his disappointment with the rebuff, he followed her lead and, now seated, went to kiss her cheek. She accepted his offering as her due, something to be endured, but made no move to bestow any peck herself.

'It's about my mum,' the woman began coldly.

'Let's leave that for now, eh, darlin'?' Eric Manson replied, glancing around the room as if to alert her to their uninvited audience. 'Tell me, how have you been getting on at uni, eh? You fixed up with a flat yet?'

'No, we'll not leave it, Dad. We'll talk about it now. She's back on the pills again and she needn't be. If you just spent more… well, if you were ever there…'

'I've a job to do, Kath, remember?' he interrupted her, his tone conciliatory.

'Yes, and so's she. Every day she goes to that crappy surgery, answering abusive phone calls, fending off drunken patients and the like and then she has to return home to an empty house…'

'It's not always empty!'

'Nearly always,' Kathryn Manson corrected him. 'And you spend a fair bit of your time in the pub, Dad, and she knows it. Think about it. She gave you a second chance, took you ba—'

'Ssshhh… Kath, as I said, not here, eh, love?' He looked at her plaintively and then nodded in the direction of Detective Sergeant Watt. The Sergeant was staring intently at his computer screen, occasionally typing a key at random, spellbound by the little domestic drama unfolding beside him.

'Where, though, Dad? You don't usually listen to me, but you know what? I think I've got ALL your attention right now. So let's get on with it. My mum gave you a second chance, God alone knows why, and you're throwing it back in her face. She thinks you're seeing that cow from the papers again. Are you?'

'Kath… Kath, for Pete's sake. This is my office…' Eric Manson begged.

'So, are you?' She was relentless.

The Detective Inspector suddenly stood up, but seeing that his daughter remained seated where she was, he sank slowly down again, looking at her, pleading silently with her for the conversation to end, but she returned his looks, stony-faced.

'Well?'

'Yes—no… I'm not sleeping with her…' he sounded desperate and then, anger mounting, his voice changed. 'It's my bloody business. Not yours!'

Kathryn Manson, however, was not easily intimidated. She had a mission, and was determined to accomplish it. He had raised the volume of their argument, so she would simply do the same.

'It is my business, Dad. Because it hurts my mum. She only came back because you promised to lay off that woman,' she shouted.

'And I have… I am, for fuck's sake!' Eric Manson raged in return.

At that very second DCI Robin Bruce walked into the murder suite with the Assistant Chief Constable, Laurence Body, in tow. Body, quick to sense the tension in the room, instantly marched over to the time-line to inspect it, leaving his Chief Inspector glaring at the antagonists. Kathryn Manson, dignity intact, rose to leave, but as she did so she bent towards her father's ear and hissed, *sotto voce* but still audible to all, 'You'd better have, Dad. Or I'll be back. Back here, I mean.'

⸻

Alice knew as soon as they arrived at the Astra that the journey *à deux* to the Scowling Crags site would be an ordeal. Manson, fury still bubbling, slammed the driver's door so hard that the wing mirror came loose. They then exited the pound, tyres burning as if in hot pursuit of a gang of international thieves, before rattling over the cobbles, heedless of comfort or safety. Every red light was treated as a personal slight, obeyed with ill-grace, accelerator depressed, roaring, for a racing start. On finding himself unexpectedly ensnared in a queue at Blackhall, he thumped the steering wheel loudly with both hands before, on impulse, screeching into the bus lane in an attempt to evade the jam. Discovering that he was now trapped between two stationary double-deckers he swore, while jinking out straight into the path of an on-coming heavy goods vehicle. Alice, eyes tight shut, cursed Kathryn Manson and her domestic concerns. Thanks to continuing discord within that dysfunctional household she would soon be deprived of her life, or limbs at the very least. With the Forth Road Bridge in sight, the Detective Inspector swivelled his neck from left to right, attempting to work out which stream of cars was moving fastest through the booths. A rapid swerve to the left and they were in the chosen lane, having missed, by inches, a collision with a red Mercedes and a motor cycle. Rigid with fear and flattening imaginary brakes with her feet, Alice smiled weakly at the motor cyclist, fist now raised at her, snarling, and signalling her responsibility for his near-death encounter.

As they bumped rhythmically over the bridge, Alice looked westwards, up the Forth estuary, seeking any distraction from this unpleasant situation. Between black clouds, shafts of sunlight were falling on the water, casting a silvery sheen on the vast expanse of tranquil, grey sea. In seconds the sun itself began to emerge from behind the dark clouds shadowing it, drifts of a borage blue sky exposed in its wake, and, as the car crossed the border into Fife, Alice became aware that her chauffeur had, finally, begun to relax. The car was no longer hurtling along at breakneck speed, and other vehicles were even being permitted to overtake them. Eric Manson lowered his shoulders and leant back into the driver's seat, letting out, as he did so, a deep sigh.

'Families, eh? Who'd have them!' he said ruefully.

'Sometimes more pain than pleasure, but not usually.'

'You travel light, though, Alice. No commitments anywhere.'

'I'm not an orphan, Sir.'

'You've no man yet?' Him and Mrs McLaren. Great minds, she thought, determined to side-step the question, certain that it was yet another volley in his little war of attrition. On the other hand, this time her interrogator was, himself, bruised and battered, unlikely to intend to commence hostilities on such a loaded subject. So instead, she smiled at him indulgently and shook her head. No reason for him to know. After all, he had met Ian Melville and their mutual antipathy had produced combustion on first encounter. His views on her lover's suitability were all too predictable and unwelcome, and his dislike had been, as far as she was concerned, a positive endorsement of Ian.

Like the weighted, spherical toy clowns once favoured by little children and impossible to knock over, Eric Manson's spirits soon bobbed back up, and by the time the Dunfermline turn-off was reached he was busy ripping the wrapping of a packet of cigars with his teeth, ready to smoke his companion out of the vehicle. Hands free of the wheel, he struck a match, sucked hard, and began to exhale acrid fumes into the enclosed space. His reluctant passenger wound down her window, aware that any complaint, or reminder that the car was her workplace, would be met with derision, the man's delight in annoying her having been re-awakened with the resurgence of his normal, bumptious mood.

They turned right off the Carnbo road up a track marked 'Blackstone Mains' and began to climb into the Ochils. Within minutes the wheels of the Astra had sunk deep into its rutted surface and a strange swishing noise came from the car as its undercarriage compressed the undergrowth. After about quarter of a mile they arrived at the Mains, an austere farmhouse surrounded by a quadrangle of steadings, and saw a hand-made wooden sign directing them further up the hill to 'The Cottage'. The gradient of the final slope was steeper yet, their route resembling a dried-up river bed, little more than pebbles and shale with occasional boulders washed up here and there. Where the road ended they parked their motor, glad to stretch their stiff limbs, and both feeling as if they had travelled into some more remote past, a sanctuary untouched by the new century.

They looked around themselves in all directions, and saw laid out before them the glory of the place, a one hundred and eighty degree view of undeveloped countryside. Somehow they had reached paradise. Not the gaudy sort promised in every travel agent's brochure, but something altogether finer and rarer, the true abode of the blessed. In the foreground were low undulating hills, scattered clumps of whin still yellow in bloom, and, sparkling in the bright sunlight, a series of burns bordered with flag irises and meadowsweet, culminating in marshland, larks and curlews calling high above. Beyond, in the distance, was a vast area of flat, fertile ground dotted with woodlands, the whole scene dominated by the great, shining expanse of Loch Leven. Looking on such a sight, the meanest spirit would have felt elated, a poet's soul inspired.

In its condition as a moss-clad ruin, the cottage in the shade of the huge sycamore tree had once enhanced the rural idyll, but it was being restored, and its appearance now jarred, reminding the onlooker that, somewhere within the garden, the snake would be coiled. New PVC windows had replaced worn, wooden ones, and grey, cement tiles were edging out old, red pantiles. Even its sandstone facade had been marred by a patch of harling; metal gutters had been removed, plastic imposters taking their place. And all around lay the detritus of the DIY man: half-filled syringes of mastic, broken slates, soggy plasterboard and sheets of torn polythene. An unsightly yellow Portakabin had been dumped in the lee of the building, and the sound of drumbeats began to come from it. A whey-faced, teenage girl emerged. She saw the two strangers, but showed no alarm at their unexpected appearance.

'Who yous after?' she enquired dully, brushing a strand of dark hair out of her eyes with her hand.

'Mr Norris. Colin Norris,' DI Manson replied.

'He's out, away for the day.'

'Where?'

She shrugged her shoulders, 'You'll need to ask ma mum.'

'And where's she?'

'Shops. She'll be back soon. You'll just have to wait.'

A tall, thin boy, dressed all in black, leapt out of the cabin and flung his arms around the girl. She giggled and the two of them then returned, twined around each other, into their den. Instantly, loud laughter could be heard, followed by an increase in the volume of the music, which made the air vibrate to the pounding rhythm. Fleeing from the noise, an Indian runner duck waddled out of the cabin followed by its five upright ducklings, the family finding refuge through the open door of the cottage.

'This place is a fucking pigsty,' DI Manson muttered, lighting up another cigar.

'I'd live here tomorrow,' Alice said, knowing as soon as the words left her mouth that such a remark would be incomprehensible to her companion, a truth so impossibly unlikely that to utter it could only be a form of provocation.

'Yeah, right,' he said, '—and on your bloody own, I'll be bound.'

Noticing a small outhouse with a corrugated iron roof, Alice went to explore it, bending double to go through the low doorway and finding herself in a foetid, unlit space. A loud moaning sound followed by a chorus of high-pitched squeals frightened her, and she peered into the blackness trying to make out the creatures responsible for the din. As her eyes became accustomed to the darkness she saw the curved outline of a large, prostrate pig. It was lying on its side, multiple teats exposed, and a mass of tiny piglets were tugging at them and scampering over each other, desperate to get their share. Delighted, Alice called out to her companion, 'Come and see this, Sir.'

But DI Manson did not follow her into the hut. When she left it, eyes now dazzled by the sunshine, she found him sitting on the edge of a stone water-trough staring at the sole of his shoe, mobile phone in his left hand.

'Thanks, Alice!' he said. 'Thanks to you I have stood on a massive bloody nail, and it's gone straight through... and this place is covered in shit. I'm taking no chances, I'm going to get a tetanus jag right now at the surgery in Kinross. I'll be back to pick you up in, say, two hours' time. Norris himself is elsewhere, after all.'

As the rear of the car disappeared from the view, Alice noticed a ripple in the water of the trough as a stray raindrop fell from the sky. Soon, ripples collided with ripples as a summer downpour began, and she looked around for shelter, unwilling to intrude into the Portakabin, but keen to avoid a soaking. The porch would have to do; some refuge there, and as she ran towards it a red Escort bumped up the slope, coming to a halt with a heavy grinding noise. A woman got out, head bent against the rain, weighed down by four full carrier bags, and began to drag herself and her cargo to the doorway. Alice watched her slow, lurching progress, bags swinging against her legs, until finally they came face to face at the front door.

'Hello. Where've you come from?' the woman asked, surprise at Alice's presence unmistakeable on her face.

'Edinburgh. We got here about twenty minutes ago. I'm from Lothian & Borders Police.'

'We? And how did you get here? I don't see any car.'

As she spoke, the woman deposited two of her bags on the ground before shouldering the door wide open and entering the cottage. Picking up the remaining bags, Alice followed her inside, and they trailed together through a tiny hall into a cramped kitchen. The inside of the house, like the outside, was a work in progress. Nothing seemed to have been finished. The floor was covered with sheets of newspaper, but in the gaps between them bare chipboard could be seen. A few stacks of logs lay beside the stained wood-burning stove, and on either side of it were cupboard units, exposing their innards to all, each carcass doorless. Despite its shabbiness, the place felt homely, inhabited and warm. Odd touches testified to its owners' affection for it: pots of fresh herbs on the window sills and a vase of wild flowers on the kitchen table. As Alice put the shopping on the floor, a black cat wound itself between her legs, purring loudly as if reacquainting itself with an old friend. Mrs Norris, now bagless too, turned her attention back to her visitor.

'So who are "we"? And, like I said, how on earth did you get here?'

'I'm sorry, Mrs Norris, I should have explained. I'm DS Rice, from St Leonard's Police Station in Edinburgh. I did have my Inspector with me, only he injured his foot on a nail outside. He's taken the car—the one we used to get here—off to the surgery in Kinross. For a jag,' Alice replied.

'OK, but what do you want from us? By the way, would you like some tea, coffee or something?'

'That would be lovely. Tea, if possible.'

Mrs Norris boiled the kettle, and then dunked a single, used teabag in both mugs before offering the watery mix to Alice.

'So, how can I help you?'

'Perhaps,' Alice said, extracting the photocopy of the specimen handwriting from her jacket pocket, '...you could look at this for me.'

As the woman examined the paper, Alice studied her. She had a sort of worn beauty, and neither age nor experience had yet robbed her of its brilliance. Her hair was brown, threaded with white, and her eyes were of the lightest grey, pupils sharp against their faded colour. Her complexion, though, had been ravaged, as if she had been exposed to all weathers, a faint network of broken veins travelling across the bridge of her nose and her cheeks. Her hands were swollen, tight-skinned and red, with short, clean nails. The woman began biting her lip, and she continued doing so even after she had raised her face from the paper.

'Mmm. What do you want to know?'

'Can you identify the handwriting, please?'

'Er… yes, but I'd like to know why, first, if I may.' Blood had been drawn from the bitten lower lip.

'Because we need to know the identity of the writer for the purposes of an ongoing investigation.'

'Oh. Well…' she hesitated, 'it's Colin's writing, I think.'

'Colin Norris. Your husband?'

'Yes. My husband's writing.'

'Can you tell me where he is at the moment, Mrs Norris?'

'Why, has he done something stupid again?' Alarm was evident in her voice.

'Again? Maybe. I don't know. That's why I'd like to speak to him.'

Mrs Norris sighed. 'He's in Edinburgh, helping his mother for a day or two. She lives in Gayfield Square.'

———

Mrs Norris was kind. Learning that her uninvited visitor could not be picked up for a further hour and a half, and seeing the discomfiture this state of affairs produced, she suggested that the policewoman entertain herself in the sitting room. She would find magazines for her, leave her in peace and attend to some household chores. Afterwards, they would have some lunch. A few copies of *Which* magazine, plus an old *National Geographic*, were handed over before Mrs Norris disappeared, her industry confirmed by the ensuing smell of furniture polish. Alice padded about the room, taking in her surroundings. On a mahogany sideboard sat a large silver cup, tarnished, and engraved with a short inscription. 'Kilgraston School – 1971 – Senior Tennis Champion – Hilary Morrison', and directly

141

above it was a faded photograph of the 1971 tennis six, with a youthful Mrs Norris in the centre, holding a silver shield above her head. Further along the same wall was another framed photo, this time depicting the Glenalmond First Fifteen, and one of the names below the array of sturdy adolescents was that of Colin Norris. Elsewhere in the room the observant would have noticed, in amongst the frayed covers and thin curtains, relics of a more privileged existence, when shopping was done at Jenners and Forsyth's rather than Ikea and B&Q.

Hearing the sound of the table being laid in the kitchen Alice entered it, intending to offer her services, to be met with cool stares from the boy and girl from the Portakabin. Mrs Norris, busy, and clearly flustered, introduced them.

'DS Rice, this is my daughter, Rosanna, and her... er... boyfriend, Jason.'

Rosanna and Jason, as if no introductions had been made, sank into their chairs and began helping themselves to the bread and soup laid out before them. But when Alice took the chair next to her, Rosanna stopped eating to speak.

'A policewoman, eh... maybe you could help Jason?'

'How?' Jason asked, glaring angrily at his girlfriend.

'With the charge.'

Jason nodded, mollified, looking now at Alice expectantly.

'See, Jason's on a charge,' the girl continued, 'and he's already up for something else. Maybe you could get it dropped for us, eh?'

Curious, Alice asked, 'What's the charge?'

'You tell her, Jason, eh?' Rosanna giggled.

The youth blushed before answering, 'Er... peein' in folks' letterboxes.'

⸺

Eric Manson arrived back at exactly the time promised, and from his breath it was apparent that he had consumed his lunch in a pub. Hobbling out of the car he instructed his Sergeant to take the wheel, disability now to the fore, and then reclined on the back seat, legs up, eyes closed, snores vibrating his torso before they had even reached the motorway. On waking at the City boundary he became irascible, demanding that Alice ferry him to his house, rest having been advised. But on passing a service station he ordered her to stop and teetered unsteadily out, clambering back into the car clutching an undistinguished bouquet which he then transferred uneasily from hand to hand until his final disembarkation at 'The Hollies'.

Consequently, Alice arrived alone at Gayfield Square, delighted to have shed her companion, still pondering on the slow smile she had noticed lighting up Mrs Manson's face as she escorted her lame husband through their doorway.

—

A departing resident let her into the tenement building. The stone stairs leading to the topmost flat were worn and uneven, and as Alice trudged upwards she was assailed by scents of cooking: wafts of a curry-scented breeze on the first floor, bacon frying on the second and, she hazarded, chopped onions on the third. Now breathless, she rang the old-fashioned doorbell and the door, after a short delay, was opened by an elderly woman, well-spoken and immaculately turned out in a polo-neck jersey with pearls and a tweed skirt. In the drawing room, Colin Norris, unshaven and clad in a paint-spattered boiler-suit, was standing on a wooden stepladder admiring his own handiwork. Only about one square foot of the old cream paint remained on the ceiling, the roller tray now empty of Snowdrop White. Unaware that his mother had company he shouted: 'Who was that at the door, Mum?'

'It's a Police officer, dear, it seems she wants to speak to you. I'll get some tea and leave you both to it.'

As the man descended the ladder Alice glanced at him. Everything about him looked wary, on guard. The second their eyes met, he covered his with his hand, massaging his temples and sighing audibly for her benefit. When he lowered his head once more to discard his roller, she noticed that the few grey curls left on it were thin, unwinding before taking their final bow and leaving his scalp forever. Although he must have been well over six feet, he appeared smaller, as if trying to minimise his presence by stooping, camouflaging his physical bulk. Because of his diffident manner Alice was taken by surprise when he took the initiative, leading her to the sofa and then sitting close beside her, an action too open and hospitable for such an apparently timid creature. She showed him the photocopy and the caption and he identified both writings as his own, seeming puzzled at the need for doing so.

'I need to ask you, Mr Norris—where were you between seven pm and ten pm on Monday 12th June?'

The man waited a few seconds before answering. 'I've no idea, Sergeant. Does it matter?'

'Yes, sir, it matters. Can I ask you to think again?'

Again, there was an unusual delay before he spoke: 'Well, that's ages ago now, and I'm sorry but I haven't a clue.'

'What about between eight and eleven pm on Wednesday 5th July?'

'Last week, eh? I don't know, but I'd probably be at home. I don't go out much nowadays.'

'If you were at home, sir, would anyone have been with you?'

Colin Norris looked the policewoman directly in the eye as he answered. 'My wife, she'd have been there, I expect. I can't be sure, I'll have to think about it, but we're both normally there. What's all this about anyway? Couldn't you just cut to the chase, please?'

'Of course, sir. The specimen of writing on the photocopy was extracted from a series of letters written to Sheriff Freeman.

You may have read about him in the papers. He was recently murdered.'

Had the man harboured any genuine doubt about the nature of her enquiries, it was now dispelled. He began to pat his curls and run his fingers through his little remaining hair.

'In the papers,' he repeated, nodding.

'Yes, and I understand that you wrote those letters—threatening letters—to the Sheriff.'

Again, Alice caught the man's eyes, and this time he held her gaze.

'I did write them, yes.' Although hoarse, his voice sounded unashamed, unrepentant.

'Could you tell me why, sir?'

He nodded again, apparently keen to take up her invitation.

'Yes. I wrote them because I was, quite frankly, desperate… DESPERATE. I wanted him to stop the wind farm development. He could have, you see. It was in his power. He owned the access strip, and without it, without his co-operation, the whole thing would have foundered… and then, of course, I'd have been all right.'

'Why were you so desperate for the wind farm not to go ahead?'

'Because,' the man sighed, '…because if it did, my life would be over.'

'What do you mean "my life would be over"?'

'I expect you have been there, Sergeant, to my house, I mean?'

'Yes, I was there this morning.'

'Then you may understand. A tiny bit. That cottage is… well, my last chance really. I used to be in shipping, highly-paid too, then I lost my job. Our office in London was "downsized". Actually, I was the only casualty, through no fault of my own. Naturally, I picked myself up and managed to land a job in insurance but… well… I'm not a salesman, so after two years they "let me go". Next I tried selling wills, it was a kind of franchise, and… in a nutshell, it didn't succeed. But Hilary, my wife, kept my spirits up, she's always believed in me. You know she even got a job herself. Bloody good effort… Christ,' he shook his head, 'and I've led her a bloody dance. Eventually we used everything we had, every last penny, to buy the cottage, and since then I've worked day and night to do it up. So has she. When it's finished… well, how could it fail? As a bed and breakfast, I mean. It's such a perfect spot. You've seen it, it's Shangri-La, the real thing. How could we fail there, how could anyone fail there…'

'And the wind farm?,' she reminded him.

'In that wonderful place, they plan to dump thirty turbines. The view from the cottage, instead of being… unsurpassed, would be totally blighted. Then who, in their right mind, would want to come to a place like that on holiday? To look out over a mass of those ugly great things and listen to their perpetual clicks and whirrs. Nobody, that's who. But I'm not going to let them destroy everything.'

'So that's why you threatened the Sheriff?'

'Yes, that's why I threatened him. But what else could I do? What would you have done?' he pleaded, and, getting no response, continued. 'It was nothing to him. A bit more money for an already rich man. I tried, just once, to speak to him about it, but he brushed me aside, said he was in a hurry, had to go to a meeting or something and then he left. Rude bugger! But, you see, without him, his participation, the thing can't go ahead, however willing every other landlord in the scheme is. I've fallen pretty low, you know. I can't even educate my own child properly, as I'd like. As Hil would like. But I can't… I can't hit rock bottom. I'd take her with me. And the worst of it is, believe it or not, she'd stay with me. But we are going to make a go of this. I'll grow the vegetables, do the general maintenance, even be the butler, and she'll cook. She's a cordon-bleu, you know. Eventually, we'll maybe be able to send Rosanna to public school, just for her last two years…'

'You threatened the Sheriff. Maybe you killed him, too?'

'You think I murdered Sheriff Freeman?' the man asked, disbelief patent in his voice.

'You threatened to put "a stop" to him, didn't you?' Alice answered.

'I know, I know I did.' He seemed irritated. 'I had to. Obviously. I had to threaten him otherwise he wouldn't stop it, would he? The wind farm, I mean.'

'So did you do it? Kill him?'

'Of course not,' Colin Norris was now speaking fast, 'of course not. It's a ridiculous idea. They were only words. Words on paper. I wouldn't do that, and if I had, you'd be the last person I'd be telling…'

' Quite, sir. What about Nicholas Lyon?'

'What about Nicholas Lyon, whoever he is?'

'Did you kill him?'

'Jesus Christ!' the man laughed out loud, 'what are you going on about? I don't even know who he is. What in heaven's name do you think I am? I only wrote letters, silly letters, for God's sake!'

Abruptly, Colin Norris stood up as if to stop any further questioning.

'Have you got a car, Mr Norris?' Alice rose beside him, maintaining eye contact.

'Yes, a white Vauxhall Corsa. It's parked in the square.'

13

As instructed, Alice lowered herself down the buoy chain, hand under hand, until she became aware from the solid ground beneath her fins that she had landed on the sea-bed. An arm gripped hers and she manoeuvred herself along the line of student bodies until she reached the last link, the beer-bellied waste entrepreneur. This undersea world was indeed, as they had been promised, a silent one, and also, unfortunately, a sightless one. In the turbid waters around Oban that Saturday, visibility was non-existent, and without a tight hold on a companion, any of the students could have become lost in the murk in seconds. Shoals of colourful underwater life might well have been gliding inches above their heads or grazing on their flippers, but in that cold, grey, impenetrable liquid they would have been unaware of it all, eyes near useless.

A message was passed in sign language from diver to diver, hand touching mask, that a circle was to be formed; and, obediently, the students huddled in a tight ring with the instructor in the middle. Each of them then, in turn, flooded and cleared their masks and demonstrated some vestigial understanding of neutral buoyancy. Alice attempted to hover motionless in the water, awaiting her go, and became aware of an unwelcome sensation. Cold water was trickling down the neck of her dry suit, weaving between her shoulder blades, headed for her buttocks. Sticking a thumb up to signal her impending ascent, she attempted to catch the instructor's attention, but he, too, could only see things in front of his nose and was concentrating on assessing Bridget's cack-handed attempt to buddy-breathe with him. The trickle of water now becoming a flood, Alice decided to make for the surface, freeing her hands roughly from her startled companions and rising at an increasing speed. She broke the water about five metres south of the buoy, blood seeping from her nostrils, overjoyed to rejoin the fresh, clear, sunlit world.

In the warmth of the Harbour Cafe she sipped her coffee, teeth still chattering like castanets, whilst Bridget busied herself examining their open water certificates.

'What nnn... next,' Alice asked, '... you... you going to become an advanced one... or even a dive master... er, mistress?'

'Not likely,' Bridget replied perkily, 'I told you, I am going to check out electrical engineering classes. I need some sparks in my life.'

'So you're not going to do more of this... ddd... diving stuff, then?'

'God, no! It's far too cold and unpleasant for me. Did you hear what they've promised us next? Coldingham! I don't care if the water is as clear as crystal there, which I doubt, wild horses wouldn't persuade me to attend for another jolly minibus excursion with...' she hesitated momentarily, 'our new friends. If I can't get into electrical engineering, plumbing sounds...'

'Congratulathions, ladieth!' Uninvited, the waste entrepreneur took a seat at their table and beamed broadly at them both, exposing toothless gums. 'Unfortunately, I failed thith time, broke my dentureth on my regulator, thadly. Ith the thelery thoup good, Bridget?'

Bridget caught Alice's eye, gave the extended arm diving signal for 'danger' while ostensibly stretching for her shoulder bag, muttered, 'My phone's going, I'll have to answer it,' and jerked her head in the direction of the exit for a joint retreat.

Alice, however, remained seated, smiling fixedly at the man, concerned that he should not be publicly abandoned, leper-like, among their mutual acquaintances. He had chosen to join them after all.

'Tho… eh… eh…?'

'Alice,' she reminded him.

'Indeed, tho Alith…' he smiled again, apparently keen to please, 'have you got your friend Bridget'th number?'

'I'm afraid not,' she lied. Kinder to extinguish all hope.

He took a gulp of his cappuccino, surfacing with the creamy lips of a black-and-white minstrel, and then scanned the entire room. 'Oh… there'th Thuthan, I'll think I'll go and join her, thee how she got on.'

So saying he picked up his tray and lumbered off in the direction of a plump blonde, leaving Alice, leper-like, alone amongst their acquaintances.

—

Rain had transformed the cottage and its surroundings. The dried-up river-bed was awash with torrents of muddy water, and the yard in front of the cottage had become a quagmire, a patchwork of puddles in which the duck and her offspring were dabbling, raindrops bouncing off them as if they were made of plastic. Alice stepped carefully out of the vehicle, inadvertently landing in a runnel of rainwater and sinking heel-deep in mud. Although only seconds passed before she reached the shelter of the porch, she was drenched, hair sticking to her forehead, legs splashed to the knee. Mrs Norris appeared quickly and recognised her from their previous encounter.

The old sheets of newspaper on the kitchen floor were now torn, sodden with muck from outside, and she was busy replacing them, a dry stack ready beside the ancient Raeburn. Her dejected state became obvious the moment she opened her mouth, her voice sounding flat, drained of all vivacity.

'I know Colin's still at the station helping you, his mother told me, and she warned me to expect another visit.'

Alice smiled, attempting to reassure her. 'It's simply that you may be able to help us with our enquiries. Possibly, help Colin too.'

Loud music, all heavy drum rhythms and shrieking electric guitars, could be heard coming ever closer, and Jason and Rosanna traipsed in, radios in hand, and began grappling with chairs at the kitchen table as if they intended to have their breakfast there.

'Out, out to the cabin, please, sweetheart, and you too, Jason… you can collect any cereal or whatever you need from here, but I have to talk to the Sergeant again and in peace and quiet.'

Neither of them made a move, the music continued to blare and Jason began to pour milk into a mug.

'I said OUT!' Mrs Norris shouted, and the teenagers' startled expressions testified to the rarity of such an outburst. The boy, having recovered his *sang froid* first, made a revolving gesture with his index finger by his temple and they slouched out in unison, staring at Mrs Norris as if she had sprouted horns, increasing the volume of the music in defiance.

Mrs Norris sat down and Alice took a chair opposite hers.

'I need to know where you were between about seven and ten on the night of Monday 12th June, if possible,' she began.

'Can't you tell me first what this is all about?' the woman beseeched.

'Not at the moment. I'd rather, please, get your answers to my questions, and after that I'll explain what we're concerned about.'

Hilary Norris walked over to the Raeburn and removed a grimy calendar from a shelf on the extractor hood.

'I live by this. I'd be lost without it. We write down any appointments, social stuff… everything on it. Colin hasn't got a diary either, and Rosanna relies on me completely.' She turned

151

back the pages to June and read "WI. Smoke." Yes, I remember… I went to my WI meeting, there was a talk about dyeing and spinning wool, I won the garden gem competition that evening. Then I drove to Perth and waited outside Smoke— it's a club—to pick up Rosanna when she came out.'

'So you were away from the house. Between what hours?'

'Probably left at about 6 pm and… well, Rosanna is always reluctant to leave, so we wouldn't get back until, maybe, 2 am or so.'

'Did Rosanna leave to go to Smoke from here?'

'No, she was at Jason's house, in Kinross. They had tea and then left there together.'

Alice nodded. 'Do you know where Colin was that night?'

'You saw, Sergeant, there was nothing in the calendar for him. So he'd be here.'

'And on the night of Wednesday 5th July, can you tell me where you were between about eight and ten?'

The woman sighed, picking up the calendar again. 'Riding. Film.'

The telephone rang and she picked it up. 'Yes, speaking,' she rubbed her forehead distractedly. 'Has it not been paid? No, no. I see. And how much for did you say? Mmm. Well, I'll send off a cheque today and I do apologise.'

'Riding. Film?' Alice reminded her.

'Of course. Rosanna goes riding at 7.30 on Thursdays for an hour, and after it, for a treat, she and I went to see "The Devil Wears Prada". Not really Colin's kind of film.'

'So he stayed at home. When did you get back from the film?'

'I don't know, but I could work it out, I suppose. The riding is supposed to stop at 8.30 pm but it never does… usually at least quarter of an hour late. Then we'd have to get to Dunfermline. The film started, I think, around 9.30 pm, and we wouldn't get home before, say, 11.45 pm.'

'And was Colin there that night?'

'He'd be here, yes. Otherwise there would have been something in the calendar. He was home when we got back.'

'Anyone else with him? Here, I mean?'

'No, no-one. I don't think so. Just ask him anyway. Please, Sergeant, please… can't you tell me what this is all about?'

'Well, you'll have seen in the papers about Sheriff Freeman. His murder, I mean. Your husband has been writing threatening letters to him.'

'What—Colin? Don't be ridiculous! Are you sure it was Colin?'

'You identified the handwriting. So did he. So have the graphologists. Can I ask you, have you ever heard your husband mention Nicholas Lyon?'

'No. It doesn't ring a bell with me. Should it? Who is he?'

'He was Sheriff Freeman's partner, and the victim of a hit and run accident.'

'You know,' the woman began, looking directly into Alice's eyes, 'Colin would never hurt those people. But he is living on the edge. He hated, and that is the word, the right word, James Freeman. So did I, actually. All our hopes had to be dashed so that he could become richer and he knew that, you know. Knew what would happen to us. Colin had explained it to him but… well, I don't suppose he did it very well. It meant too much to him. He probably came across as a madman with a glittering eye…'

Tears began to form in her eyes and she closed them, slowly allowing the drops to trickle down her cheeks unmopped, '… but he wasn't always like that, you know. He's just had such bad luck. Honestly, Sergeant, he's not your man. He is desperate and depressed, but violent? Never. Please…' she implored, 'please don't… don't push him over the edge.'

Every time his shoe came to rest on another step, a sharp pain hit the ball of his foot, shooting down the length of the big toe. He inhaled deeply, pungent cigar smoke cloaking the stench of human urine, attempting to rest his weight on the banister and spare his throbbing limb. Another sodding ten storeys to go. Only animals live in Niddrie, he thought, animals that soil their own high-rise nests. A gob of spit landed on his shoulder and he looked upwards into the delighted faces of two skinny boys suspended above him, before they danced off, laughing like drains, in search of new quarry. On the next landing he had to step over a figure, curled in the foetal position and breathing loudly, nearly losing his balance in the process and silently cursing the social work department's failure to attend to such cases. What else had they to do? And his hard-earned taxes squandered on suchlike well-intentioned lard-arses.

The wound in his foot was feeling hot; in fact, it was on fire. He became morbid. Bloody septicaemia will carry me off before the tetanus manages to lock my jaw. And no antibiotics even offered, although, God knows, they're fundamental enough for this kind of infection. All those years of contributions, and never to enjoy my own retirement. Never to wake up with one decision only to make; which course to spend the day on. Of course, she'll be all right then, living the life of Reilly and maybe, stranger things had happened, finding another man. Still, he thought, Kathryn would visit him on his deathbed, tears fairly gushing down her face, regretting humiliating him, realising only then his true worth. And for the stone, something tasteful, white marble with black lettering and, possibly, an obituary in *Stationwide*.

How would they describe the wound, though? Obviously, as sustained on active service but, unfortunately, it would have none of the glamour of a fatal gunshot injury or stabbing. If they simply used the words 'penetrating injury', omitting any reference to his foot, that would sound all right. 'Fatal injury

154

sustained in the line of duty' had a good ring to it, and was, well, would be, perfectly correct. Perhaps he should expressly stipulate no guitars for the service, otherwise that minister-boy might ruin his service with some fucking Kumbaya-like chants. There should be a few readings from the Bible, naturally, but none of those nancy poems except, maybe, that one about a ship on the horizon. 'She is gone' and everything, but maybe it should be changed to 'He is gone' or maybe it was talking about the ship? For added poignancy there would have to be flowers, possibly even a piper.

As he reached the eleventh floor, a woman signalled franti-cally to him and he followed her into her flat. Curtains of a transparent red material covered the lounge windows, letting little light into it. Relieved to take the weight off his foot, DI Manson slumped into an armchair, his hostess sitting, erect, on a small settee on his right.

'Mrs Munro, I presume?'

'Aye.'

He smiled at her encouragingly, 'You said, on the phone, that you'd information to give us about the road accident, that you'd rather give it to us in person. The one mentioned in the appeal, the one in Moray Place on…'

'Aye.'

He smiled again, nudging her to share whatever titbits of information she had, but she made no response. 'Well?' he said, his smile becoming a rictus.

'Ye're nae happy, eh, ah can aye tell.' She nodded her head sagely.

'I'll be happy enough, I assure you, if you could just tell me what you know about the accident.' His cheeks ached from his attempt to maintain a good-natured expression.

'Na… na… yer nae a happy man. Ah can tell it, ken. Ye can-nae hide it… it's leakin' oot ye.'

'Look, Mrs Munro, I came here expecting to get information

about the accident, and I'd appreciate it if you'd just attend to that, please.' His smile not yet curdled to a snarl.

'Och, Mister, ah see things. Things ye'll never see. Ah seen the accident too. A big motor whammin' intae that wee man.'

Now we're getting somewhere, he thought.

'So you saw it, the accident? Whereabouts were you at the time? Were you in Moray Place?'

'Ah wis here, here in ma' ain lounge.'

Pain, and now frustration, had taken its toll on the meagre supply of manners long ago coached into the policeman, and aggression, always lurking just below the surface, took control. 'Well, if you were in your bloody lounge, lady, how the hell did you see anything in the centre of Edinburgh?'

Mrs Munro viewed him with pity. 'D'ye never watch the telly, eh? Psychic powers. Some folk are blessed wi' them. Ah seen the accident in ma heid. OK? That OK wi' you? A wee man hit by a white motor car.'

'White? How do you know it was white?' His interest had been rekindled, but Mrs Munro was a beginner, an untalented one at that, not sharp enough to pick up crucial signals.

'White, blue, red, what difference does it make, eh?'

Clutching the change in his pockets, clicking coin on coin like worry beads, he tried one more time:

'Mrs Munro, did you see the accident in Moray Place?'

'Yer aura's black noo, ken. If it changes tae red, ye die. I telt ye, didn't ah. Ah saw the accident, in ma mind's eye. Ah've psychic powers. Ah ken a' aboot you an' a'. Yer hurt, eh? Deep inside…wounded… There's a wurd, a wurd's coming… it's… flatfoot.'

—

When Alice smelt the smoke she expected, for an instant, to see Elaine Bell sitting hunched over the computer, fag in hand, instead of DCI Bruce's ramrod figure, upright, savouring his illicit pleasure. He looked sheepish at her entry. His fingers moved, momentarily, as if he was going to stub the cigarette out before he raised it back towards his mouth and took another, unashamed, draw.

'How did you get on, Alice?' He was daring her to say something.

'So-so. Hilary Norris can't give him an alibi, so we've just got his word that he was at home. I timed the journey. His house to Moray Place, I mean, and it took, maybe, fifty-five minutes or so. He'd have had plenty of time to leave the house and be back at it for her return. Have we got the results on the car yet?'

'That battered hulk! It's got enough bumps and scratches on it to have killed an army. Traffic, if you can believe it, still have given us nothing on the paint match, and the CCTV's a washout. No bloody resolution.'

'And the DNA?'

'Still in the pipeline. The bastard certainly seems to have a motive, eh?'

Alice nodded but said nothing.

'So, Sergeant, did he do it?' DCI Bruce enquired.

'Maybe. He felt righteous anger, for sure, and he's unapologetic for terrorising that old pair with his letters, but would he go further than that? I don't know. Perhaps the Sheriff got it right. Norris's impotent, really. He doesn't finish things, succeed at things… his wife reckons he's breakdown material. What do you think, Sir?'

'Me…' he said airily, 'I think he had the means and the motive, but until we get the results it's all so much hot air—that's what I think, for what it's worth.' Seeing Alice's surprise at his apparent humility he took a final drag, idly blew a smoke ring, and dropped the dog-end into a saucer before continuing. 'Haven't you heard, yet? And you a detective, Alice! I'm offski, away—back to Torpichen. Elaine Bell has risen from the grave, mysteriously cast off her "ME",'—he mimed the quotation marks—'and is returning here to take the reins. Her weeks of sick leave are up and she's raring to go, eager to get back into harness. Nothing to do, obviously with our… MY lack of progress in this most important case, or her coup with the Mair case. Simply, the Assistant Chief Constable assured me, a question of the best uses of resources, even if it does, strangely, involve changing horses mid-stream…'

As he was speaking DCI Bell walked back into her office, raising her head to inhale, to the full, the pungent aroma. Seeing Alice, she smiled at her before turning her attention to her colleague.

'Robin, you should try the patches. They do work, you know. I'm hardly even…' she inhaled deeply again, 'tempted now, and no worse-tempered than any other post-menopausal woman.' So saying, she repossessed her office, laying out her few photos, and putting her coffee-mug back in her drawer. Leaving, Alice made a surreptitious thumbs-up signal to her boss, returned by the slightest nod.

⟶

Oddly, Miss Spinnell's door was open that evening, and sensing his mistress' proximity Quill began to howl, whining and jerking at his tether. Wondering idly if she would find an empty flat, the phantom pilferers having somehow finally removed everything and rendered all security useless, Alice tapped on the door and headed down the dark passageway towards the kitchen. In it she could hear Miss Spinnell's voice, raised in feeble fury, in a one-sided telephone conversation.

'Indeed. And you, I need to know who you are! So I can report you to your superiors. I see. Well, "Just Paul", I'd like to speak to someone with two names if you please, a Christian name and a surname, preferably.'

'Oh!'

She dropped the receiver as if it had burnt her and turned, eyes rolling in all directions, towards Alice.

'He put the phone down on me! Well, "Just Paul", we'll see about that.'

'What's the matter, Miss Spinnell?'

'I failed it. He said that I've failed it,' she whispered, chin trembling, fear in her eyes.

'Failed what?'

'My cholesterol test!'

'Don't worry,' Alice said soothingly, 'it doesn't mean much. There are statins, blood-pressure reducing—'

'But for days and days before I had no butter, no cream, no milk even… I've never failed anything in my life, you know. The *shame*!'

Baffled, as usual, Alice patted a bony little shoulder, forgetting Miss Spinnell's dislike of being touched, her hand being shrugged off with a shudder of revulsion.

'Thank you, dear,' the old lady said coldly, moving rapidly out of range.

'Quill all right today?' Alice asked, thinking it best to change the subject.

'Well, no. Not "all right today", in fact, needing treatment, I expect. I've kept it for you.'

'Kept what?'

'His sick,' she said, beckoning her visitor towards a dustpan resting on a coal scuttle.

In amongst a revolting brown, scummy mass, scraps of wrapping paper had been regurgitated and were visible; red, gold and black.

'But you've been feeding him Mars bars, Miss Spinnell?'

'Precisely. A Mars a Day Helps You Work, Rest and Play. But not in his case.'

Walking beside the dog up the tenement stairs to her flat, Alice contemplated the strange symbiotic relationship that had evolved between herself and her neighbour through their shared pet. The old woman's day only seemed to begin with the arrival of her life-enhancing charge, and her reluctance to part with him grew on each visit. Initially, the care she had lavished on the mongrel had exceeded that of any professional kennel keeper, leaving Alice with a career, a pet and no anxieties about her dog's welfare. However, as the years were passing, Miss Spinnell's repertoire of eccentricities was multiplying, impinging on every area of her life including her dog-minding abilities. Spaghetti hoops yesterday, a Mars Bar today. But, Alice thought, the balance remained in the old lady's favour. True, the now flatulent Quill would become barrel-shaped before his time, but it was unthinkable to deprive Miss Spinnell of her greatest solace and only protector. Without the dog to guard her and her fortress, the imaginary thieves might run amok, make her life unbearable. And, anyway, Quill loved her with or without her marbles. Somehow, the status quo must be maintained for as long as possible.

———

Everyone could feel it and in small ways showed it: the team was complete again with DCI Bell back in charge. For over an hour they had exchanged information, explained leads followed, cursed over dead-ends and, at the close, had their tasks allocated to them by her.

'Alice, you and Alistair can go to Nicholas Lyon's funeral,' she instructed. 'It's at the Warriston crem. Starts at eleven o'clock.'

Then she turned her attention to DI Manson. 'By the way, Inspector, you haven't told us how you got on with that Munro woman?'

Open laughter followed her query, and she raised her eyebrows quizzically.

'Well, Eric?'

'A malicious nutter, ma'am. I had to climb eleven storeys in a tower block to be told that she'd seen the accident, but only in her fucking head.'

'And I gather you've a sore leg?' Elaine Bell said sympathetically, looking at his left foot, now shod in an oversized tartan slipper.

'I have,' he replied with dignity.

'Well, maybe today you could mark up statements, eh? Stay in the office?'

The Inspector nodded before limping off, turning round angrily on catching a whispered chant of 'Pieces of eight, pieces of eight' from Alistair Watt.

—

Little groups of people wandered uneasily about the car park, conversing in low voices, peering around anxiously for their allocated place, no allowance made in the crematorium's rigid timetable for the bereaved getting lost. The notice stated that the 'Lyon' funeral was to be held in the Lorimer Chapel, a building more fitted to a bus-station complex than any religious purpose, its architecture low-key and utilitarian, carelessly hostile to the numinous.

Mrs Nordquist was standing alone in the front row, the place otherwise completely deserted. Feeling the need to stick together and somehow manufacture a congregation out of thin air, the others took their places beside her as if such proximity had been necessitated by a shortage of space. She acknowledged their presence by no more than a slow-motion blink in the shade of her broad-brimmed black hat.

'When's kick-off?' Alastair whispered.

'Eleven o'clock exactly. Three minutes to go.'

An aged man crossed in front of the altar, genuflected while making the sign of the cross and made for a pew towards the back. He was joined, seconds later, by a couple of elderly women, ankle-fat sagging over their too-tight shoes. The sound of piped music became audible as if to herald the entry of a group, pensioners all, whispering to each other irritably before cramming themselves in single file into a middle pew. Last to arrive was a thin man, evidently unused to such chapels, placing the kneeler on his seat as if it was a cushion.

The service itself was uninspiring, all the motions simply gone through. Prayers were murmured in reverential tones and the paltry congregation's attempt at hymn singing was bolstered by another hidden music system, miraculously providing an angelic choral accompaniment. Eventually, to the sound of the Trumpet Voluntary, the coffin, swathed in an embroidered sheet, sank down before juddering its way into a concealed opening, its last few feet in silence except for a strange squeaking sound from the rollers.

A few more desultory devotions and they were free to go, the black-hatted undertakers almost outnumbering the bereaved. Alice recognised one of the old ladies as the gossiping shopkeeper, and the family resemblance with the other one was so marked that she had no doubt that they were sisters. Their escort, the aged man, dawdled nearby, fidgeting, eventually cupping their elbows and easing them into the car. The pensioners helped each other clamber back into their minibus, a battered van with 'MOODY'S COACHES–CARNBO 866644' in gold lettering on its unwashed rear. Two attempts at ignition and its engine spluttered into life, the vehicle weaving its way between dazed mourners. Only the thin man remained unaccounted for, gazing at the bouquet of flowers propped up against the chapel wall, reading the inscription on the card.

'Excuse me, could we talk to you for a minute?' Alice asked hesitantly. The mourner looked up, surprised to be approached, more so again when they showed him their identification.

'Are you a relation or friend of Mr Lyon?' Alistair began.

'Yeah, relative. I'm Ivan McKellar, his nephew. My mum's his sister.'

'But she's not here?'

'No. They don't get on.'

'Sorry to intrude, here of all places, Mr McKellar, but could you tell us why?' Alistair continued.

Seeing the man's disquiet at the query, Alice indicated the Astra and the three of them then sat inside it, as if in some way a post-funeral Police interview in an enclosed space was more seemly than an open-air one.

'Why do you want to know?' Ivan McKellar enquired.

'We need background information about your uncle. He died as a result of a hit-and-run accident. His death is being investigated, but we know very little about him. Anything you could tell us might be of help.'

'Okay,' the man nodded, 'but I haven't much to give you. They fell out, him and my mother because… well, he was gay wasn't he? She's religious, Catholic, devout, blah, blah, blah, blah. She thinks hell-fire's his destination…' he shrugged. 'Mine too, if she but knew it. She cut him off thirty, maybe more, years ago. I was only about six but I remember him well. I loved him, thought he was the world's best uncle. One day she said we were never going to see him again. She'd discovered that he was involved in a gay relationship with the man he lived with. Obviously, nobody else would ever have assumed anything else but… jeez, otherworldly or what? Anyway, all contact ended then, but I never forgot him. I missed him. So when I was older I started writing to him, just now and then, but he always answered. Dead quick, too. After I moved to Edinburgh, got a teaching job at the University, we used to meet up. Not often, he wasn't in the city much. I eventually told him I was gay, but he didn't say a lot about it. Old school maybe, you know, the "don't flaunt it" attitude. And perhaps there is a gay gene, because I've certainly got it. Soon, I'll tell her too, and then she'll cut me off as well. None of that loving the sinner crap for her.'

'Are you his only family then, your mother, brothers and sisters or whatever?'

'I think so. There were just the two of them and there's just the one of me. Not good breeders, you see, my family. Yeah, we're pretty well it.'

'Nobody else?' Alice asked.

'Nobody else. Too many dead ends. Me and him for a start.'

———

Elaine Bell could not conceal the pleasure she felt on returning to St Leonards and her command. The weeks away had felt like an eternity. She was conscious that she was smiling too much, an almost imbecilic grin periodically escaping, and had to stifle the impulse to sing under her breath. But this was the way it was meant to be for her. Destined. Alive again, truly living. And those familiar station smells were most welcome. No more cooking, cleaning and manufacturing outings simply to get herself out of the house. No more awkward exchanges with neighbours or, God forbid, day-time television. All the pains remained, but here they were no more than a distraction, there they had somehow magnified, engulfed her.

Through her open door she saw Alice Rice and called her, telling her to close it behind her.

'How did you get on at the Lyon funeral?' she enquired.

'There was almost no-one there, Ma'am. Mrs Nordquist, she'd arranged the whole thing, a couple of neighbours from near Geanbank including his cleaner, a group of pensioners from Carnbo and a solitary relation, a nephew. Lyon's sister didn't come. There'd been a family rift over his homosexuality. Apparently she's an ardent Catholic.'

'OK Alice, well done. Now, about Colin Norris—Eric seems to think though that he'll get a confession out of him, that we should caution…'

The Sergeant interrupted. 'Even if Manson—sorry, the Detective Inspector—got one, I'd be very ginger about it ma'am.

Unless it disclosed something only the murderer could know, it wouldn't be worth much. The man's a wreck… the last time I saw him his hands shook so much that he spilt his own coffee. In his state the defence would have a field day and we won't get another bite at that cherry.'

The DCI nodded her head. 'But all this wind farm stuff, it may be… well, just wind. Let's go back to basics. Look at the family, eh? Lyon's got none, apparently, except for the sister and nephew. That right?'

'Yes. And no clear motive there,' Alice said, thinking as she spoke. 'The rift was maybe thirty years ago, I can't see that figuring in any way.'

'And the Sheriff, Freeman, what about him? Any family?'

'There's a brother, that's all. No reason, though, to suspect him.'

'Nonetheless, let's check him out. Thoroughly. And I don't think we'll discount the nephew yet, either.'

—

But before the Scowling Crags chapter comes to an end, Alice thought, one last enquiry to pursue. She found Vertenergy's number without difficulty and dialled it, noting as she did so that their office was in Edinburgh. To dot the i's and cross the t's properly, a check had to be made in case the company knew of any particularly hostile anti-wind farm campaigners, any individuals displaying more than the average level of hostility. And the news she received from the woman at the other end of the line surprised her.

'Scowling Crags? That one's not going ahead.'

'Really? The protestors at the Perth meeting seemed unaware of that fact. Are you quite sure?' Alice said in disbelief.

'Hang on a minute and I'll double-check.'

She waited, patiently, for two minutes, ears assaulted by a hideous loop of 'Soave Sia Il Vento' on the flute.

'No,' the voice returned. 'It looked as if we were going to have to withdraw the application, but we're not going to now.'

'Do you know why it was going to be withdrawn?'

'Yes. That's what I've been talking to my superior about. Apparently, James Freeman withdrew permission for us to use the access strip but then that was countermanded…'

'Countermanded by whom?' Alice interrupted.

'By his brother, Christopher Freeman.'

'Sorry, when did all of this happen?' Alice enquired.

'Can you give me just another minute? I've got the file here in front of me.'

This time, fortunately, no travesty of Mozart to raise the blood pressure before the voice returned.

'James Freeman withdrew his permission for the development in a letter. He sent back all the contract documents too.'

'What was the date of that letter?' Alice asked.

'Erm… 7th June, this year.'

'Okay, and the countermand?'

'That was in a letter from his brother, Christopher. Do you want to know its date?'

'Yes, please.'

'It's headed 13th June.'

14

By the time Alice arrived all the food had been laid out and the trouble that he had taken amazed her. China plates had been provided, glasses, napkins even, and dish after dish of her favourite things, including Scotch pies and strawberries. Two bottles of champagne rested on the grass, one unopened, the other with half its contents consumed. A late picnic supper on the banks of Dunsappie Loch with the sun still high in the sky was a treat underrated by the majority of the residents of the city, but not by Ian Melville. He fully appreciated the extraordinary good fortune that the burghers enjoyed, having in their midst Holyrood Park in all its pristine beauty. A breeze rippled across the loch, disturbing a pair of mallard, and they flew off, wheeling round towards Duddingston and the shelter of the reedbeds by the church. What a place, she thought, what an unbelievably wonderful place. And that was not all that he had for her. Shyly, he eased out from under the rug a parcel wrapped in newspaper and handed it to her. He was confident this time she would love it, not be surprised or disconcerted by the gift. After all, in creating it, in every line and in every shadow he had caught her essence. A slumbering cat could not have looked more elegant, perfect, ineluctably itself than she had, naked and asleep, that morning.

A little more champagne and with it, a lot more courage. Sufficient alcohol to loosen his tongue, allow the truth to escape yet let him withstand the consequences. Good or bad. With the Krug's assistance, he would be able to look into her eyes and say what was on his mind, express what had remained on it for far too long. Unsaid. But how would she react to such a declaration? That she liked him was certain. And if she was half as attracted to him as he was to her then he need have no anxieties on that score. But love? That was another matter altogether, stronger, more elusive by far.

Having refilled her glass, he topped up his own, the champagne beginning to convince him that whatever he said would be understood. And here, now, with the waters of the loch lapping at their feet, no misunderstanding could arise between them. They were as one. True. He had said the words before, although not often. Elizabeth Clarke had silenced him, stopped him dead in his tracks; but this, surely, was a mutual passion if such a thing had ever existed.

A sudden doubt assailed him, pricking the expanding bubble of his happiness. Perhaps she would think that it was the drink talking, rendering valueless whatever he said. And, of course, it was the drink talking, but *in vino veritas*, and sober he might find himself unable to voice this most pressing concern.

'Alice, I love you,' he said quickly, but his voice was drowned by the whine of a passing car, and seeing him speak, but not hearing his words, she smiled contentedly at him before placing another strawberry in her mouth. No. This will not do, he thought. Such a declaration would have to be made with him stone cold sober. His restraint would have to be overcome not by champagne, but by the force of his clear will to say those three, difficult words to her.

As he agonised, Alice sipped her drink, saying nothing, pre-occupied by Freeman's death and only dimly aware that her companion had sunk into silence. It was a benign silence, though, the sort usually only achieved in the company of dumb animals or small children, a stillness not requiring to be broken and replaced with chatter, however inane. A few minutes later she picked up the picture that lay, now unwrapped, at her feet and studied it. Where, she wondered, should she hang a naked portrait of herself? It would have to be somewhere prominent, otherwise he might be hurt, thinking it disdained, uncherished. Better that she be thought an exhibitionist, displaying her unclothed self to a critical world. A small flock of gulls swept over the water, wings spread wide, calling shrilly in the dusk. They encircled a lone swan, their quick, jerky movements contrasting with its slow, dignified progress. When Ian Melville suggested walking back to her flat Alice was not surprised, keen to walk with him, until she remembered the car. So she handed over Quill's lead, kissed him and watched as he set off, running, the dog free beside him, leaping up and yelping with joy, both racing down the uneven slope in their haste to reach Broughton Place.

—

DCI Bell inspected the edges of the nail on her index finger, then chewed them while on the move, pacing to and fro in the murder suite, waiting for her troops to arrive. Most of the changes wrought by her predecessor, in her office and elsewhere, had been undone by her early morning industry and she was impatient now to start her briefing. DC Lowe dawdled in, cigarette drooping from his lips and, to her amazement, allowed it to remain there in her presence. She ratcheted up her quizzical expression to no effect, resorting eventually to a hostile stare directed at the cigarette itself.

'Would you like one, ma'am?' the bewildered constable asked.

'No, dunderhead. Put it out, it's against the law, duh?'

She shook her head in disbelief as Lowe, now flushed, dunked it in his mug of cold tea. Surreptitiously, she inhaled its fast-fading fumes before resuming her pacing, watching out of the corner of her eye as Lowe read the instructions on his nicotine gum paper before cramming a strip into his mouth.

Alistair Watt's arrival was preceded by a murmur of jazz before, still swaying to the rhythm, he unplugged himself from his MP3 and sat down, looking expectantly at his boss as if she was about to speak. By nine o'clock all were present except for DI Manson, who could be heard shuffling up the stairs in his tartan slippers, tapping each step with a newly acquired stick. When he appeared his complexion was uncharacteristically sallow, yellowish, as if he had recently fainted.

'Go home, Eric, you look awful!' DCI Bell said instinctively, panicking for a second that his condition might be infectious and her squad fall like flies, and then remembering the likely cause of his malady.

'I am fine, ma'am. I saw the doctor yesterday, got some new painkillers from her. The last ones went for my guts. I'd rather stay on the job, if it's all right with you.'

His mind was still churning over the previous night's events. An evening of near continuous weeping and wailing, interspersed with threats to leave him. Terminating with exile to the spare room to sleep in an unmade bed, covered only by a candlewick bedspread. And all because of that siren from the tabloids. She certainly owed him now. In spades. It had begun peacefully enough, his wife's armchair close to his own, his foot placed solicitously on a stool by her. But then their viewing had been interrupted by the sound of the telephone. He had known immediately from the very first ring that trouble was on the other end of the receiver. And had it not been for his fucking foot he would have handled the emergency like a professional. Just another dratted wrong number, dear, and then back to *Coronation Street*. Instead his wife had jammed her ear to the phone, neutral expression gradually changing into that of a rabbit transfixed by a stoat, and then, hands shaking, had handed the instrument over to him. Every word of the conversation he had with the siren was now branded onto his mind.

'Er... hello,' he had begun tentatively, paralysed by his predicament.

'C'mon Eric, it's only me. She'll never know. So, how are things?'

'Fine.' Nothing had been given away.

'Not seen you at the Balmoral lately. Not out of sorts?'

As if she cared. 'No, no. I've been very busy.'

'Eric... Eric, it's me, remember? I've missed you. I was wondering how things have been going on the Freeman murder?'

Her real concern had been flushed out quickly enough. 'Fine.' Cheeky cow.

'Don't be like that... talk to me, lover!'

'Well, I'll see you in the office first thing tomorrow, Constable.'

Frowning hard as if impatient with a subordinate, he had put the phone down, limped back to his seat and resumed watching the television, but Enid had not been fooled. A squawk as unique as that one could not be explained away. And the subsequent interrogation, using the female weapons of choice, tears and tantrums, had forced an admission from him. Indeed, all contact with the woman had not ceased but, he had explained weakly, it was only for his work. Well, mainly. The thought of further recrimination, more pained disappointment, would have been intolerable even if his foot had not been throbbing fit to burst. The office promised respite. A sanctuary.

'Okay, people,' the Chief Inspector began '...we've got the forensic result. It seems that the paint flakes from the locus don't match those taken from Norris's car, and it looks like it wasn't his DNA in Moray Place either. We know he's got no alibi and he has admitted writing the letters but... well, I'm not sure. We'll keep him in our sights, but not hold our breaths. Torphichen Place has passed on information about two back-street garages, worked exclusively by moonlighters. One's in

Newhaven and the other's along the canal, so I want DC Lowe and…'

'Yes,' Lowe piped up, interrupting her flow, suddenly alert to his own name.

'and DC McDonald,' she glared at him, 'to go along and see if either of them has had a white car in since the hit-and-run. Alistair, I need you to help out with Holmes this morning, and Eric… well, let's see. You could prepare the report for the Assistant Chief Constable. Have you made any progress with Christopher Freeman yet, Alice?'

DS Rice shook her head. 'I'm going to see him now, Ma'am; they've been away. But I have discovered that, somehow, he learnt that his brother had changed his mind about the wind farm. And I intend to find out how, precisely, he made that discovery.'

——

Sandra Freeman let her in, grasping the poodles' diamante collars to prevent her dogs from tearing off into the road and then, on closing the door, releasing them to jump all over her visitor. Alice was assaulted on all sides by them, pink tongues emerging from their dark heads to lick her, untrimmed claws laddering her tights. In the kitchen an open bottle of nail varnish sat on the table, and Mrs Freeman immediately busied herself removing black curls from her wet nails before, sighing, she collected a paper hankie and began wiping off all the polish, ready to start her task afresh.

'Could I speak to your husband, please, Mrs Freeman?'

It was as if she had said nothing. The woman continued attending to her nails, brows furrowed with concentration, tongue protruding, intent on producing a flawless surface. Just as Alice was steeling herself to repeat the question a response arrived, flat in tone.

'No. He's still in bed.'

'When is he likely to get up?'

'Mmmm—' the woman buffed the nail on her ring finger furiously, 'well, he's probably...'

Her sentence remained unfinished, hanging in the air, as the man waddled into the room, unshaven, Paisley-patterned dressing gown flapping open to reveal stained, striped pyjamas. Spying an open packet of cigarettes on the dresser, a hairy hand emerged and scooped them up, and in seconds he was drawing deeply on one, sucking in his cheeks as if taking in the first life-giving oxygen of the day. A smoky kiss was bestowed on his wife.

'Coffee, darling?' she enquired, still preoccupied with her manicure.

'Of course, my love.'

'I'll just let this dry and then put it on for you. She wants to talk to you again, sweetie,' Sandra Freeman said, uncapping a Nescafe jar cautiously as if her nails might stick to the lid.

'Does she indeed...' her husband replied. 'Well, she'll just have to wait until after my bath.'

⟨━⟩

Smelling of Imperial Leather, and clad now in a viyella shirt and patched cavalry twill trousers, hair slicked down with water, Christopher Freeman showed his unwanted guest into his sitting room. It was small, bedecked with cheap ornaments, and cold. The fireplace had a dusty bowl of potpourri in it and the only two armchairs present were each draped with an antimacassar.

'I don't suppose you've come to tell me who killed my brother or his "partner" by any chance?' the man began.

'No, sir, I'm afraid not. I'd like to ask you some questions though, to help us with our continuing enquiries.'

'Fat lot of use I'll be, I'm sure, but on you go.'

He extracted a flask from his pocket and poured a tot of

whisky into his milky coffee, sniffing the unappetising mix before taking a loud gulp from it.

'I was wondering, sir, when did you get your new car?'

The major looked deeply affronted. 'I really don't see what that has to do with anything, Sergeant. I'm more than happy to assist you but I don't want our time wasted. Sandra needs to hoover in here, you know, it's her invariable routine.'

It struck Alice, not for the first time, that the man seemed unnaturally detached from the murder investigation being pursued round about him. His own brother was the victim, but, for all the concern he showed, it could have been a tadpole killed rather than his own flesh and blood. The man's co-operation, she decided, was no longer optional.

'If you would prefer it, sir, we could easily move this talk to St Leonards? No problem there with housework,' she smiled, with her mouth only, not her eyes.

'No, no. Carry on…' he shifted in his chair uneasily. 'Just thinking of the wife, you understand.'

'The new car?' she reminded him.

'I don't know. A couple of weeks ago, probably.'

'And what did you do with the old one?'

'Sold it.' He nodded his head sagely.

'Which garage did you sell it to?'

'Er… no garage, actually.'

'No? How did you sell it then?' Not that old chestnut, surely. A sale over a pint in a pub to a stranger.

'On the street. You know, with a sign in the back. Car for sale, telephone number, etc.'

'And were you paid by cheque?'

'No, of course not! From a complete stranger? Wouldn't be worth the paper it was written on.'

'Cash, then. I expect you put it in the bank.' The Major shook his head emphatically. 'Hardly worth it, we only got a couple of hundred anyway.'

'Presumably, you got the buyer's name, you know, for registration purposes?' He shook his head again.

'Scrap. No names, no pack drill.'

'Well, perhaps you could give me its registration number?'

''Fraid I never remember that kind of thing… a type of dyslexia, I expect. Gave them all the papers too.'

'Could you remind me, sir, of the make of the car and its colour?'

'Naturally. It was a Volkswagen. A Volkswagen Polo, whitish, cream-coloured. More my wife's toy really.'

Mrs Freeman came into the room, Hoover trailing behind her, and sat on the padded arm of her husband's chair, smiled encouragingly at him and casually rested an arm around his neck. They fitted well together; both past their prime, ordinary, comfortable, leaning thigh against shoulder, touching each other. Seeing a loose hair on her husband's collar she picked it off, tossing it into the empty fireplace.

Alice's phone went and she was relieved. The call would, whatever its actual content, provide a pretext for her to leave. She did not intend to interview the Major in the company of his wife. She wanted them kept apart when spoken to in order to minimise the leakage of information from one to the other. In fact, DCI Bell was calling to bring her back to the station, and she was pleased that she could leave with an honest excuse.

Having asked to use their loo, she was shown into a cramped, windowless cubby hole off the kitchen, the noise from the over-size fan deafening any occupant, obscuring any unwanted sound effects. The place had been done up as a gentleman's convenience to Mrs Freeman's specification, cream paint, smutty prints on the wall and a few ancient copies of the *Shooting Times* cobwebbed onto the cistern. Passing her hosts' bedroom and seeing the major's ivory hair brushes on a dressing-table, on impulse, she dashed in and speedily combed through one of them with her fingers, gathering together a good crop of grey hair from its bristles.

—

'I said there was some kind of gay connection in all this, didn't I?' DC Lowe said excitedly, slamming down the telephone receiver.

' Yes, you did,' Alice conceded.

' Well, the boss says we're to go to see that Georgie boy again, Sarge. Great, eh?'

'What are you going on about, Kevin?'

Her patience was at a low ebb, weeks of overwork taking its toll.

'Sarge, we've to go back to the bookstore or whatever. We've to find that guy. He's been at it again, bragging in the pub and all. Only this time he's talking about Mr Lyon, like he knew him too or something. He's been mouthing off about the big house and the man's sister. Stuff he couldn't know unless he'd been seeing Lyon himself.'

'Fine,' Alice said and, briefly, closed her eyes. For days the squad had been treated to an intermittent dialogue between Eric Manson and Kevin Lowe, speculating, piling one shaky supposition on another, all founded on the simple premise that two gays could never be monogamous, faithful, like good, old married heterosexuals. Sex would hold the key to this case. Georgie would be implicated in it one way or another. Sometimes their conversation centred on the investigation, often it roamed free, covering subjects as diverse, and complex, as human nature and normality, usually wrapped up in a few heated minutes.

On this matter, an unexpected meeting of minds had occurred. One, Alice thought ruefully, informed by inexperience and the other by prejudice. And all the vilified 'political correctness' courses in the world could not make up for their lack of grey matter. Only yesterday she had listened as Alistair Watt, exasperated into participation, challenged their joint conclusion that a side effect of 'gayness' was promiscuity. Casanova, Don Juan, Alan Clark, Hugh Hefner had not all been gay, he had suggested—promiscuity incarnate tended if anything to be resolutely heterosexual. Yes, Eric Manson had countered, undeterred, but they have a choice. Gays don't. They are constitutionally incapable of fidelity. Undisguised laughter had greeted this new thesis, and Alice having dismissed it, enquired whether her two colleagues would then condemn, as they appeared to do, other unchangeable genetic traits such as left-handedness and whether, perhaps, having a choice and still being unfaithful could be viewed as more culpable. DC Lowe had asked her to repeat that one, then observed that his girlfriend's cousin was a gayboy and actually seemed quite nice. Good at football, too.

—

A mousy assistant in the bookshop re-directed the Police officers to Georgie's lair in Cumberland Street, a basement flat on the humbler, east side of the street. Having descended the stone steps to the front door they entered, finding themselves serenaded by Dusty Springfield's smoky tones, belting out 'Preacher Man'.

The kitchen table was covered in punnets of loganberries, and the man pulled out chairs for them, all the while explaining that he was having a dinner party that evening and had a mass of de-husking to do. Favouring them with one of his brightest smiles, he declared that he would continue with his task while they spoke, if that was all right with them. They both nodded, dazzled by the smile's warmth into immediate, unthinking assent.

'Mr De Thuy…' Alice began, but she was instantly corrected.

'Georgie, please. I'm always known as Georgie, by everyone. Everyone. I prefer it.'

'Well, Georgie,' she tried again, accustoming herself to its informality and feeling, unaccountably, that her professional status was diminished by its use, 'I hear that you've been saying, at the Boar's Head, that you knew Nicholas Lyon.'

Georgie, now biting into a loganberry, shook his head. 'I'm afraid you've been misinformed, Sergeant, I've never said I knew him. I wouldn't have claimed that. Your informant, whoever he, or she, is, has got it wrong.'

'OK,' Alice persisted, 'but you were talking about Geanbank, and about Mr Lyon?'

'I may have done.'

'So can you explain…' the question remained unfinished on her lips as the kitchen door opened, and a figure, face and body hidden by vast armfuls of flowers, barged in, dropping his cargo at one end of the table.

It was Ivan McKellar. And he seemed every bit as surprised to see DS Rice as she was to encounter him once more.

'Mr McKellar… I didn't realise that you knew Mr De… er… Georgie.'

' No,' he hesitated before continuing. 'Well… Edinburgh's a small place, eh?'

'But how d'you know Mr De Tea?' DC Lowe butted in, unable to contain his curiosity, 'How come you know him?'

Georgie took control, smiling beatifically at the company and displaying, once more, his even white teeth. 'We met, officers, in the "Grape and Grain", you know, on the High Street. We'd both gone there for a bite to eat and, well, Ivan was on his own. It was after his uncle's funeral, actually. Not so very odd, really… to make a new friend.'

As he was speaking, two young women, both hauling carrier bags and talking noisily to each other, drifted in, deposited their burdens on the floor and continued nattering together until they became aware that their conversation was being listened to by all the others present in the room.

'Lorna and Eileen, meet DC Lowe and DS Rice,' said Georgie brightly, breaking the tense silence that had replaced the girls' chat.

—

Emerging back onto the street and before they were out of their host's earshot, Kevin Lowe began to talk.

'Sarge, I think I've got it. Really. See, that Nicholas guy was… well, gay, eh, and so's his nephew. Maybe they, him and that "Georgie" fellow, killed the two of them… he's Nicholas's only living relative. He'll cop the lot.'

'What about his mum?'

'Yeah, but they'd fallen out and all… they didn't get on, but a gay nephew, that's quite different. There'd be a lot in common. And you can't deny it's odd, I mean Georgie sleeping with the uncle and then, coincidentally, meeting the man's nephew! And the smiler's got no alibi either. We should really check them out.'

'If Georgie did sleep with the uncle…' Alice mused.

'Well, he said he did… he admitted it. Why should you doubt it?'

'I just do. And, if Georgie was involved, he's far too intelligent to drop himself in it. So, you'd expect him to deny any relationship with the Sheriff, not boast about it and then repeat the same story to me. Unless he's a positively pathological exhibitionist, of course.'

'A what?'

15

Three pages; one, two and four. She searched her desk in case the missing sheet was hidden beneath the patchwork of paperwork that covered its entire surface, temporarily losing page two under newly disturbed documents in the process. No page three and nothing on the computer either. She shouted across to DC Littlewood, now busy tending a pot plant.

'Tom, there's a page missing.'

'Sorry, Sarge. I'll check the fax in case I overlooked one.'

While waiting she read the traffic department's efforts and her attention was drawn by a diagram of the accident locus. Tyre marks were shown in red with a cross at the point of impact. The final position in which the body had been found was also depicted together with a rectangle, representing Nicholas Lyon's car. The first two pages gave a factual account of all observations made at the scene, including measurements taken, and, tantalisingly, the final line of the second page was headed 'Conclusions'.

The third sheet was handed sheepishly to her and she studied it eagerly. On the basis of the evidence available its author had concluded that Nicholas Lyon had been deliberately run down; the length of the tyre marks and the injuries sustained by him being consistent with a high-impact collision, maximum acceleration having occurred whilst the victim was near stationary, within the driver's unimpeded line of vision. This judgement was fortified by the only relevant witness testimony available, which had referred to sounds consistent with sudden acceleration followed by another single sound suggestive of impact. A catalogue of the contents of the victim's car appeared below the last paragraph, and Alice scanned the list quickly. Attached to the report was a photocopy of a handwritten note and the words 'Meet' and '5th' were legible, although the name, or initials, between them was not.

In her excitement Alice did not knock on DCI Bell's door but strode straight in. The Inspector, her top few blouse buttons undone, seemed to be trying to pull an electrode off an area of skin below her right collarbone, and she looked up, furious at the interruption, a single unplugged electrode swinging limply in her hand.

'Alice, what the fuck are you doing?'

'Sorry, Ma'am, I should have knocked, I know. But there's something important in the traffic report…'

'Shut the bloody door, then!'

The Chief Inspector slowly peeled a further electrode off her shoulder and returned the lead together with a mass of others to a small pouch.

'A tens machine, Alice, since you didn't ask. I don't want any strange rumours circulating in this station. It's supposed to help muscular pain, chronic pain. I borrowed it from a friend who used it when she was pregnant. So, what's so urgent then?'

Alice placed the traffic report on her superior's desk, page three uppermost.

'Look at the conclusions, Ma'am. Nicholas Lyon was murdered, as we suspected, but there's more than that, and I think we should get forensics to check out Moray Place again.'

Doing up her buttons and still plainly annoyed, DCI Bell muttered, 'Why?'

'Because Mr Lyon must have, surely, been meeting someone there that night. Look at the note. I can't make out who, I can't read all of the writing, but we should follow it up…'

Elaine Bell examined the photocopy carefully, 'Maybe. OL… GL… F… No, I can't make head or tail of it, either.

But suppose he did meet someone there, that wouldn't necessarily lead us to whoever ran him down...' the Chief Inspector parried, still truculent.

'No. There may be no connection whatsoever. On the other hand, there may be.'

Diligently, Alistair Watt trawled through the statements taken from the neighbouring residents. Only Mrs Nordquist and her housekeeper reported seeing or hearing anything immediately before the accident, but it was not clear that any of the interviewees had been specifically asked by the uniforms if they had noticed any signs of occupation in number seventy-three before nine pm.

———

Loud knocking on Mrs Nordquist's immaculate white front door evoked no response other than a volley of deep, echoing barks, sufficient to wake the dead. Mrs Gunn, however, was at home, an apron concealing most of the décolletage on display despite her dress. Blackened marigold rubber gloves were discarded together with a cloth onto a kitchen table laden with tarnished silver. Having washed her hands at the sink she led her visitors into her drawing room.

'Can't think what more you can possibly want,' she said conversationally, as if to break the ice.

'It's about the night of 5th July,' Alice replied. 'You told the constables that you saw and heard nothing of the hit-and-run.'

'Correct,' she nodded.

'But,' Alistair broke in, 'we need to know if you saw anything beforehand. In particular, did you notice any lights or anything in the Sheriff's house to suggest that someone might have been in it before the accident occurred?'

'Mmmm... let me think.' She paused for a few seconds, before continuing. 'I'm awfully sorry, but I can't remember a single thing about it now. Nothing sticks in my mind about that date. Apart from the accident, of course.'

Alistair caught Alice's eye and she removed Mrs Gunn's signed statement, now folded, from her pocket and handed it to the woman. She ostentatiously unfolded it, looking bemused, disturbed even, as if touching it might, in some way, soil her.

'Oh, how interesting,' she purred on reading it. 'It's what I remembered when I spoke to that young WPC. Of course! I'd been to drinks at Helen's that night. You know,' she paused, 'there were lights on... in Freeman's place, I mean. But nobody asked me about that, they just wanted to know if I'd seen anything of the accident. Or heard anything, obviously. No-one asked me about the house. I did see lights on. I thought it was you people actually as, goodness knows, you'd been practically living there.'

'Iona,' a voice bellowed, and Hamish Gunn hobbled into the room, doubled up, head almost parallel with the floor. On seeing the visitors, he attempted, briefly, to straighten up, groaned and relapsed back into his crooked state.

'It's jiggered, darling. Completely jiggered!' he said, shaking his head, addressing his wife.

'How did it happen?'

'I parked the car in George Street, was just getting out of it, when suddenly, "snap!" and it had gone. Completely gone.'

'No golf with Freddie at Muirfield this afternoon, then. I'll phone him for you.'

As the woman left the room her husband lowered himself carefully onto a sofa, looking up at the Police officers.

'What can I do for you, Sergeants?' he said, eyes closed tight shut, as if the effort required to show good manners had become too much.

'In the circumstances, sir, we'll be very quick. It was just to see if you remembered seeing any signs of life in Sheriff

Freeman's house before Mr Lyon was hit in the accident?'
Alice said.

'Christ knows!' He grimaced, clearly in pain.

'It was the night...' Mrs Gunn shouted, 'remember, darling, of Helen's drinks party. We walked home from Douglas Gardens. There were definitely lights in his house.'

'Well, I don't remember any,' the man replied cantankerously.

'Well, they were there, sweetheart.'

'Maybe! Maybe! But I don't remember any, and I'm off to bed. Give me a hand up the stairs will you, Iona?'

———

Eric Manson was in a quandary. Should he peek again? But if so what might he find? He might scare himself to death. Preparing himself for the worst, he gently removed the tartan slipper, peeling off the heel, then easing the toe end forwards, minimising any unnecessary pressure on the forefoot. A finger at the top of the sock and it, too, could be removed without pain. Slumped on the lavatory seat he raised the sole for inspection and was horrified to note that the puncture mark was not only red but ridged too, a clear zig-zag pattern extending from it in all directions. Bloody Hell, he thought, this is SERIOUS. Spying his sock down on the floor he bent over to retrieve it, repelled by the prospect of its contamination, but relieved to note on examination that it was textured, replicating precisely the ominous pattern he had observed on his foot. Good. So far, no red line extending from the wound upwards to his heart. Presaging death.

'Complete wanker!'

The voice, by his cubicle door, alarmed him. He had been so absorbed in the inspection of his injury that he had not heard anyone joining him in the gents.

'Pussy footing about in his tartan baffy!' A different voice this time.

'Marilyn, not Eric. Marilyn Manson. Marilyn. Happy Birthday, Mr Chief Constable… Happy Birthday to you. Boo Boo Be Do,' the first voice crooned.

Incandescent with rage, but unable to risk clambering off the loo seat, infected bare foot exposed to the filth on the toilet floor, Eric Manson fumed impotently. Little bastards!

A word from him, though, and they would be off, he thought. Unpunished. Stifling little mewls of pain, he pulled his sock on and laid the slipper on the floor, toes pointing like a ballerina, ready to put his foot into it. But the sound of heavy footsteps signalled his tormentors' premature exit, the door swinging behind them.

In front of the mirror he gazed at his reflection. Too pale. Ghostly. And only yesterday his pleas for a different course of antibiotics had been refused yet again. If that sodding doctor has got it wrong, he thought, bile overflowing, I'll… I'll… I'll… I'll die! And no painkillers left. Inspiration came quickly, and he fished in his pocket for the Boots bag. Inside it was a small bottle of Calpol, an errand completed for his daughter-in-law. A sweet, strawberry flavour coated his taste buds and he swallowed half the contents, impressed by his own ingenuity, reassuring himself with the thought that babies don't feel pain.

———

On Alice's desk was a note in DC Littlewood's meticulous hand.

'Lab rang this morning. Report not available for a further week or so due to backlog. Results are through. Analysis of hair follicle samples and comparison with alien door handle samples from Moray Place reveal the DNA is from the same source.

P.S. Bob says he prefers Glenfiddich.'

Too many roads, Alice thought, were beginning to lead to Christopher Freeman. His DNA was in the Sheriff's house, but his wife had said that the brothers had not met for years. Somehow, too, he appeared to have known of James Freeman's change of mind about the access strip almost as soon as the wind farm company did, countermanding the instruction immediately. Yet he had given the impression that he had not been in recent contact with his brother. Urgently, she checked Holmes to see if the statements from their neighbours had been put on the system. Four residents of Frogston Road had been questioned and none of them recalled seeing a 'For Sale' sign on the Volkswagen Polo, although every single one of them said that they were familiar with the vehicle, aware that it was owned by the Freemans.

___

Her arrival at the bungalow was greeted coolly; the Major was present and on his own. His wife, he explained, had gone to collect their dry cleaning. He showed Alice into the sitting room, ostentatiously switched the cricket off and then they sat in the armchairs, facing each other. Both now tense, conscious that a duel was about to begin.

'This seems to be becoming rather a habit, Sergeant,' the man began dryly.

'Yes, sir, but I had to leave prematurely last time, our talk seemed unfinished.'

'Well, let's finish our "talk" this time, shall we?'

'Can you tell me how you knew your brother had decided not to go ahead with the wind farm, to keep Blackstone Mains out of it?'

The man blinked and swept his slick-backed hair with this hand.

'The company. Vertenergy told me. Obviously.'

'How did they tell you? By phone, letter or what?'

He paused before answering, 'By phone, as I recall.'

'When?'

'How do you mean "when"?' he said crossly.

'When did the company inform you by telephone of your brother's decision?'

A longer pause. 'The day before I wrote the letter.'

'That letter was dated 13th June… one day after your brother's death, and we informed you of the killing on that very day.'

'So, what are you suggesting? That I'd be too paralysed with grief to attend to a business matter? I think you'll find I've never pretended to be close to James. On the contrary, I told you that we didn't hit it off.'

'No, what I was wondering about, sir, was the land. It belonged to you and James, both of you. On James' death…' her sentence remained unfinished.

'On James's death, it should by all rights have come to me,' Christopher Freeman said, before correcting himself, 'well—normally.'

'But,' she continued, 'it went to Nicholas Lyon. Your brother's partner, and before we spoke to you, as I recall, you were unaware that your brother had a partner at all…'

'So?'

'Can you tell me, Mr Freeman, what Blackstone Mains being part of the Scowling Crags development would mean to you in financial terms?'

'None of your bloody business, Sergeant!'

'You won't tell me?' she enquired evenly, eyes never moving from his.

'Correct. I won't tell you. It's got nothing whatsoever to do with you, with the Police or any so-called investigation. It's a purely personal, financial matter.'

Alice nodded her head slowly before continuing, 'Obviously we can get such information from Vertenergy, sir.'

'Well, get it from Vertenergy then.'

'Going back to the car…'

'The car! The car! What is it with the bloody car and you people?' he interrupted, exasperated.

'Going back to the car,' she continued, 'you told me, sir, that you sold the car as scrap to a stranger. When exactly did you buy your new car?'

'I don't see what that has to do with anything…'

'Maybe not, sir,' she said firmly, 'but I'd still be grateful if you could try to remember.'

'Oh, I don't know precisely. After I'd disposed of the old one.'

'And when was that?'

'I told you before, weeks ago, I can't remember exactly.'

'No, sir, I appreciate that, but perhaps you could give me the name of the garage from which you bought your new car? Otherwise, I suppose I could get the same information from DVLA.'

'Tooles Garage. Tooles in Liberton.'

'Finally, sir, can you tell me where you were between about seven and ten pm on Monday 12th June and eight and ten pm on Wednesday 5th July?'

'No problem. I was here with Sandra. Sandra will back me up in that. You'd better ask her. So that's it, is it? You lot sure that I did it, eh!'

Alice shook her head 'No, sir. If we were, we'd be in the station right now and I'd have cautioned you long ago.'

⌒

Walking up Comiston Road, polythene-encased dry cleaning flapping on two coat hangers, Sandra Freeman became aware that every so often the hems of the clothes were sweeping along the pavement, and rued her decision not to take the car. Worse still, friction seemed to be attracting the swinging load towards her legs, impeding her movement and making her gait thoroughly abnormal, constant stops and starts required in order to untangle her limbs. At this rate it would take at least another quarter of an hour before she was at home, she thought, looking up at the sky anxiously for signs of impending rain.

Her mind drifted, returning as it habitually did to domesticity and the practicalities of life. Dog food was needed; Chris could get it from the local pet shop this time. He could exercise his charm on the fat lesbian behind the counter, suffer the usual humiliating grillings about the absence of lustre on the boys' coats. Maybe even render a cheque and see if his writing, lacking loops to the same extent as her own, was declared 'not sexy'. The cheek of it! And actually, it was probably the very reverse of the truth. A small, cramped hand meant dynamite under the sheets, the only place where full abandon was sanctioned. Her indignation evaporated on seeing the familiar figure of DS Rice, sitting in a parked car, now rolling down the driver's window and beckoning her towards the vehicle.

'I could give you a lift home, if you like, Mrs Freeman?'

The woman did not need to be asked twice, and with almost indecent haste bundled her cleaning onto the back seat and then herself into the front. Signalling to re-join the traffic, Alice said casually, 'I've just seen your husband, he said you were out and then, by good luck, I saw you. Maybe we could finish our chat on the way to your house?'

'Fine by me,' Sandra Freeman replied, lighting up immediately.

'Your car. The new one. When did you get it?'

' Not a minute to spare, eh! The day after Chris got rid of the other one.'

'Chris... er, the Major sold the other one, didn't he? Can you tell me how?'

'I really don't know. He said he needed a new one and who am I to disagree with that?' she smiled. 'I'm the driver, of course, and the other one was a rustbucket. It had a hole in the floor, water actually came in, if you can believe it.'

'Can you recall a sign in the car, a "For Sale" sign?'

'No… but that's how Chris sold it. I remember now. He told me.'

'And on Monday 12th June between about seven and ten pm and on Wednesday 5th July between about eight and ten pm, where were you?'

'That first date, that's the night James died, eh?' the woman asked, inhaling deeply.

'Yes.'

'I was at home with Chris…' a cloud of smoke issued from her mouth. 'The second date, I don't know. Is that the date Nicholas Lyon was hit?'

'Yes. Do I turn left here?' Alice asked.

'Yup, left now. I was there with Chris. He was with me.'

'Are you sure?'

'Yes, I'm sure,' Sandra Freeman said tartly, distrust now evident in her voice.

'Here all right?' Alice enquired, drawing the car to a halt.

'Here's ideal.'

'And you said you were the driver?' Alice asked, hardly expecting an answer, the woman, cigarette dangling loosely from her lips, now wrestling open the car door, ready to extract her load from the back.

'Yes. Chris lost his licence a while ago. But he gets it back at the end of the month.'

———

She assembled everything in her head before leaving her desk and this time she knocked, although the impulse to barge in was stronger, if anything, than before.

'Come in.'

Alice advanced through the door and was disappointed to see the Assistant Chief Constable, Laurence Body, seated in the Chief Inspector's office.

'Yes, Alice,' DCI Bell said.

'Well, Ma'am,' she began, disarmed by the unexpected presence, 'it's about Mr Freeman… sorry, Sheriff Freeman and his partner, Mr Lyon.'

'Yes.'

'I've new information that might help us, but I could always come back later, tell you when you're free. You know, after the Assistant Chief Constable, Sir, has…'

Wordlessly, Laurence Body rose from his seat, went to the window, collected from beside it another chair and then placed it beside his own. He smiled reassuringly at the Sergeant and, with a courtly gesture, indicated for her to take the seat. Oh fuck, she thought, worried that in such august company the power of speech might desert her or, at least, the power to persuade. Treat it like a presentation, she told herself, but a subversive answer in her own head replied that she had not prepared for any such thing, expecting instead some form of dialogue, ideas exchanged, tested, accepted or rejected, all in the course of an ordinary conversation.

'Well Ma'am, Sir…' she began, voice sounding weak already. 'I think Christopher Freeman murdered the Sheriff and the Sheriff's partner, but we may have great difficulty in proving it.'

'Go on,' Body said eagerly, clearly rapt.

'First of all, motive. James Freeman, the eldest son, inherited all of the Freeman wealth, the vast house in Moray Place, land and so on, except for a single farm, Blackstone Mains, which was shared with his brother, Christopher. Originally, the elder brother was pro-wind farm and seems to have got Vertenergy involved or at least acceded to their wind farm plan. From Alistair's enquiries with Vertenergy it seems that their lease of Blackstone Mains for a twenty-five year period would've netted the brothers a sum in excess of one and a half million. And for Christopher Freeman—almost anyone I suppose—that's a huge amount of money. As far as I can see, he lives in pretty reduced circumstances. He doesn't seem to have had any sort of career and his house in Frogston Road West reeks of genteel poverty. But the money won't have mattered so much to the Sheriff: he was already rich, and he'll have got a fat pension from the government. Also, he knew he was dying. Nicholas Lyon said that when James Freeman entered into negotiation with the company he was keen on renewable energy, global warming and all that. Over time, though, he changed his mind about wind turbines, possibly due to some extent to his partner's arguments, appeals or whatever. Christopher Freeman, however, didn't know that his brother had a partner, male or female. If his brother didn't have a partner then it wouldn't be an unreasonable assumption, even taking into account their strained relationship, that in the event of the Sheriff's death the land would remain in Freeman hands, that it would be left by James Freeman to Christopher Freeman…'

The telephone rang, breaking the spell, and the Chief Inspector's irritation could not have been missed by her caller.

'Yes, Eric. Go home. Get better and, please, please don't come back to the office until you're mobile again. Okay. That understood? Fine. Bye.'

'Suppose…' Alice started again.

'How do you mean, "suppose"?' the Assistant Chief Constable interrupted.

'It is only a supposition, Sir, but reasonable, I think.'

'Go on then.'

'Suppose Christopher Freeman called on his brother on the night of the murder. We know that the Sheriff had, by that time, told Vertenergy that he didn't intend to allow Blackstone Mains to be included in the Scowling Crags scheme. Surely he must have communicated his decision to his brother, by some means? Anyway, we can check his phone records on that. If he did tell his brother then it seems quite plausible to me that

Christopher Freeman might want to visit him. To talk to him. Persuade him to change his mind again and allow the scheme to go ahead. After all, his brother's DNA was found in number seventy-three.'

'Is that right, Alice?' Elaine Bell asked, clearly surprised by the news.

'Yes, Ma'am. Well, the lab says the stuff from the hairbrush matched…'

Laurence Body interrupted, 'What on earth are you talking about, Sergeant? "The stuff on the hairbrush"?'

Alice's eyes met her superior's with dumb entreaty, then Elaine Bell spoke: 'Ah, Sergeant Rice used her initiative, Sir. Collected some hair samples, granted in a slightly unorthodox fashion, from Christopher Freeman's house.'

'Well, that will be of no use in court,' Body said coldly.

'I know, Sir,' Alice said, 'but we'll be able to get one we can use once we take him in.'

'Bloody stupid thing to do, though. Carry on.'

'So Christopher Freeman's DNA is in his brother's house. He must have been there about the time of the murder. The Sheriff had a cleaner after all. But he's denied being there, and his wife said that the brothers hadn't met for years and he, standing right beside her, made no attempt to correct that impression.'

'They're brothers, for heaven's sake,' Body interjected. 'If he knows that his DNA was found at the scene then he'll suddenly "remember" a recent innocent visit to explain it away. Then what will we have left? There was no DNA on the truncheon thing.'

'Sir,' Alice said, determined to keep going, 'we can make it more difficult for him than that. He doesn't know about the DNA he left in the building. And he's not a bright spark either. If he did murder his brother in Moray Place he's going to be determined, on all occasions, to deny going anywhere near the house whenever he is given the opportunity. If in his interview under caution we get him repeatedly stressing that he hasn't been near the house for years, and he's bound to say that to protect himself unless he knows about the sample, then he'll find it very difficult indeed to explain all those denials on the record at his trial if he chooses to give evidence at all. The jury won't be convinced by him if he's consistently denied being near the place until confronted with the forensic evidence linking him to it…'

'Maybe,' Elaine Bell said, musing, 'but the interview under caution would have to be handled incredibly carefully.'

'What else have you got?' Body said testily, plainly unconvinced.

'It's all circumstantial, Sir, about the Nicholas Lyon killing too, but again a sort of picture is beginning to emerge. I think so, anyway. Traffic concluded that Nicholas Lyon was not accidentally run over. The driver of the car seems to have accelerated at him, having been able to see him clearly. Tooles Garage sold Christopher Freeman a new, well, new secondhand, car on the afternoon of 7th July. Alistair got that information from them today. Mrs Freeman, and the Major, admit that they bought their new car two days after Nicholas Lyon's death, and they both said that the old car had been sold the day before they got the new one. Mrs Freeman's pretty vague on the sale. Either she doesn't know anything about it or she doesn't want to talk about it. Christopher Freeman said he sold the car to a stranger for cash, conveniently enough, scrap value only. A "For Sale" sign was, supposedly, in the back of the car. Only neither his wife nor any of his neighbours remember anything about any "For Sale" signs. It seems likely that Nicholas Lyon met someone at the Moray Place house and Mrs Gunn saw lights in the house before the accident. Suppose Forensics find more of Christopher Freeman's DNA in…'

'Hold on. Hold on. Hold on,' Body said, 'Forensics are

checking Moray Place again, are they? Suppose they do find "more" of Christopher Freeman's DNA. What exactly can be done with that?'

'Yes, Alice,' DC Bell added, concerned, aware of the potential problem.

'It's difficult, I know. I did say that. The Defence will, no doubt, suggest that any "more" DNA found was always there, missed by Forensics the first time, and then attempt to cover it by exactly the same explanation as will be proffered for the original stuff. I see that, but it might be useful for us to know. Suppose…'

'Suppose this. Suppose that,' Body said sarcastically, patience clearly frayed.

'Suppose,' Alice battled on, 'Nicholas Lyon and Christopher Freeman met in Moray Place that night. I don't know why, but suppose they did. Both of their phone records could be checked to see if either called the other. The Major might have wanted to talk about the inheritance or whatever… their affairs on any view had suddenly become linked. Suppose Christopher Freeman leaves the house, presumably not having achieved whatever he wanted, and kills Nicholas Lyon, runs him down with his car. It would explain the absence of the white—and I saw it myself—Volkswagen Polo, the timing of its disappearance, and the new DNA, if it's there.'

'For Christ's sake,' Body said angrily, 'this is no more than a mass of conjecture, one theory on another. And the little hard evidence that exists will probably melt like spring snow in the hands of a half-competent counsel.'

'Has Christopher Freeman got an alibi for the killings?' DCI Bell asked quietly.

'Yes, Ma'am,' Alice conceded, adding desperately, 'but only from his wife.'

'And no car's been found,' the Assistant Chief Constable added.

'Thank you very much, Sergeant Rice, I'll speak to you later,' DCI Bell said, and Alice, now dejected, waited to be dismissed.

'I think, perhaps, Sergeant, you might more usefully go and see Mr Du Thuy and his friends. Too many coincidences there for my liking,' Laurence Body added, escorting her to the door.

16

'Whereabouts do we go, Mum?' Alice asked, worried that they would be late. Peering round in all directions as if still trying to find her bearings, her mother said, 'Keep going to the top of this road and then, I think… take the first right.'

'And you're sure they'll have a space there? The place seems to be jam-packed.'

'Yes. Yes. I've got a reserved one in the oncology car park, a privilege I could well do without.'

As the car drew up at the barrier, a fat man in a peaked cap, sweating profusely, peered in at the driver's window, frowning as if to repel any interlopers. Hastily, Alice's mother passed across her appointment card and the bouncer, pudgy fingers obscuring most of the writing, examined it.

'Busy today?' Mrs Rice enquired politely.

'Aha. The pole's already been up n' doon like a hoor's breeks,' he muttered, head still bowed, engrossed in his inspection, before continuing, 'Okay hen. In ye go. Furst oan yer left.'

The radiotherapy staff trooped out, one of them putting a comforting hand on Alice's shoulder as he passed. Seconds later the red light above the door went on, signalling that the treatment had begun. Inside, Olivia Rice lay semi-naked on a hard metal bed, with little more than a paper towel to preserve her modesty. She stared up at the ceiling, willing herself to relax, conscious that her neck muscles were on the edge of spasm. Everyone had said that she would be fine, the rays would cure her, not kill her. And the small tattoo on her breast, delineating the target area, had been minutely aligned with the machine. 'One thousand and one… one thousand and two,' she began counting, but before she reached 'One thousand and five', her six seconds of radiation were up and she heard a strange clicking sound followed by a passage of whirring, announcing that her first session was complete. The middle-aged nurse returned and freed her from the bed and the contraption above it, directing her behind a screen where she was reunited with her clothes.

Seated in the corridor, Alice crossed, uncrossed and then re-crossed her legs before, on automatic pilot, beginning to recite a Hail Mary. Self-consciousness returned with the first 'Holy Mary, Mother of God' and she laughed at herself, parroting mumbo-jumbo, but found that she was unable to leave the prayer incomplete. Just as she had decided to rise from her seat and investigate the magazine table, her mother reappeared, calm and smiling, chatting animatedly with the radiographer about the virtues of pink fir-apples.

—

It was just too unlikely, she thought. And, looking at Georgie, affable, amusing Georgie, she could not imagine the James Freeman that his partner had described forming any kind of alliance with him, never mind a one-night stand. He poured more tea into her cup, before resuming his stool amongst the books and beaming, magically, at her again. Although she returned repeatedly to the original meeting in the Boar's Head, he took no offence, patiently answering all her questions. She knew it was the lynchpin, without it little more would be left than a chance meeting between two gay men, both of whom worked in the same area of Edinburgh. Ivan became a suspect because of Georgie, and Georgie became one because of Ivan.

'So you're sure it was him, the Sheriff, because of the like-ness to the newspaper photo?' Alice asked.

'Yes. I never bothered reading the actual obituary. But I re-member his looks all right.'

'Not because of anything he told you?'

'No.'

'Did he say anything much?'

'Well, we chattered for a bit, as you do, got to know each other... Not so different, really, from the heterosexual world, you appreciate.'

'I'm sorry, I didn't mean to suggest...'

Georgie quickly touched her elbow, grinning again to reas-sure her. 'That's all right, Miss Rice, I didn't think you did.'

She tried a different tack. 'James Freeman, you know, was not far off eighty.'

'No!' The man seemed thunderstruck.

'The chap you met, I take it, didn't seem so old?'

'Certainly did not. No. Let's change that. Was not. I'm not some kind of gerontophile, I can assure you. No wonder Ivan seemed a bit taken aback when I told him about the liaison. It's a miracle he didn't run away screaming.'

And then the light dawned. The photo, used in the papers, and which she had not seen, must have been an old one. She racked her brain for anything else she could remember about the dead Sheriff.

'When you talked, did the man have a speech impediment?'

'Christ almighty! What else? No, not that I can recall. What did you have in mind?'

'Ws for Rs. You know, "Wound the wagged wocks, the wagged wascal wan..."'

'No. Definitely not. I'd have noticed that.'

'What about a scar—on his body. Cutting right across his chest?'

'This is beginning to sound as if I picked up an aged

monster… er, no disrespect to the Sheriff intended. No, no scar either. I take it all back. The man I slept with was normal, normal body, normal voice and not Methuselah. I did not, repeat did not, sleep with the deceased judge! I take it all back!'

Then he ruffled his hair with the tips of his fingers, laughed and said, 'What I want to know, detective, and this could be your next assignment, is who the hell did I bestow my favours on? As my old flame used to say—

"You know it's mad and bad as well,
To copulate when stocious.
You do not know your lover's name,
And the sex will be atrocious!"'

A single trail remaining, and all that was needed now was a phone check. It was the obvious thing, except that permission from on high would be required, and those breathing the chilly air had seemed singularly unimpressed by her theory. An alternative, albeit imperfect strategy would now have to be deployed. She searched for Vertenergy's phone number and found it scrawled on a Post-it attached to the front cover of her diary.

'Detective Sergeant Rice here. I understand that my colleague, DS Watt, spoke to a Mr Vernon from your company yesterday. Could I speak to him, please? There are a number of new matters that have arisen.'

The receptionist, boredom unconcealed, said that she would send someone to find him; he was certainly in the office but had not been answering his phone. In the meantime, Alice would have to be put on hold. A minute or two of complete silence and then she was unceremoniously cut off. Re-dialling, fortunately, produced another receptionist, one abashed to hear of the mishap and prepared to leave her desk to find the Director.

'Hello, Sergeant Rice. What can we do for you today?' The man's voice was cheery, eager to please.

'It's in relation to the Scowling Crags wind farm, Mr Vernon. I understand that all of your dealings, originally at least, were with the late James Freeman, but that later his brother Christopher Freeman became involved...'

'That's right. Christopher Freeman informed us that permission would be granted to use Blackstone Mains as the access strip for the development.'

'After you received the Sheriff's letter withdrawing permission for the inclusion of Blackstone Mains, did someone from your company contact Christopher Freeman to tell him of the withdrawal?'

'No,' the man sounded puzzled, 'I wouldn't think so. You see, at that stage, we dealt solely with James Freeman. I doubt anyone here was aware, then at least, that the land was jointly owned. Even if they did know it, the assumption would have been that Freeman was consenting on behalf of all the landowners of Blackstone Mains. We'd have no cause to contact Christopher Freeman. I'm not sure anyone then knew that he even existed. Normally, we would have tried to tie up the "legals" before embarking on the quest for planning, but we couldn't this time, too many applications to risk being barred by "cumulative effect".'

'So you're pretty certain that no-one from your company phoned Christopher Freeman for that purpose?'

'Well...' Mr Vernon hesitated before replying. 'Yes. I'm in charge of the Scowling Crags development. I didn't talk to him and I can't think of anyone else who would have done so. I could check it with Roger I suppose...' he paused again. 'No. It's pointless. He was off on holiday then, so there'd be nobody. I bet my life on it that no-one from here contacted Christopher Freeman. We were very relieved when he contacted us.'

Alice replaced the receiver and breathed a long sigh of relief. DC Lowe strode to her desk. 'The boss wants to see you,

Sarge, and it's urgent,' he said, frowning and jabbing his finger at her as if to convey added force to the order.

—

The scent of coffee in the small office reminded Alice that she had missed her breakfast cup. Too much of a rush if the appointment at the Western was to be kept. DCI Bell looked up on her entry, busy brushing a mound of spilled sugar off her desk into a waste paper bin.

'Ah, Alice,' she said, and the relative warmth of her tone reassured her subordinate that she was not facing the dressing-down she had begun to anticipate.

'I've been thinking things over...' she continued, 'and I'm persuaded by your... reasoning. I just hope to God that your unofficial sample of the man's DNA proves identical to the official one we'll get on arrest. That it's not his wife's, for example. Otherwise, I'll be for the high jump. Anyway, after you left I got the ACC's grudging permission for a check to be run on James Freeman's telephone calls for two weeks prior to his death. We'll see if he called his brother. A verbal result should be available either late this morning or early afternoon, the printout will follow later. We've got permission to do Vertenergy too.'

'Excellent, Ma'am. I've already spoken to a Director of the company, a Mr Vernon, the chap that Alistair talked to yesterday, and he's pretty positive that they didn't tell Christopher Freeman about his brother's change of mind. But a check would put it beyond doubt.'

—

The absence of the poodles from the bungalow made it appear, somehow, larger, more commodious, as if the grand proportions of the beasts had distorted the scale of the house. It also seemed unnaturally quiet, dull and lifeless, and Sandra Freeman herself seemed subdued, immobile and absorbed in the business of smoking her cigarette. Without much thought Alice enquired politely as to the dogs' whereabouts.

'He's got the boys, both of them, up at the Mains for a good long walk,' she replied, distractedly.

Slowly but surely the significance of this ostensibly innocuous piece of information began to sink in. Blackstone Mains was a remote destination, one off the beaten track, and a couple of Shetland ponies would be more welcome, less disruptive, on a bus than those two massive, ill-disciplined poodles. Anyway, few buses, if any, would pass on such obscure back roads, and only the closest friend would allow his vehicle to be soiled by the dogs and their messy ways.

'I didn't see the car outside,' Alice said. Her hostess, briefly, showed some interest and then, expelling smoke forcibly through her mouth, said calmly, 'No. It's back in the garage, the one we got it from. In Liberton.'

'What's the matter with it?' Alice shot back, allowing little time for thought or, more importantly, fabrication.

'Mmm…' Sandra Freeman paused. 'The carburettor—dirt, yeah—dirt in the carburettor, I think.'

'The garage,' Alice said, while removing her mobile from her pocket, 'that would be Tooles, wouldn't it?'

'Yes! Yes! Tooles.' Mrs Freeman was becoming vexed. 'Why on earth do you want to know that?'

'Because I need to check that the car is there. At the garage, I mean. You see, I think that your husband must have it, up at Blackstone Mains.'

Mrs Freeman rubbed her eyes with her thumb and index finger, and then forcibly stubbed her cigarette out.

'Oh very well…' she said, exasperation having replaced her previous irritability. 'Very well. He does have it. There. He shouldn't have it, of course. I know that. But… well, he does. Now, are you satisfied? Going to go up there and charge him now? That'll be the toast of your enquiry I expect, eh? "Murdered Sheriff's brother caught driving his own car without a licence".'

'Or insurance,' Alice added, then continued '—but it's not the first time, is it? His driving whilst disqualified, I mean?'

'What exactly are you getting at?' Sandra Freeman asked, her face creased with concern, brows furrowed, blinking rapidly.

Quickly, Alice thought things through. It would be a gamble, she knew that, but one that would surely pay dividends. If she could project sufficient certainty, then the woman's own surprise would prevent her from making false denials, protecting her husband and painting herself into a corner.

'On the night of his brother's murder your husband had the car. That's correct, isn't it?'

The woman's expression revealed that she had, indeed, been caught off balance, but she said nothing, playing for time, so Alice repeated the question verbatim, emphasising her assertion and then waiting patiently for a reply.

'All right, all right. I was staying at my mother's that night, down the road. So he kept the car, to go to the pub he said. The next morning he told me that he was worried that someone had seen him, reported him, a neighbour or some other do-gooder. And they would do that here, you know, in this neighbourhood. I said I'd help him. He needs his licence back. He's a man, he needs to be independent.'

'Same again on the night of Mr Lyon's accident, eh?'

'Yes, he took the car then, as well. But he wasn't away that long. He said he had to get out, cabin fever or whatever, and we needed ciggies too.'

'Mrs Freeman, you lied...' Alice began.

'I know I lied,' the woman interjected. 'Of course I bloody lied. I had to. Wouldn't you have done it? He's perfectly safe, you know, been driving for years, and it's only a matter of days before he's allowed to drive again. Legally. If either of us had told you the truth… well, what then? You'd probably have him disqualified for life!'

—

Climbing the flight of stairs, each upward step felt easier than the last, as if her legs were on springs, but on arrival at the office she found it empty of all life except for DC Lowe. He was on the telephone, receiver clamped between shoulder and ear, attempting to write something down whilst simultaneously flicking through a telephone directory. No. Not him, she thought. Too much of a liability. DCI Bell was in her office, puce in the face, struggling to fend the Press off, fiddling crossly with a rubber band.

'No. I appreciate that. What do you expect me to say? If you are not getting satisfaction from Fettes or from here then, obviously, it's your prerogative to go elsewhere. Indeed. The Chief Constable may well, as you suggest, view matters differently. Yes. It is entirely up to you. I expect that your Editor does know him well. Goodbye.'

She slammed down the instrument and began massaging her shoulder and neck. 'A RIGHT FUCKER' she mouthed silently at Alice, before, breathing out slowly and calming herself, she turned her full attention to her Sergeant.

'Good news…' she began, 'the Sheriff spoke to his brother on the phone the day before he died, and there's no record of Vertenergy contacting Christopher Freeman following their receipt of his brother's letter.'

'Yes, Ma'am. And Mrs Freeman lied…' Alice replied. 'Her husband has no alibi for either of the nights. A friend's giving her a lift to the station and I'm going to ask DC Lowe to look after her when she arrives, get her tea and so on. If we go to the Mains he can keep an eye on her until we get back. The others are all out and about, and DI Manson's not back yet.'

Heavy rain started to fall, overwhelming the tattered wipers on the Astra, reducing visibility in the city to a few yards. Crossing the Dean Bridge the traffic ground to a halt, filthy water streaming from blocked gulleys on either side of the road, flooding the slight depression opposite Eton Terrace. They stopped again at the lights by the Bristo Baptist Church, rainwater now beginning to drop through the roof onto Elaine Bell's lap, ingeniously deflected to the side by the use of a laminated map adopted as a shield. Headlight to bumper the line of traffic flowed on, the Astra trapped mid-stream, until at the Barnton roundabout, the shower having finally dissipated itself, black sky gave way to blue and the sun emerged from its hiding place.

No tickets. No money. No purse even, Alice thought, instantly cursing herself, visualising her bag on her desk at the station. And everything, everything she needed was in it, including, critically, her identification. Surreptitiously she glanced at the fuel gauge. Full, thank Christ—that humiliation, at least, avoided—but the towers of the bridge were looming nearer, her crass ineptitude about to be exposed.

'I don't suppose you have a pound coin for the bridge, do you, Ma'am?' she asked lightly, attempting to disguise the acute discomfort that she felt.

'No, Alice…' the DCI replied. 'I assumed that you would have come prepared, so I didn't bring my purse.' The car reached the booth and the toll man extended his hand in automatic anticipation of payment.

'I'm sorry, we've no money between us, but we're Police officers—on Police business,' Alice said, but hearing her own voice and taking in afresh the shabbiness of the unwashed car, the hollowness of the assertion struck her.

'Well, well,' the man sounded doubtful. 'Must be some mighty big operation on over in Fife, eh? You're the third car of polis I've had this morning. Do us a favour, eh? Prove it! Go on, hen, gie us, gie us a flash o' yer blue light or something.'

'Show him your identification, Sergeant,' the Detective Chief Inspector said testily. Alice caught her superior's eye, and shook her head, dumb with embarrassment. Instantly, looking daggers drawn, Elaine Bell extracted her card from her jacket and flashed it at the official. With a mock salute the barrier was raised, just as a lorry behind, lights glaring, began to hoot its horn, impatient for progress.

No-one appeared to be about, but the Freemans' car was parked at the top of the first track, near the farmhouse. The building itself was clearly unoccupied, with metal shutters protecting its windows and fallen slates perched perilously in the rhones. Instinctively, the two women stuck together as they began searching the sheds that formed the quadrangular steading. The first one, cobwebs frosting the windows, appeared to be some kind of feed store with piles of old hessian sacks stacked against one wall and empty grain bins on either side of the door. Attached to it, fortunately with electric light installed, was a workshop, half the floor removed to form an inspection pit, and the concrete of the remainder blackened, coated in a thin veneer of ancient oil. Old Shell tins lay about the place, and on a rough-hewn work bench rested spanners, wrenches and other tools, beside a yellowing newspaper, as if someone had been interrupted mid-task and never returned. Next, Elaine Bell prised opened a stable door which creaked noisily, and as they peered in a rat scuttled, hunchbacked and lame, across an old table, then jumped, landing heavily in a pile of sawdust. Quickly, the door was slammed shut, ensuring that the creature remained incarcerated, unable to reach them. Over the excited twittering of sparrows perched on the roof, distant shouting could be heard.

'Pepe… Chico, you bloody dogs. Come here!'

Following the direction from which the voice had come the two policewomen ran towards a patch of scrub woodland, finally stopping for breath on reaching a large haystack built on an old bonfire site. A few bales had fallen from the stack and lay, burst and broken, on the cold ash. Sitting beside them, incongruously, was a rusty can of petrol, and the stench of fumes from it filled the air, obliterating the gentler scent of the hay.

Suddenly, Alice felt two huge paws thudding on her back as an exuberant poodle welcomed her, then slid to the ground to shake itself vigorously, showering her with a fine spray of mud. Chico, not to be outdone, immediately bounced up on her before turning his attention to Detective Chief Inspector Bell, the flustered woman now engaged in a losing battle, ineffectually attempting to fend Pepe off with an extended knee. When this ploy failed, she turned in a circle hoping to baffle the dog and unbalance it, but inadvertently created a game, as with each turn the poodles revolved with her. Eventually, having lost interest in the visitors, the two dogs raced up the stack, chasing each other all over it, causing little falls of hay in their path and emitting high pitched yelps like excited puppies.

'What the hell are you doing here?' Christopher Freeman said, striding briskly towards them, stick in hand, staring at Alice and then at the Chief Inspector. He looked dishevelled. His jacket was torn, stems of dry hay protruding from the tweed, and it and his corduroy trousers were heavily stained, as if water or oil had permeated deep into their fabric.

'Looking for you…' Elaine Bell replied calmly. 'I am DCI Bell of Lothian & Borders Police. Major Freeman, we'd like you to come back to Edinburgh with us, to St Leonards Street.'

Christopher Freeman said nothing, but stroked his chin between his thumb and forefinger. Just as the silence was becoming oppressive he said, 'And for what reason exactly?'

'To interview you about the murders of James Freeman and Nicholas Lyon.'

'Oh for God's sake,' he exclaimed, evidently astonished. 'You've got absolutely nothing on me. If you had a shred of evidence I'd have been pulled in long ago. I have an alibi. I was with Sandra, both nights, remember? She told you. I told you.'

'No,' Detective Chief Inspector Bell said quietly, 'you were not.'

'Have you been pestering my wife again?' the man demanded angrily of Alice.

'No,' Elaine Bell snapped back, 'she hasn't. She's been doing her job. Perhaps you should know that your wife is at the station at this very moment and she, too, is likely to be charged, obstructing us... as she has done.'

The man looked crestfallen. 'Why, for pity's sake... why are you dragging her into this?'

'Because she lied to us. And she, like you, will have to pay the penalty for that.'

'Well, do your bloody worst then.' Christopher Freeman had speedily recovered from his surprise and regained his initial confidence. 'We'll get a decent lawyer. Maybe plead guilty to some silly trumped-up little charge. You've got nothing, after all...'

A crashing sound accompanied Pepe's sudden descent from the hayrick, bales cascading to the left and right, one tumbling on top of the poodle, temporarily stunning him. A good portion of the structure had fallen with the dog, and beneath the remaining stack, a stretch of glass had begun to reflect the cloudless sky above. It was the windscreen of the white Volkswagon Polo. It took a few seconds for the impact of the revelation to sink in, and the first to react was Christopher Freeman, breaking the silence with a furious oath. Alice braced herself for threats, menace, physical violence even, and was beginning to feel the unpleasant effects of the adrenaline now coursing within her, but when she looked again at the Major she saw that he no longer appeared aggressive or defiant; panic had transformed his features, his face now pale and bloodless. Without another word, he struck a clutch of matches and hurled them towards the car, one dropping lit at his feet.

And then, mysteriously, time stood still, rendering Alice immobile, transforming her from an actor in the drama of her own life into a mere spectator. Before her eyes a man had begun to burn, snakes of flame encircling his legs, weaving sinuously upwards, twisting and turning, the heads of the serpents seeking out his face. And the brightness of the fire, its brilliant intensity, mesmerised her, drawing all her attention to it, making its source seem insignificant, compelling her to watch the strange spectacle that seemed to have been choreographed for her benefit alone.

'Alice! Alice! For Christ's sake, help me!'

The sound of DCI Bell's voice broke the enchantment, revealing with hideous clarity the scene in its true colours. Christopher Freeman was standing engulfed by fire, shaking his head frantically, his hair now alight, limbs writhing ineffectually in an attempt to rid themselves of the clinging flames. From his mouth issued a grotesque noise. A continuous high-pitched squeal, like a terrified, wounded pig, and the cry echoed and echoed in Alice's brain, before reaching an unbearable crescendo. And then, suddenly, it stopped, but the silence that followed it was eerier yet, as if all life on earth had ended.

In their repeated attempts to smother the flames they used their jackets, shifting them from place to place, frantic that their only weapons should not be consumed by the enemy. Become the enemy. To begin with they did not feel pain as their hands burnt, but when it did break through they continued, determined to subdue the flames, to suffocate them and somehow return the hellish torch back to its human form.

Her lover shampooed her hair and then soaped her body gently, as if she was a child, before pouring scented bath oils into the warm water. And still Alice did not feel clean. The awful smell of roasting flesh had permeated her, clung to her skin, tainted her hair, entered every single one of her pores. Nothing would drive it away, eradicate it from her system or cleanse her. A glass of white wine rested on the bath, the opened bottle beside it, and desperate to take the taste from her mouth she took one little sip after the other, rolling each around on her tongue, concentrating on the flavour. But a single image remained before her eyes, unalterable; a man incandescent, alight, writhing and twitching on the ground as, frantically, they tried to douse the flames, sticks of charred flesh emerging from beneath black smoke. And, in the process, she had inhaled him. Literally. Minute particles of scorched human being had entered her nostrils, probably her mouth too.

Exhaustion having made her careless, she reached for the plug, withdrawing her hand the instant the first moisture soaked through the bandage. The stab of pain in her fingers was excruciating, robbing her of breath and bringing tears to her eyes.

Walking slowly into her bedroom she found that it had been festooned with flowers: freesias, lilies and roses, the air now laden with their innocent perfumes. Clean sheets had been put on the bed and the covers turned back.

'Live with me?' Ian Melville said, coming close and lying next to her. She did not hesitate, needed no time to think or fashion an evasive reply. 'I'd love to,' she said, and it was no less than the sober truth.

17

Christopher Freeman seemed to have been drifting for days, waking every so often to be greeted by agonising pain and then, just as it seemed unbearable, relief would wash over him from somewhere on the tide, carrying with it the gift of unconsciousness, until the next breaking wave of agony. Once more his body sensed oblivion's approach, was beginning to cry out for the sweet euphoria that the morphine brought, but until its touch there was something he knew he must do. Sandra was there, beside him, he was sure of it, he could feel her familiar presence even if he could no longer see it. Somehow, he must speak, explain everything to her before he died, and death seemed to be creeping closer every day in the guise of sleep.

'Sandra,' his voice sounded unfamiliar, dry, like the hissing of a snake. 'I want you to know why I killed James...' He stopped, briefly gathering together all his strength before continuing, 'I went to beg him, tell him... to change his mind about the wind farm... ah... the money... the bastard was drunk... slurring his words... DRUNK. He started on about the way I'd lived my life... alcohol... ah... you, everything. We argued. It was nothing to him and... ah... everything to me. He turned his back on me... Then I hit him... my cuff around my hand... with that trun...'

His voice tailed off, the effort of speaking having drained him of the little energy he possessed, but, thankfully, he could make out a woman's voice, talking softly, answering him, protesting even, attempting to console or maybe silence him. An immense sense of relief flooded over him, as he imparted the reasons to her. But he must finish, explain all or be lost again on a tide of painkillers, unable to speak.

'Sweetie,' he tried again, hearing the same ugly rasp as before, 'the Lyon man... ah... he invited me to Moray Place to choose mementoes... stuff not left to me in the will... ah... it was all really mine. He offered me things he'd chosen—nothing decent but... ah... it was all my family's... not his...' He stopped, momentarily, to lick his lips. 'Said no to the wind farm, too... James's wishes to be sacrosanct. If James... ah... then who was he to override them... the hell with me...' He hesitated again briefly, marshalling his resources to continue. 'I thought... after his death everything... come back to me... the land... I'd be the only Freeman left. James was old-fashioned that way... and if it was to go elsewhere? Well... nobody else would refuse that huge sum of money... no, they'd co-operate with me... When the car hit him... ah... wro...'

His mouth was moving, he was sure of it, enunciating the words, but no sound was coming out and he cursed himself, for leaving the most important thing to last when there was nothing left to say it with. That he had loved her. But already he could feel the pain lifting, easing, the awful aching in his limbs melting away, and it was impossible not to welcome it, surrender to it, whatever remained unsaid.

Seeing his eyes gradually closing, Alice hurriedly signalled for the doctor to approach, fearful that the man might die before his wife returned.

'Thanks for staying with him, Sergeant. I don't know where the hell Mrs Freeman's got to. The nurses have looked everywhere they can think of. But don't worry, this sometimes happens. A short, lucid interval and then oblivion for hours or even days.'

'Will he survive?'

The doctor shook his head. 'No chance. Anyway, he doesn't

213

want to, and no wonder. Half his body burnt and the prospect of a trial. Then God alone knows what.'

Unpleasantly aware that Christopher Freeman's message had never been intended for her ears, Alice left his side, determined to track down his spouse and relay it to her. It no longer had anything to do with the law; the man was way beyond all that now. Minutes later she put her head out of the main doors and spotted the woman sitting on a bench, mouthing smoke rings and staring into space. Taking a seat beside her she carefully repeated every word she could recall, apologising all the while, trying to explain how she had ended up as his involuntary confessor.

'So now you know... everything that I heard, I mean...' Alice concluded.

As Sandra Freeman listened impassively, she rolled a ball of silver paper backwards and forwards between the fingers of one hand before, suddenly, flicking it away. Then, dropping her cigarette onto the tarmac, she left without a word to resume her vigil by her husband's bedside.

━━

A decision must be made. He would like what she did not, that was the invariable rule in all dealings between them. If she stuck to that she could not go wrong.

'I'll take a box of the dark chocolates, please,' Alice said, trying, vainly, to remove some pound coins from her purse without hurting her damaged hands. The assistant, seeing her predicament, extracted the money for her and put the box into a carrier bag. If only I could carry it in my teeth I'd be all right, she thought, as the weight of the small load began to cut in, reminding her just how tender the burns still were. An old man smiled at her as she stopped at the end of his bed to cast her eye around the ward, still searching for her quarry. As she was scanning the male patients, a nurse tapped her on the shoulder.

'Who are you looking for, dear?'

'DI... er... Mr Manson.'

'The foot or the elbow? They're both Mansons.'

'Eric, the foot. Is he all right now?'

'Fine. Everything's under control. He'll be out in the next day or so. You'll find him in the second to last on the left.'

Bag swinging uncomfortably, Alice made her way to the bottom of the ward, but stopped a few beds away from the man. He was lying asleep, snoring gently, with both his hands above the covers, his wife holding each of his in hers. It was a picture of marital devotion, and one she was reluctant to disturb. So she handed her gift to an auxiliary and left the hospital, deep in thought, wondering if she would ever be loved as he appeared to be. All imperfections accepted.

———

'Everything done?' Ian Melville asked, opening the car door for her.

'Everything done.'

'To the beach, then?'

'To the beach. The beach at Tyninghame.'